BAITING THE BEAR

THE NOBLE NORSEMEN

VIRGINIE MARCONATO

OLIVER BOOKS

PROLOGUE

"Oh! So beautiful!"

Björn frowned. Who was in the hayloft? A child, evidently, judging from the fluted voice but who? And who was she talking to? Silently, he crept forward and saw a young girl he didn't recognize crouched by the wall in the far corner. Ah. At least one of his questions was answered. She was talking to Barley, his tabby mouser, who had given birth two months ago. But who was she and what was she doing here on her own? She could not be more than two or three years old and did not live in the village.

He coughed to catch her attention. Surprised, the little girl turned huge amber eyes on him. Björn inhaled sharply. He had only seen irises of that color once in his life. His heart started to drum, but before he could ask the question already on his lips, the little girl beckoned him forward.

"Come see, there are *kittens* here!" She said the word with as much enthusiasm as a gold panner would have reserved for his biggest flake. He could not help a laugh. Kittens did not elicit the same enthusiasm in him.

"I know."

"There are five of them!"

"I know," he repeated, kneeling by her side. "But you have to be careful. Barley, their mother, is very protective of her babies. Don't try to touch them. You wouldn't want her to hurt you, would you?"

"No." The little girl, who had already extended her hand to stroke the kitten nearest to her, froze. "How do you know her name?"

"She's my cat. I rescued her a few years ago when she got herself trapped in a hole in the forest. She was just skin and bones then, almost starving."

"You're a hero then!"

Björn tilted his head in amusement. No one had ever called him a hero before and he quite liked it. "I don't know about that. But I certainly saved her life."

"What's your name?"

The change of topic caused a smile to bloom on his lips. With a heart-shaped face and a dimple on her right cheek, the girl was adorable.

"I'm Björn. It means Bear." Why he felt compelled to add that detail, he had no idea. Perhaps because, unlike the children in the village, the little girl appeared to be Saxon, and therefore wouldn't know his name's meaning.

He sat back on his heels, wondering. Her not being of Norse descent made her presence here all the more mysterious. How had a Saxon child ended up in his hayloft?

"You are called *Bear*?" The little girl's eyes grew as round as coins. It seemed he had said exactly the right thing to attract her attention. His smile broadened and he nodded. "Oh, you are so lucky! I want to be called Bee, but Mama told me it was not possible to have an animal name! She calls me Dawn."

Björn's heart resumed its drumming. Perhaps he knew what a Saxon child was doing in the Norseman village after all...

"Your mother. Is she here with you?" he asked, taking advantage of her willingness to talk.

"Yes. She is visiting her sister."

This time his heart leapt. That was exactly what he had hoped to hear.

In all his life he had met only one woman whose eyes were of a molten gold color and who might have a reason to visit the Norsemen village. A woman he had obsessed about for years. Could he dare to hope?

"What is your mother's name?" he asked the girl, trying not to sound as if his life depended on the answer.

But she had already lost interest and was trying to catch one of the little kittens, the one that was as white as snow.

It happened in the blink of an eye. Barley pounced. The little girl shrieked.

The opportunity was lost.

CHAPTER ONE

EAST ANGLIA, AUTUMN 1041

"Toland is dead."

The words were spoken without emotion. Dunne didn't see why she should pretend to be devastated, or even saddened by the death of her husband. Her sister knew the man had not been of her choosing, but rather imposed on her by their father. Life with him had not been easy to say the least. At the start of their marriage, she had even hated him. But after the birth of their only daughter they had started to drift apart, which, as far as she was concerned, had been a blessing. The less time they spent together, the better. Now when she thought about him, which was not often for a newly-widowed woman, she felt nothing but indifference.

Frigyth stared at her. Clearly the news was more of a shock to her. "What happened?"

Dunne shrugged. "He went to town one night, no doubt to meet one of his many conquests, and he never came back."

That had been one of the reasons their marriage had become more bearable over the years. He'd started to go find his pleasure elsewhere. Far from being offended by this disregard for her sensibilities, Dunne had been relieved. Now someone else had to deal with Toland. Enduring his rough handling in bed had been bad enough, but she'd also had to bear his insults.

"Jesus, but you've grown fat since our wedding day. What man in his right mind would want a woman like you? Can't you move when I bed you? Or at least moan? What have I done to deserve a woman who doesn't know what to do with her hands? Or mouth?" The list of recriminations had been endless, each more hurtful than the last.

It seemed in the last year he had found more accommodating women, women who moved under him, who moaned, who used their hands and mouths the way he wanted. Good for him. Except that his dissolute way of life had ultimately proven to be the death of him.

Well, it just went to show that sometimes you did reap what you sowed.

"On the way back home one night he lost his way in the darkness and broke his leg in a hole he didn't see," she told Frigyth dispassionately. "I wouldn't be surprised if he was drunk as well. That night, it was unusually cold. Unable to walk, he was forced to lie on the frozen ground without a cloak. A farmer and his son found him in the morning. Dead."

Her sister didn't pass any comment or offer her condolences. Frigyth was no hypocrite and she probably didn't feel sorry for the man's death either. The few times they had met, the tension between them had been palpable. Dunne had often wondered if her husband had not tried to press his advances on her sister. She knew he had lusted after her, and that would have accounted for her coldness toward him, as well as the way her husband, Sigurd, never left her side for even a moment whenever they visited. The Norseman always hovered in the background, as if ready to intervene and stop Toland from bothering her. Not that it signified much. Sigurd was utterly besotted with his wife and every inch the jealous protector. He might well have acted in the same way even if no lecher had been lusting after Frigyth.

It was better not to dwell on this overmuch anyway. Toland was dead, and he could not hurt her anymore. It was all that mattered.

After a few days on her own, wondering what to do, Dunne had decided to leave a house which was only associated with bad memories and find a new place to live. Her first port of call had been her sister. Frigyth was now happily married and lived in a village of Norsemen not too far from the town where they had grown up. After a few weeks spent here to adjust to her new freedom, Dunne would try and make a new life for herself and her three-year-old daughter.

She looked around, frowning. Where was Dawn, by the way? She had been here just a moment ago, playing with her puppets. Panic flared inside her. "Where has Dawn gone?"

Frigyth placed a soothing hand over her arm. "Fret not. The village is not so big. Most likely she saw a dog or a squirrel and followed it."

"Yes." Unfortunately Dunne knew all about her daughter's love for animals. But if she had followed a stray mutt, or a wild animal, it meant she could be anywhere, even in the woods. Damn it, she had only lost sight of her for a moment! Dunne started to run. "I have to find her, she is too—"

It was then that she heard the cry.

Ouch!

Her daughter's voice, unmistakable.

"In the hayloft," she cried, veering in the direction of the tall wooden structure, Frigyth close on her heels. In the hayloft she found her daughter. Dunne saw everything in quick succession. First the blood, then the way Dawn was holding her injured hand. Finally, the man who was standing next to her, tall and menacing. He was so imposing she should perhaps have seen him first, but she had been too focused on Dawn, too shocked by the blood on her hand. Why was her daughter bleeding?

Not stopping to think, she fell on the man. "What did you do to her, you animal!"

Her fists met muscles that were as hard as steel. It didn't take her long to realize she would not inflict much damage, but, as the man was not even trying to stop her, she carried on hitting him anyway. It was oddly satisfying. She had been too worried at finding her daughter missing, then too irate at the notion of anyone hurting her, to be in full control of her emotions. She needed to let the fear, the relief and the anger out, and attempting to beat a tall Norseman to a pulp was a surprisingly efficient way of accomplishing it.

"Mama, how did you know he has an animal name?"

The unexpected question, as well as the awe in Dawn's voice stopped Dunne in her tracks. Her daughter did not sound distressed in the least. Perhaps the man had not hurt her after all.

She turned to face the little girl. "I-I beg your pardon?"

"He's called Bear. I told you it was possible to have an animal name! Now will you call me Bee?"

What was this? Dunne had thought she was defending her daughter against a vicious attacker, and she was being told that they were friends. In view of this information, she had no choice but to let go of the man. Not that, as predicted, she had inflicted much damage. He appeared more amused than hurt by her outburst.

Frigyth came forward with a smile on her face. "This is Rorik's son. He lives here in the village. Don't worry, he's not going to hurt anyone, much less an innocent little girl."

"Of course, I'm not! What do you take me for, preying on children!" The Norseman, who was much younger than she had first supposed, looked so offended that Dunne instantly knew he had not been the one to hurt her daughter.

"What happened then?" she asked, taking in a deep, calming breath. "Why are you bleeding, Dawn?"

"Bee!" the little girl protested. Dunne threw her a glance that made it clear she had better answer without delay. After having been made a fool in front of a stranger, her patience was running thin. "I wanted to pet one of the kittens, but the mama cat scratched me."

"I told you Barley might do that." The man's voice was deep and beguiling, stroking over Dunne's frayed nerves. She looked at him again. Perhaps he was not as young as she had thought. He exuded a calm confidence she did not associate with youth. "Mothers are very protective of their young."

This last comment was aimed at her, without a shadow of a doubt. She had pounced on him, baring her claws like this mama cat called Barley had. Well, what else was she supposed to do? She'd thought her daughter was in danger, of course she would want to defend her, even when it was clear she had no chance of winning the fight.

"I'm sorry, but we have to leave. We've had a long day."

She felt out of sorts, without quite knowing why. Perhaps it was the relief of seeing that her daughter was not injured after all, perhaps it was the odd draw she felt toward the man. Up until today Dunne had thought her brother-in-law the most attractive man she had ever set eyes upon, and one of a kind. Now she could see that Sigurd was not unique, but simply a Norseman, which was to say as different from Saxon men as night was from day. From what she had seen, the men in the village all boasted impressive physiques and harmonious features, and none more so than "Bear."

Was that really his name or just another of Dawn's fanciful musings? They had seen the massive animal just once, a year ago, when a bear baiter had paraded it in town in front of awed onlookers. The blond man staring at her was just as massive as the animal and just as beguiling.

She shook her head. Why was she gawping at a stranger, compelling though he might be? She had better things to do, like finding a place to stay for the next few nights. Frigyth had told her a man called Wolf would help her. She had better go find him before nightfall instead of fawning over someone she might never see again.

"Dawn, say goodbye to your new friend," she said, lifting her daughter into her arms.

"Goodbye, Bear."

A chuckle answered her. "Goodbye, Bee. I hope to see more of you in the next few days."

"THE CASK OF ALE IS EMPTY," Sigurd said, looking into the cup in his hand. "If you wait a moment, I'll go and see Björn. He might have another one ready."

Dunne's ears pricked up at the name.

Björn. In other words, "Bear." Frigyth's husband had told her yesterday evening that the man Dawn had met in the hayloft was one of the most well-liked young men in the village. He lived with his sister Ingrid. At the death of their parents a few months back, he had taken over the making of the ale and had started to supply a few lucky friends with his production. Such a task was usually reserved to women, but Björn had apparently helped his mother as a child and developed a talent for it.

"No one makes ale quite like him," Sigurd had added, throwing an apologetic glance toward his wife. "Sorry, Birdie, you are the most talented cook I know, but—"

"No need to apologize." Frigyth had laughed. "The ale I make is palatable at best, it is agreed. We are much better off drinking what Björn makes." As usual, the discussion had been concluded by a kiss. As far as Dunne could tell, her sister and her husband were incapable of arguing.

Sigurd walked over to the door. "Let me go get a fresh cask before we eat."

Dunne was on her feet before anyone had time to blink. "Let me go."

Both Frigyth and Sigurd arched a brow at the statement.

"Are you sure?" her sister asked.

"Certain. I owe him an apology for the way I behaved yesterday," Dunne explained hurriedly, not sure why this was so important to her. After all, he had seemed to understand her impulse to defend her daughter. "This will be my chance."

"Very well. His hut is the one by the hayloft."

As she made her way to Björn's hut, Dunne could not account for the way her heart was fluttering in her chest. She was merely going to apologize to him, nothing more. There was no cause for such silliness.

She found him outside, stirring the contents of a large boiling vat with a wooden paddle. Up until that moment, Dunne would not have cited ale-making as a licentious activity, but she was forced to reassess her opinion there and then.

Because Björn was bare-chested, and the sight was the most arousing thing she had ever seen.

As he moved the paddle back and forth through the thick grain mash, the muscles on his back twisted and pulled, betraying immense strength. There wasn't an ounce of fat on his body; everything was taut, golden, and smooth. The man was sculpted perfection, from the expanse of his broad shoulders to his trim waist and impossibly tight buttocks. Dunne started when the thought crossed her mind. Never before had she noticed how tight or flabby men's buttocks were.

Then again, she had never seen Björn half-naked before.

It was impossible not to notice how perfect he was. She couldn't tear her eyes from the sight. He raised a hand to wipe his brow with the back of his hand and everything within her coiled at the way his bicep contracted and bunched. Why? There was nothing extraordinary in it. And since when had her skin grown too tight for her body? She had no idea. All she knew was that she had been struck dumb.

She must have made a sound because he spoke, his attention still on the vat.

"Ah. Just put everything on the table, thanks."

"I-I'm sorry. I don't have anything for you."

He stopped and looked over his shoulder at her. Something flashed in his blue eyes. Amusement? Annoyance? She couldn't tell. Unsure how to behave, Dunne waited.

Eventually Björn smiled and hung his paddle on a hook in front of him. "Forgive me. I thought you were Ingrid, my sister, bringing me some food."

"No. Sorry. I came to...Well, Sigurd sent me here to say he would like a cask of ale, if you have one ready" she finished lamely. This was not why she was here, not really, but suddenly she had gone all shy. In her defense, she had not expected to find him in such a state of undress. How was she supposed to think straight in front of a half-naked man?

"Of course, I can have one readied for him." Björn turned fully to her, eyes ablaze. "But I don't think that's why you came."

"N-no?"

Dunne couldn't think with his chest on full display. The back had been splendid, the front was spectacular. Short blond hairs shone on his pectorals like gold dust sprinkled on stone, ridges lined his taut abdomen, forcing the eye to follow the line disappearing under the waist of his braies. Dunne had to bunch her fists to stop herself from reaching out to him. Never before had she had the urge to pet a man.

But a golden bear? Apparently she did.

"Why else would I have come?" she whispered when she finally tore herself from the contemplation.

He walked over to her and leaned in, stopping close enough for her to smell something both earthy and floral she assumed came from the grain he had been stirring. Did all the women who took care of the making of the ale smell like this? She had never noticed before. Either way, it was as potent as the drink he was mixing.

"I think you're sorry for hitting me yesterday and you came to apologize," he said in a low purr. "As well you might. Look at what you did."

He hunched a shoulder to show her a series of small bruises at the back of his bicep she had noticed before without thinking of attributing them to her clumsy attack on him.

"*I* did that?" She was aghast. Never had she imagined she would actually hurt such a strapping man.

"Yes. Surprising what protective mothers will do, as I told your daughter before you arrived. You lashed out at me for hurting your child the same way my cat lashed at Bee for touching her kitten. Imagine what you would have done if you'd had claws as well. I might well have been shred to ribbons."

"But you didn't hurt her," Dunne whispered, disconcerted by the admiration in his voice. He sounded as if he were impressed by her courage when she was sure he should be outraged. Any other man she knew, save perhaps Sigurd, would have made her feel his ire.

"Of course, I would never have hurt her, but you didn't

know that at the time. I was just a strange man alone with your daughter and she was bleeding."

She nodded. Seen like that it did make sense. Still, she knew he was being more reasonable than most. "In any case, I apologize for hitting you and I thank you for not hitting me back."

He recoiled, all traces of amusement gone from his face. "You think I would do such a thing? Hit a woman?"

"Well, I was attacking you. It would have been only fair if you'd defended yourself."

"By grabbing your wrists, perhaps, and preventing you from hitting me, not by hitting you back!"

He looked so shocked by the idea she could not help a smile. "No. I see that you would never do such a thing."

The mere idea of hurting Dunne sent a chill down Björn's spine. He would never hit a woman, no matter what she did to him, and if he ever touched *her*, the woman he had been dreaming about for years, it would not be to inflict pain. If she allowed him to, he would cradle her heart-shaped face while he kissed her full on the mouth, then he would run his hands along her flanks, cup her buttocks and draw her to him before tumbling her down onto his pallet and making love to her.

He could not believe she was really here in front of him. It was as if after so long fantasizing about this moment, he had made her appear with the power of his longing.

And she was just as compelling as he remembered. The amazing eyes the color of liquid honey and the mass of chestnut hair she wore loose over her shoulders had not changed. She looked different than she had at her sister's wedding, though. It was hard to pinpoint what it was exactly, but she seemed to have lost the hounded expression she'd worn then, as if she didn't feel...trapped anymore.

Yes, that's what it was. She looked free.

He let out a groan of dismay. The attraction she exerted over him had not diminished in the least. On the contrary, it seemed to have grown. In the same way he had grown into a man since Frigyth and Sigurd's wedding, she had become much more than an unattainable figure of desire he'd only been allowed to glimpse from a distance. She was all too real, had become part of his life. They were talking, she had come to his hut, she had even touched him. Granted, it had been to pummel him, but still, she had left her mark on his skin. His soul, of course, had been struck a long time ago.

Hope fluttered in his chest. He had not dared hope she would come to see him but here she was, less than a day after their meeting in the hayloft. Could it mean anything?

"How about that cask then?" she whispered, clearly at a loss as to how to carry on the conversation.

"I have one here, ready."

He watched her eye the cask he'd indicated and then bite her bottom lip. His groin instantly tightened. Did she have any idea what that gesture would do to a man? Apparently not. She seemed oddly innocent for a woman who was married and had a child, as if she'd never been courted in her life and did not know the way men's minds worked. Perhaps she did not, perhaps she had married her childhood sweetheart when she was very young and had never had cause to observe men or wonder how best to appeal to them. Perhaps her husband, the lucky sod, had never needed to woo her, because it had always been assumed they would end up getting married. He pushed the disagreeable thought from his mind. The less he imagined her with another man, the better.

"Sigurd can have it," he said, nodding at the cask again. "Ingrid and I have plenty left until the next batch is ready."

"Thanks. It looks rather heavy, though."

That's when he understood why she had looked appalled

earlier. She thought she was going to have to carry it back to Sigurd by herself.

"Don't worry about the weight. I'll take it, not you." What did she take him for? First she'd been worried he would hit her, now she thought he would make her handle a full cask of ale on her own? What sort of men was she used to that she could think such things? "Did Sigurd say when he needed it?"

She reddened, as if she were loath to inconvenience him. His groin tightened further. The color suited her, making her eyes sparkle like gems. "As soon as possible, from what I understood."

"Very well. I'll see to it now then."

"Thank you."

"It's no problem."

She took a step back. Only then did he realize they had drifted closer during their conversation. It had been so natural to be next to her that he had not registered the closeness, even though it was not every day he found himself bare-chested in front of a woman who was not his sister.

"Well, I'm happy to have met you, Björn."

"Me too." Finally.

"I'm Dunne, by the way."

"I know." He crossed his arms over his chest. "It's not the first time we've met, you know."

She hesitated. "No, but I didn't tell you my name yesterday."

Björn shook his head. That was not what he meant at all. "You don't remember me, do you?"

Dunne blinked, looking caught out. "Should I?"

"No," he said bitterly. Why would she remember a youth she'd met so long ago, who had not exchanged a single word with her? "You have no reason to remember me, but I saw you here at the village three years ago when your sister married Sigurd."

"Oh. And you remember me?"

Remember her? He almost let out a laugh. He had dreamed about her countless times, imagined her face, her body when he gave himself pleasure at night. Up until now he had felt no guilt over it, because he'd never thought to meet her again. She had been as unattainable as the goddesses in his parents' stories, a figure of beauty and fascination, nothing more.

But now she was a woman of flesh and blood standing in front of him, looking at him expectantly, and he did feel guilty. If she knew what he'd done to her in his imagination as he'd discovered the pleasure his body was capable of giving him, she would flee as fast as her legs could carry her...She had filled his every lewd thought for years, been her wildest, favorite fantasy. Her name had been on his lips, her face in his mind every time he'd reached the pinnacle of pleasure. No other woman, real or imaginary, had ever been able to replace her.

"Yes, I do remember you," he said curtly.

He'd been obsessed with her.

But how could he not? She was the most beautiful woman he'd ever seen, gloriously feminine. Unusual. Intriguing. Sensual. The list went on and on. She was also married—and utterly out of bounds. He took another step back, for more safety.

"Is your husband here in the village as well?"

He winced when the question left his lips. He hadn't meant to ask her that. Would she balk and answer that it was none of his business?

She did not, and her answer almost sent him reeling backward.

"No. My husband is dead."

CHAPTER TWO

"Thanks, Björn. What would you like?"

Björn looked at Sigurd in incomprehension. His brain seemed to have stopped working the moment Dunne had said she was widowed. In other words, free.

"What would I like?" he repeated dumbly.

He had not expected the question, but the answer was simple. What he would have liked was for Dunne to see him as a man who could be part of her life now that she was not accountable to anyone. She was not a married woman anymore, but a widow, and that changed everything. A single woman who knew his name was not an unattainable goddess. Now she might consent to mingle with mere mortals such as he.

Now he finally had a chance to woo her.

"What do I owe you as payment for the ale?" The Dane looked at him oddly, which was no wonder. Björn probably looked like a blurry-eyed fool right now. But how was he supposed to think when Dunne was looking so lovely in the background?

Today she had donned a deep green dress that made her

eyes glow and it was taking all his concentration not to stare at her.

"Don't worry about payment," he mumbled. His friend had already repaid him a hundred-fold by sending Dunne to get the cask. It had given them a chance to get properly introduced, away from mingling daughters, protective cats, and suspicious sisters. "Although…There's one thing you might do for me."

"What is that?"

"Not you, but your wife rather. Ingrid would like to improve her sewing and learn to make clothes. Perhaps Frigyth could teach her?"

Sigurd twisted his lips while his wife shook her head slowly. "I'm sorry," the Saxon said. "I'm afraid what little I could show her, Ingrid will already know. I'm not the best seamstress."

In truth, Björn knew she had little talent for sewing, which was exactly why he had asked. With luck, Dunne would be volunteered in her place. If, of course, she knew how to sew. He was taking a gamble but there was little risk. If she did not know how to handle a needle, he would have lost nothing.

He didn't have to wait long to find out. Frigyth stole a glance toward her sister, who had retreated in the distance during their discussion. "Dunne. You're good with a needle. Would you agree to show Björn's sister what you know?"

She seemed to hesitate then she nodded. "Of course. It will be my pleasure."

Björn's chest expanded in relief. He'd gambled—and won the most perfect prize he could imagine. Time with the woman of his dreams. Now he would have to utilize it well.

"Perfect. I'll see you tomorrow then?"

Dunne watched Björn walk away pensively. Before leaving his hut earlier, he had donned a shirt and, as he moved, his gait predator-like, she tried to imagine the muscles rippling over his back.

"Come. Let us break our fasts."

Tearing her gaze from him, she followed Frigyth back inside the hut. They got the food ready while Sigurd tapped the cask and poured everyone a drink.

Frigyth took a long draught of ale and sighed. "Mm. Still as good as ever. Be careful, sister. If you stay at the village too long, you might well acquire a taste for Björn's ale."

"I'm not too worried," Dunne replied, accepting the cup Sigurd was handing her. As far as she was concerned, ale was ale, one was much the same as another. But she might well acquire a taste for the brewer, she reflected, which was little wonder considering the way his body was sculpted and how his eyes burned when he looked at her.

She placed her lips on the brim of the cup and inhaled. The smell, yeasty, fresh and floral, reminded her of Björn. To hide her unease, she drank—and felt her eyes widen when ambrosia hit her tongue.

Damn it, she'd been wrong. Ale was not ale after all. It seemed that some could be the best thing she had ever put in her mouth.

"What did I tell you?" Frigyth had not missed her reaction and sounded very pleased to have been proved right.

"Yes. It's delicious," she said honestly. "To think he didn't even want any payment for it. It makes no sense."

"Well, you'll be able to repay his generosity by helping his sister. Their parents died in the spring and Ingrid will be glad of the help. She is still young and I think she misses the guidance from her mother."

"Yes."

Though that comment made her feel like she was nearing fifty rather than thirty summers, Dunne was glad she would not need to make up an excuse to see Björn. Because she did want to meet the enigmatic Norseman again.

She spent the whole day thinking about their next encounter.

Finally, the morning came, bitterly cold for the season. Wrapping herself in her cloak, Dunne made her way to Ingrid and Björn's hut alone. She had wanted to take Dawn with her as protection against any unwise impulses, but the little girl had understandably preferred to stay behind and play with her cousins. In any case, she reflected as she rounded the well, it was unlikely Björn would be bare-chested in this weather and anyway, surely he could not be as appealing as she remembered? She had only been overwhelmed yesterday because she had never seen a man's chest before, other than Toland's, and the contrast with her husband could only have played in Björn's favor. Yes, that had to be it.

Except...

Except that it was not only his chest that had captured her attention. It was his face, his voice, his hands, the way he moved, the way he laughed, the way he—

She came to a skidding halt. She had to stop this before she was in front of him. Björn was not for her, he was only a boy. Sigurd had told her this morning he was nineteen, in other words a whole decade younger than her. She'd been married, she was a widow, and she had a child. His sister was looking for someone to teach her what their mother had not had time to teach her. In such circumstances, he would never see her as someone he could take an interest in.

Comforted in her resolve to act with composure, she knocked on the door. A young woman opened. Dunne's heart fluttered. Who was she? His sister or his sweetheart? Before now she had not even considered the possibility that he could have one but, now that she thought of it, she could not imagine how he would not. Before she could start imagining the worst, the girl beckoned her inside.

"You must be Dunne." She smiled. "Come in. I'm Björn's sister, Ingrid."

"This is hopeless!"

With a sigh, Ingrid placed the shirt on the table. Dunne picked it up to examine it.

"It's not that bad," she said carefully, not wanting to discourage the girl even if, in truth, the stitches along the hem were not only uneven but too tight, causing the fabric to pucker at odd intervals. It was quite an achievement, really. Even at the age of eight, Dunne could not remember being so clumsy with a needle. But then someone who had never been shown properly could not accomplish miracles. "I expected worse."

Ingrid stared at her for a moment, then burst out laughing. "Oh, you really don't know how to lie! I defy you or anyone to want to be seen in such an awful garment and I wouldn't blame them!" She gestured at the shirt she had attempted to make for herself from one of Björn's old ones. "This is awful."

"Yes, it is, rather," Dunne agreed. There was no point in lying, they could both see the hem was not right. "But that is why I'm here, to show you. With practice you are going to improve."

"Let's hope so."

By the end of the afternoon Ingrid had made noticeable progress. Her stitching was painfully slow but at least the result was acceptable.

"Well, now all I have to do is repeat this a thousand times and I should be fine." Ingrid made a grimace, clearly not excited by the prospect. "Thank you for your patience, Dunne. Do you have time to come again in the next few days?"

"Yes, of course. I don't have much to do in the village,

anyway." The smile budding on her lips vanished because at that moment Björn entered the hut. She had refused to acknowledge until then that this was precisely what she had been waiting for all day.

"Good afternoon. How is the sewing going?"

Ingrid gave a big sigh. "Not as well as I would like. I can already tell that sewing will never be a favorite activity of mine."

"Ah, sister." He leaned in to place a kiss on the top of her head. The gesture was so natural, so tender, that something within Dunne melted. Not one used to witnessing gestures of intimacy, much less being on the receiving end of them, she could not help but envy the easy affection between brother and sister. "You will improve, I'm sure."

"Yes. And Dunne has agreed to help me. She's really very good."

Two pairs of blue eyes turned to her, one framed by long lashes, one ablaze with a secret fire.

"I thank you for your help," Björn said, his voice deep with gratitude.

"It's not a problem. I like to be useful."

It wasn't a lie. It felt good to help someone else—and more to the point, it felt good to be appreciated for it. Nothing she had ever done had been good enough for Toland. It was a nice change to be considered skilled at something.

The following day Dunne was back, as promised, but when she knocked on the door, it opened on Björn.

"Ingrid is abed I'm afraid," he said when he saw her surprise.

"Oh? Nothing too bad I hope?"

He gave her a slanted smile that set her heart aflutter. "No. Only she suffers badly on the first day of her woman's cycles. It's been like that for years and there's not much we can do, unfortunately. She just needs to sleep it off."

The ease with which he talked about this most feminine of afflictions took Dunne by surprise. Most men didn't want to hear as much as a word about the phenomenon. Toland had forbidden her to ever mention it, demanding she only indicated she was unavailable to be bedded. She could tell the mere idea of her bleeding, though perfectly natural, disgusted him.

Björn did not appear disgusted. On the contrary he seemed sorry not to be able to bring his sister comfort. He really was unlike anyone she knew, at ease with all things associated with women.

"Oh," she said again, not quite sure what to say. Mercifully, she had always been the very picture of health, and never suffered during her womanly flux, so she didn't have any advice to offer poor Ingrid.

"Listen, seeing as you're here..." He rubbed a hand over the back of his neck, the gesture betraying intense embarrassment. She couldn't help a smile. Surely what he was about to say could not be more personal than what he had just revealed about his sister. "Would you do me a favor?"

"Of course."

"My shirt caught on a nail this morning and it ripped. I was wondering if you could see to it?"

She nodded and allowed her eyes to wander up and down his chest, wondering where the rip could be. "I don't see any tears?"

He cleared his throat. "No, it's at the back. But come on in, don't stand in the door thus. Ingrid will be pleased to see you, even if she won't feel up to sewing today."

While Dunne knelt next to Ingrid's pallet, Björn hastily went to the back of the hut, away from the two women. There, he hooked the back of his shirt on a nail that was sticking out of the wall and took a step forward. The fabric tore with a worrying sound. Damnation, he'd meant to ensure Dunne stayed a while longer, not to make her labor all day over his ruined garment. Still, there was no helping it now, it was done.

He went back to the hut and found her standing by the table, a needle and thread at the ready.

"Would you mind going outside to sew?" Ingrid moaned. "I would like to try and sleep in the dark if I may."

"No, of course not. You just get the rest you need."

Björn placed the wooden panel he'd made for that express purpose over the window and led Dunne to the bench outside.

"Let's see this tear then," she said, placing her ball of thread on the seat.

Björn turned around and heard her inhale sharply. "Is it that bad?" he asked with an inward wince. "I thought it might be, considering the noise it made."

She gave a small laugh. "Well, let me put it this way. I'm amazed I didn't see anything wrong with your shirt before."

Björn was glad to have his back to her because his face might well have given the truth away otherwise. She hadn't seen anything wrong because there hadn't been anything wrong. It had been a spur of the moment thing to pretend he had something to repair. Had she guessed as much? Was that why she was laughing? He dearly hoped not.

"Do you think you can repair the damage?"

"Yes. But you'll have to take you shirt off."

Even better. Björn had not missed the way Dunne had ogled his bare chest the other day. She seemed to find his body to her liking. Presumably her husband had not been as muscular as he was. He liked the idea. Anything that could play in his favor, he would shamelessly use. Without waiting for further instructions he grabbed the back of his shirt and pulled it over his head. There was another inhale of breath behind him and Björn could not help teasing her.

"Don't tell me the nail scratched my skin also?" he asked in mock concern, placing a hand over the small of his back to force Dunne's gaze to land on it. Not that he didn't think she wasn't already ogling him. "Could you check please? Is it bleeding?"

There was a silence and then she whispered, "N-no, your skin is just...perfect."

Perfect, hey? That was promising. He turned around—and almost knocked her over in the process. In her bid to check the imaginary scratches on his back, she had apparently bent over and so was a lot closer than he'd anticipated.

"Forgive me," he said, straightening her.

"No. It's me. I..." She took a step backward, cheeks flushed. "I will see to your shirt now."

Björn nodded and watched as she settled herself on the bench to thread her needle. When she started working, he leaned a shoulder on the wall of the hut.

"I might as well watch how you do it and learn some tricks. I'm not too gifted at sewing myself," he said to justify his staying here. The way her fingers moved was mesmerizing.

"You can't be good at everything."

He arched a brow at her unexpected answer. "What am I good at, in your opinion?"

The rhythm in her stitching faltered ever so slightly as if she'd realized she'd revealed too much. "The ale you make is very good," she finally said, not looking at him.

"I'm glad you think so." He'd received compliments for the drink countless times, but he had always brushed them off as nothing. Dunne's approval warmed his chest in an unprecedented way. It was another step in the right direction.

She liked his chest, she liked his ale. What next?

For a moment neither of them spoke. Then two male voices reached them from just beyond the hedge.

"Do you understand what they're saying?" Dunne whispered, leaning in toward him. His heartbeat picked up, as it always did when she was near.

"Yes. But I'm afraid it's not terribly interesting," he added, picking up on her curiosity. "They are saying they need a new rope to replace the one at the well which is frayed."

"Oh. Indeed it's not very interesting." She made a grimace he found adorable. "It sounded more exciting in Norse."

"Do you think so?"

She nodded as if she could not believe he did not. But he was so used to the language that it held no special appeal to him.

"So you understand Norse. Can you speak it as well?" she asked.

In that moment he dearly wished he could speak the language with ease, because he could tell she wanted to ask him to say something. But he knew he was far from fluent and the last thing he wanted was to appear ridiculous in front of her when he stuttered and hesitated. Although she would not understand the mistakes he made, she would hear the difference between his halted speech and the other Norsemen's ease. Perhaps he should ask Sigurd to teach him to speak better.

"I don't speak it as well as the other villagers," he answered gruffly. "Unlike them, I was born here and my parents encouraged me to use the language of their new home, as they wanted me to blend with the local Saxons as much as possible."

Dunne nodded. "I understand. Unfortunately, it can be difficult for foreigners to be accepted. Still, it's a pity. You could have learned both languages. I'm sorry, I didn't mean to criticize your p-parents," she stammered, as if fearing she had offended him. He gave her a reassuring smile. She had not. "Frigyth told me they died in the spring."

"Yes. An awful accident. Their horse took fright when a dog shot between its legs and bolted, overturning their cart while they visited the market in town. At least they died together. It was better that way. Better for them, at any rate," he said in a low voice.

The whole village had been hit hard by the sudden, shocking loss. The two of them had set off at dawn, hale and hearty as usual and before dusk had been reduced to a mangled, bloody mess. His sister had spent weeks prostrate in bed, staring at the ceiling. He was only just now starting to hope she would recover from the grief.

"Thank you for helping Ingrid. She misses our parents dreadfully, and feels she didn't have time to learn all our mother would have taught her. I know she thinks herself a failure for it."

"She's not a failure!"

"No, she's not, and with the support of someone like you, I'm sure she will see that."

Something tightened in Dunne's chest. Ingrid, who was barely seventeen, was seeing her as a mother figure. Did Björn feel the same? He was only two years older than his sister and he had just asked her to mend his shirt. Hardly what a man would do to woo a woman into bed...

She started. Men trying to woo her into bed? Since when was that something she worried about? Her decision had been made at Toland's death. She wouldn't let anyone try to entice her into bed, since it could never lead anywhere. She was determined never to marry again. Unexpectedly, she had been given a chance at a satisfactory life, and she would live it without a husband lording over her.

She resumed her stitching, glad to have something to focus her attention on other than Björn's bare chest. When he had removed his shirt so casually, only inches away from her, she had almost passed out. There had been such grace in his movements, it had felt so intimate to witness such an act, so evocative...

And then he had handed her the shirt, still warm from his body and smelling of dried flowers and herbs. She had barely resisted the urge to bring it to her nose and inhale.

"I think I should go back to my hut soon, see what's to be done about it."

It was only when Björn sat down next to her that Dunne realized she had spoken out loud. "You don't sound so sure. Perhaps you should wait another few weeks."

"Oh, I don't mean go back to live," she said. "I don't even want to see the place anymore. But arrangements will have to be made. With the price I can get from the sale I will be able to buy something else and start anew."

Something tightened in her chest at the idea of leaving the Norsemen village, but she could not stay here forever. It was not her home. Sigurd's Icelander friend Wolf had found her a hut to stay in momentarily, but she had no reason to outstay her welcome.

"When are you going?"

"The sooner the better. I want to put it all behind me, build a new, happy life for Dawn and me."

"A happy life," Björn repeated slowly. "Were you unhappy with your—"

"There you are. All finished," Dunne jumped on the opportunity to cut the personal question short. She did not want to talk about her marriage to anyone. Conversations with Frigyth were taxing in the extreme; with anyone else they were unthinkable. Mercifully, Björn seemed to take the hint. Instead of insisting, he took the shirt she was handing out to him.

"This is incredible work," he said as he examined it.

She shrugged. Her skill with a needle was not incredible, only a consequence of her misery. During her marriage to Toland, she had done little other than mend his awful-smelling shirts and create pretty clothes for Dawn, the only source of joy in her life. She was barely allowed out of the hut and, anyway, she had no appetite for anything else. Dealing with her husband seemed to suck all of the energy out of her. In those circumstances, it was little wonder she had become proficient at sewing. Yes, she was skilled, but only because she had been so dreadfully unhappy. Instead of living her life, she had sewn the tedium of her days away so it was hardly a cause for congratulation. Except...except that it now allowed her to spend some time with a man who intrigued her more with each passing moment.

The irony was not lost on her.

"Thank you."

With a nod, Björn slipped the shirt back on, hiding his bare chest from view. She could not help but think she should have lingered over the task some more.

"I will accompany you when you go to the hut."

Dunne started at the unexpected declaration. Björn wanted to accompany her? Why? "You don't have to—"

"No, I know, but I want to. It will be my way of thanking you for what you're doing for Ingrid."

"There's no need. I'm enjoying it. Besides, I'm doing it to repay you for the ale, as you well know."

"Sigurd and Frigyth should have been the ones repaying me for the cask. You don't live with them."

"I've been drinking the ale as well, so it—"

"Listen, we can argue the matter over until dusk and still not agree." He crossed his arms over his chest, looking every inch the determined male. She should have bristled. Instead she shivered. "If you don't want me to accompany you, then I won't. Just tell me as much."

What was she doing? Why was she hesitating? It should have been simple. Did she want to go to the hut alone? No. Did she want to spend a day with Björn? Yes.

"No please, come with me," she said eventually.

He nodded as if he'd not doubted this issue for a moment. "I will come to you at dawn tomorrow. Be ready for me."

Dunne's heart skipped a beat. The words sounded more evocative than he probably intended. Or perhaps it was just her. "I will."

CHAPTER THREE

"This is Demon, my horse." Wolf gestured to the black stallion tethered behind him. "Björn told me you intended to go to the village beyond the forest. He will take you there."

"Thank you." Dunne placed a hand on the animal's rump gingerly. Not that there was any need to be wary. The horse seemed rather placid, just like its huge master. "Erm. He's... impressive."

The Icelander smiled. "I know. You're not the first person to comment on his size."

"I'm sorry to be so predictable," she mumbled.

A chuckle reached her from behind. "I'm glad you spoke before I did, because I was about to say the same thing." Björn laughed. "I would hate to be seen as the predictable one. Much better it was you."

She had no idea if he was lying to try to alleviate her embarrassment or if he spoke the truth but either way the show of support comforted her. She thanked him with a brief smile.

"Björn, you'll climb on first," Wolf instructed. "I'll help Dunne on once you're settled."

Apparently she was to ride pillion, something she had never done before. Two strong hands grabbed her by the waist and hoisted her up. She lifted her leg instinctively and found herself sitting on top of the enormous horse. Before she had time to prepare herself for the intimacy of the contact, she found herself wrapped around Björn like a vine. Her arms encircled his trim waist, her legs bracketed him, and her chest was plastered against his taut back. He was warm and solid against her.

She almost closed her eyes in delight.

"Do you feel secure enough?" Wolf asked. "You'll need to hold on tight while you ride."

Yes. That was the problem. She made a sound that could pass for an agreement and looked away.

After one last thanks to Wolf, Björn clicked his tongue and Demon walked on.

As they progressed, it became harder and harder not to place her cheek against his shoulder blade. There was no choice but to resist the urge, however. Holding him was justified by her position, but what would he think if she started rubbing against him in the same way cats sometimes rubbed against her, as if trying to burrow under her skin?

They reached the village too soon for her liking. She could have spent the whole day riding with Björn's warm body pressed against hers. It felt...natural, which did not make sense. They had only known each other for a week.

"The hut is out of the village, this way."

She indicated a path meandering through young saplings. Björn steered the stallion in that direction without a word. As they neared the place, Dunne's heart started a wild drum in her chest. Memories flooded her, each more unpleasant than the last. The stream where she had drawn water to cook the food Toland always disparaged, the meadow where she put his disgusting clothes to dry, the oak, at whose foot, she had cried herself to exhaustion too many times.

Why had she come? She should have sent Wolf and Sigurd to sort things out. Simply being here made her nauseous. Her arms instinctively tightened around Björn as if in search of comfort.

And then, at last, the hut appeared through the trees. A gasp escaped her lips.

She had expected to find the place deserted, but it was a hub of activity. What was happening? The hut's door was open, people were coming and going with their hands full of various objects. She saw a tall, ginger man carry the blanket her mother had made for her when she was a child and load it into a waiting cart. Her heart jumped in her throat. No! She could not be parted from that! It was the only thing she had left of her mother.

"Who are these men?" Björn asked over his shoulder.

"I recognize only one, Toland's brother. I imagine the others are his friends. But what are they doing here?"

"They are stealing your possessions, that's what they're doing!" Björn replied, urging Demon into a canter.

A heartbeat later, they came to a halt in front of Leodred. His eyes went wide when he recognized her. "Dunne!"

"Leodred," she said frostily. He had always been more affable than Toland but that didn't mean much. Next to her husband anyone would have been considered personable and right now she was not disposed to generosity. He was, after all, stealing what little she possessed.

Björn was already off the horse and waiting to help her jump down. She thanked him with a squeeze of her fingers and planted herself in front of Leodred.

"What are you doing here? Why are you taking my things?"

The man scratched his thinning hair. "Well, I thought you'd

left after Toland's death, you see, and I had no idea where you'd gone."

Was that his excuse? She'd been gone less than two weeks! "I did leave. But this is still my house."

"Actually..."

That one word sent dread along her spine. "Actually?"

The man shuffled on his feet. "The day he died, Toland had visited me to tell me that he intended to bequeath the house to me in the event of this death."

Dunne worked very hard to hide her shock. Her husband had decided to leave her and their daughter destitute? Was that what his brother was saying? But why was she even surprised? He had borne her no love. Instead of betraying her hurt and disbelief, she chose another tack.

"The day he died, he'd gone to visit one of his many lovers, not you."

Leodred did not have the decency to appear uncomfortable. Evidently he thought Toland's love life was none of her concern. As his wife, she could not quite agree, even if she had not been jealous.

"He did go to her, but first he came to me. Business first, pleasure after, I guess."

What could she say to that? Nothing.

When he saw she didn't answer, Leodred let his gaze wander over her. Dunne shivered in revulsion. The two brothers shared similar features and for the first time she had an inkling of how Toland would have appeared if he had looked at her with desire. Perhaps it was for the best he had not, because the result made her flesh crawl. The man was practically licking his lips.

"Between you and me, I never understood why Toland chose to go to other women when he had you in his bed. I told him so many times. Surely a woman like you can provide a man adequate relief?"

Behind her she heard what sounded like a snarl and suddenly she felt a masculine presence looming over her. Goaded beyond endurance by the pathetic display, Björn had decided to intervene. She was instantly comforted.

"You claim the house is yours, that Toland gave it to you in preference to his wife and child," Björn said, deliberately ignoring the lewd comments. "That's very convenient, is it not? What proof do you have of all this? Or are we to accept your word without question?"

Leodred blinked at him. "And who are you?"

Björn clenched his fists. He'd heard and seen enough of the man, who was nothing but a despicable liar and a lecher to boot. He just wanted him and his cronies gone.

"Nevermind who I am, it is of no import. If the house really belongs to you, you had better prove it to Dunne before you start stealing her possessions."

"Alas, as we know, my brother met his demise the very day he told me of his decision. There was no time to inform anyone else."

"What a shame." Björn bared his teeth menacingly, glad to stand several inches taller than the Saxon. He was impressing him without effort. "So, in the absence of proof, the house still belongs to Dunne. As does everything inside it. You had better start unloading that cart."

There was a pause as the man considered his next move but Dunne took a step forward, standing her ground. "Start with the blanket. I'll be taking it with me today."

Leodred took in a sharp breath, not best pleased to be ordered about by a woman. "There is, of course, an obvious way to solve the problem," he said, his gaze fastening onto her. The look in his eyes was predatory. Björn felt his hairs raise on end. "You and I could marry. Then we would both own the—"

"No."

The word exploded out of his mouth and he placed himself in front of Dunne to make his intent crystal clear. This man would marry her over his dead body. Not that there was any risk it would ever happen. He could tell from the way her body had tensed that she didn't want to be Leodred's wife either. Björn could only congratulate himself on having accompanied her today. The idea of her having to face the scoundrel on her own made his stomach churn.

Leodred was not so easily beaten, however. "Leave us, pup," he said dismissively. "No one asked for your opinion. Dunne doesn't need you to handle these negotiations. Why, you could be her son!"

Björn gritted his teeth. Did the man have to hit where it hurt? He knew he was markedly younger than her, but it didn't signify anything for him. Besides, he didn't have to take it lying down, did he? He could give as good as he got. "I *could* be her son, but only if she had given birth to me at age ten, after being bedded at age nine by a lecherous goat old enough to be her grandfather."

The man blinked once. Twice. Then he frowned. "Are you calling me a lecherous goat?"

"A bit slow on the uptake, are we, old man?" Björn sneered. "Must be the age."

"Listen here, you—"

"No. *You* listen to me. Dunne is not marrying you, or anyone. She is not going anywhere but back to the Norsemen village with me, and you will leave her and her house alone. Us three here know there is no validity in your claim that the house belongs to you, so you will drop it."

"You are no one, you have no right to meddle in—"

"On the contrary, I have every right. She's carrying my child."

A stunned silence followed the declaration. Dunne looked at him with eyes as round as coins. In that moment she looked remarkably like her daughter. But Björn was not going to back down so easily. Leodred was not getting his filthy hands on her property—much less on her body.

"So you see," Björn concluded, straightening up to his full height. "Unless you want to fight me for her, which I would be only too happy to do, you will back right off."

"I'm carrying your child! What were you *thinking* saying such a thing?"

Dunne rounded on Björn, torn between disbelief and outrage. What had gotten into him that he could make such a ludicrous claim?

It had had one advantage though. After having deposited her belongings back inside the house under Björn's menacing glare, Leodred and his friends had left.

For a moment she had feared they would take advantage of the fact that they outnumbered him four to one, but mercifully they had seemed to conclude that he was more than capable of taking them on. Perhaps the men Leodred had rounded up had been reluctant to pillage her home to begin with, or perhaps they thought Björn would prove a formidable adversary, especially if she sided with him. Whatever the reason, they had not even tried to go against him from the moment they'd heard him claim he was the father of her unborn child.

Too stunned to react to the declaration at first, then too

relieved to see the men leave, she had kept her temper in check for as long as she could but as soon as the cart had disappeared around the bend, she exploded.

"How could you say something like that without even consulting with me first?"

Björn was not impressed by her outburst. "When could I consult with you? How? Leodred needed to be told in no uncertain terms that he could not lay claim to you. If I had asked to speak to you privately in the middle of the conversation, it would have looked as if we were concocting a story, a story he would never have believed."

He had a point, but she refused to acknowledge it. "So it was better to act the part of the possessive oaf?"

He twisted his lips. "Yes. And what is it to you if *I* am seen as an oaf anyway?"

She refused to be amused. "Why did you do that?"

His answer took her by surprise. "Sigurd once told me he had pretended to be Frigyth's husband to save her from a union she didn't want."

Dunne stared at him. As Frigyth's sister, she knew all about the deception that had taken place some three years ago. But that lie had ended up in a true, happy marriage. "What does that have to do with anything?"

Björn shrugged, as if the answer was obvious. It wasn't to her. "It gave me the idea of pretending we were involved. I could not claim we were married. Leodred would only have asked to see proof of the union, and there is none."

No, there wouldn't be, since they were not married. The mere idea of belonging to another man sent her heart fluttering in anguish. She had sworn to herself that she would never marry again. Dunne forced herself to focus. They were not discussing marriage, fortunately, only the lie he had spun.

"But there is no proof that I am carrying your child either," she said in a whisper.

Björn's gaze landed on Dunne's stomach. It looked so soft and inviting, the perfect place to pillow his head after making love to her and watch as a new life bloomed inside her. He cleared his throat. Why was he getting lost in such fanciful musings? Since when had his physical craving for her become a longing for more? For a family together?

Things were progressing at an alarming speed.

"It was the only thing I could do to stop the man. And there is no proof that you are *not* with child at the moment," he answered roundly. "Leodred has no choice but to take my word for it. Pregnancies do not show until a few months in. I knew the blaggard would not want to raise a Norseman's bastard or risk marrying a woman already with child."

She still didn't appear convinced. "But we never even slept together!"

"I know." By the gods, didn't he know it. Sleeping with her was all he could think of day and night. "But Leodred doesn't. And we could easily have." All too easily. Right now he was battling the need to carry her over to her pallet and bury himself deep within her, show her that he would do much more than lie to protect her from other men's lust.

"But..." Dunne hesitated.

He steeled himself. "But what?"

Please don't let her say that she agreed with Leodred, that she thought him young enough to be her son...Please, let her not see him in that light. He was a man, damn it all! Never had he felt more like one than in front of her, a woman he desired.

"Don't you have a sweetheart back at the village, a girl who could take exception to the lie?"

He let out a breath. She was only worried about the possible damage to his love life. If she assumed he had one, it meant she didn't think him too young to even think about bedding women. The relief was palpable.

"No, I don't have a sweetheart," he growled. "Don't worry about me. What matters is that you won't have to marry yet another man you don't want."

There was a pause as she absorbed what he'd just said. Then she nodded. "Yes. That is all that matters. I suppose I should thank you."

"I suppose you should." He arched a brow. "Whenever you're ready."

She pinched her lips at his provoking words. "Thank you, Björn."

"You're very welcome. After all, lying didn't cost me anything."

No, perhaps not. Still. Dunne was grateful for his help. There was no denying she would have had a hard time dealing with Leodred without him. She had not even thought to doubt the fact that her brother-in-law now owned the hut. Had Björn not been there she would not have realized that, without proof, he could not dispossess her.

"Shall we? I would like to reach the village before nightfall if possible, and see Dawn."

He nodded and led her back to Demon. After stuffing the blanket in the saddlebags he had insisted on bringing with them, he helped her back into the saddle. It was only when he climbed on himself that she realized he had put her in front this time. At first she was glad of the change, as it meant she wouldn't have to press herself against his back or feel his body rub the tender place between her legs. But then she saw how utterly engulfed in his embrace she was. With his strong thighs cradling her buttocks, his chest supporting her back and his arms holding the reins around her, she was not going anywhere.

"I thought we might try it this way since Wolf is not here to help you into the saddle," Björn said, his voice reaching her from somewhere above her head.

"Yes." She could not have uttered more than that one word if her life had depended on it.

The horse started to move and it all became even more intimate. No longer able to keep her back straight she had no choice but to mold herself against Björn's solid chest.

To hide her unease she started talking about a girl from the Norsemen village called Gertrud. She'd had the impression that all the men in the village lusted after her. Perhaps Björn was one of them. Talking about a girl he was attracted to might distract him and make him forget how intimately he was holding her.

"She has the palest, bluest eyes I've ever seen. And that's saying something, since I have seen more blue eyes since I arrived at the village than I thought possible." She gave a little laugh. Could Björn hear how nervous she was? Probably. But at least he could not see her face, which had no doubt become flushed. "I think Frigyth and Merewen, and Dawn and I, of course, must be the only people there with eyes that are not blue. Gertrud's really are extraordinary."

They were. But Dunne found herself thinking that she preferred the blue to be deeper, like...Well, just like Björn's. It was more arresting, less crystal-like, almost velvety. She shook her head. Velvety eyes...What was she thinking?

Seeing that he didn't respond, she carried on with her rambling, talking about the first thing that came to mind. Anything would be better than silence.

"I heard that Magnus the smithy broke his anvil the other day. I cannot imagine how one might do that, but evidently it is possible. Can you fathom such a thing?"

There was no answer.

By THE GODS, he was going to come. Here, out in the open, whilst fully dressed and sitting on a horse, just from holding Dunne in his lap and hearing her talk about...Björn gritted his teeth. What was she talking about exactly? Blue eyes and the village smithy's anvil? He had no idea and he didn't care. All he knew was that he had been hard from the moment he had settled her between his legs. Why had he suggested she might want to swap and sit in front of him?

Every movement of the horse sent him closer to explosion. When it walked, the gentle rocking was impossible to withstand. When it trotted it was even worse, and he did not dare canter, knowing he would be unable to focus properly. The last thing he wanted was to send them both toppling head over heels. To make matters worse, he had not stroked himself in days, too ashamed to picture Dunne to bring himself release now that he knew her and he had met her young daughter.

But now...The unusually long abstinence was taking its toll. The way her buttocks were rubbing against him was sweet torture, the warmth of her body, the softness of her curves cradling him was beautiful agony. It was all...too much...He was going to...*Ah!*

In one powerful rush, he erupted, warmth flooding his braies. A groan escaped his lips, almost a whimper. Never had anything so delicious felt so excruciating.

Dunne stopped talking about whatever she was talking about and looked at him over her shoulder. "Björn, are you all right?"

No, he was not all right, never had he felt worse, or more humiliated. Had she heard him groan? Had she...Damnation, had she felt anything? His hardness, the heat blooming between their two bodies?

"Yes," he breathed. "I'm all right. Only I need…"

He needed to get her off of him before she realized what had happened, if by some miracle she hadn't already. Pulling on the reins, he jumped from the saddle as quickly as if he had been scalded by his release and hurried toward the undergrowth.

"I'll hold Demon while you see to your needs," he heard Dunne say.

Oh, now she thought he was going to shit himself. How much worse could it all get? This was a nightmare.

He looked at his wet lap in consternation, not sure what to do next. Never before had he come in his braies, or even come close. Thankfully, he was wearing dark clothes so nothing showed, and his erection had subsided. He might be able to get away with it if he behaved as if nothing was amiss. In any case he could not remain here all day. At some point he would have to leave his hiding place and face Dunne.

Dunne patted the stallion's neck, trying to calm the beating of her heart. What sort of a wanton creature was she turning into? She had no idea, but feeling Björn behind her, with his member hard as rock, had created havoc with her senses. At first she had thought that the protuberance she felt pressing against the small of her back might be part of the saddle but then she had understood it was not. Heat had flooded her veins at the realization. The man holding her in his arms was aroused.

Impressively so.

Of course, this had nothing to do with her, could not have anything to do with her. Gertrud was most probably the reason. Why, oh, why, had she talked to him about the girl who roused all the men's interest when in all probability the motion of the horse was enough to stir a man's lust? Why did she have to add to the problem? She had never ridden with a man before, but she should have seen it coming.

She should have refused to sit in front of him. It had been marginally less intimate being at the back. At least she had been none the wiser about his body's response to being in the saddle.

Björn soon reappeared, a look she could not decipher on his face. Then she understood it was embarrassment. Yes, that had to be it. He probably feared she would end up noticing his hardness if they carried on as they'd been earlier. Well, too late, she had already noticed. Not that she would tell him as much, of course. But she could spare him further humiliation, at least.

"I will sit behind you for the rest of the journey, if you don't mind," she murmured, not quite able to meet his eye. "It was more comfortable than in the front."

Had he just groaned? With her gaze on the ground, she could not be sure. She waited, still not looking at him.

"Very well," he said gruffly. "I'm sorry I suggested the change."

Oh, now he would take her for an ungrateful wretch. "It's nothing to do with you," she specified hurriedly, "only, I felt as if I hampered your handling of the reins placed where I was. You would be more comfortable, no doubt, if you were able to see where you're going."

She had to stop talking now, before she admitted that the feel of his hardness rubbing against her had roused unholy feelings within her.

"Yes," he agreed slowly.

"And here I can use a log or a rock as a mounting block. No need for Wolf to help me up."

Nodding, Björn led Demon to a fallen tree. He climbed on first, then held out his hand to her. Placing her left foot on the stirrup, she hoisted herself up as best as she could.

"Hold me tighter," Björn instructed, his voice gruffer than ever. He was angry with her, and no wonder. She had insulted him moments after he had helped her get rid of Leodred. "Otherwise you are going to fall as soon as we move."

She tightened her arms around his trim waist and felt her breasts flatten against his back. The heat of his body warmed the place between her thighs. Again.

Mm. Perhaps she should have offered to walk.

CHAPTER FOUR

"**M**ama, wake up!"

Dunne bolted upright, jolted from the most licentious, forbidden, exquisite dream she had ever had. The interruption was as welcome as having the contents of an icy bucket thrown in her face while she was luxuriating in the sunshine.

"What's the matter?" she panted, looking at her daughter.

"Are you all right? You were moaning, like I do when I have a tummy ache. Do you have a tummy ache, too?"

Mm, no, the ache was situated lower. In fact, her whole body felt afire, on the brink of something she had never experienced before. As if that was not bad enough, the place between her legs was throbbing, urging her to put an end to the discomfort. But how? She had no notion of how her body worked. She suspected the place where a man joined with her was the place that could give her the satisfaction she was after, but she had no idea how to achieve that satisfaction. Should she squeeze her legs, use her hand? In what way?

In any case, she was not alone in the pallet, but next to her innocent daughter. She had better wipe such licentious thoughts from her mind.

"I'm all right, sweetie, don't worry. I...Maybe I ate too much of Aunt Frigyth's bread last night. It's nothing, anyway, I will be fine." She kissed the mop of curls. "Go back to sleep, it's the middle of the night."

Thankfully Dawn did not argue and shuffled back to her side of the pallet where she promptly fell back to sleep. Dunne collapsed back onto the furs with a sigh. She had been dreaming of Björn and was on the verge of...something. Something she didn't quite understand but knew instinctively would have been glorious.

His hands had been all over her, caressing her, his lips at her neck, his tongue licking her skin, his—

Dear God. He had been making love to her in a way that bore no resemblance to what she had experienced in Toland's bed and, as a result, the sensations in her body had been unprecedented, delicious. Although it had only been a dream, she could still feel the embers of the brazier glowing, even long after the flames had been extinguished by Dawn's interruption. The caresses had been a product of her overheated mind, but the burning they had created in her body was all too real.

This had been caused by their ride that afternoon no doubt —and possibly his talk of her carrying his child.

As irate as she had been at the time for the liberty he had taken, the idea had inflamed her imagination, there was no denying it. Because, to be with child, she would have had to lie with him and welcome him inside her body, the most intimate act a man and woman could share together.

How would she bear to face Björn after what they had done in her dream? His fingers had been inside her, for heaven's sake, stoking her need! Well, not truly, but...It felt as if they had. She would not be able to look at his hands, his mouth, his groin, without blushing like a young maid. Not that she should be looking at these in the first place, or try to imagine where to place her lips on him when she looked at him...

Oh, what a silly, silly goose she was being.

Why would Björn, who was the epitome of male beauty, be interested in someone like her, an older woman of unexceptional appeal, a widow with a child, when all the girls in the village lusted after him?

When the sun rose, she still didn't have the answer to that question.

She decided a good dunking in cold water would help restore her to her senses. Leaving Dawn with Frigyth, she set off for the river. It was chilly, but the sun was shining.

With luck, she would emerge from the water with her blood—and her imagination—cooled.

BLOODY BLEEDING HELL.

Björn had never been one for swearing out loud but if ever there was a time to emulate Sigurd, who had always been some sort of a role model for him, this was it.

In front of him, standing on the riverbank, was Dunne. Stark naked. No. Worse than naked, or rather *better* than naked, his frazzled brain amended.

Somehow the wet, transparent shift plastered to her body made the vision even more spectacular, even more tempting. He could see almost everything, the pebbled nipples, the generous breasts, the soft stomach, the rounded hips, the dark curls at the apex of her thighs. And what he couldn't see he could all too well imagine. The smooth skin, the tight buttocks, the soft petals hidden between her legs.

Head thrown to the skies, back arched, arms up, she was

wringing water from her glorious hair. How was he going to get this image of pure decadence out of his head? It had been bad enough trying to forget her when he had only seen her dressed but now…Now he had no chance.

He was as hard as he had ever been, so hard it ached. In an effort to alleviate some of the tension twisting his body, he put his hand over his straining member and squeezed. Damn it, he was ready to burst.

He should go, stop spying on her, leave before he did something he regretted, but his feet were glued to the ground. His mind had gone blank. His limbs felt heavy and light at the same time. His throat had forgotten how to swallow. The only parts of him that seemed to work were his eyes, which looked their fill at the goddess in front of him, and his cock, which demanded immediate release.

He squeezed harder.

Just then Dunne opened her eyes and saw him. Her gaze fell to his hand, which was still wrapped around his shaft and her lips parted in shock. And little wonder…It would have looked as if he was stroking himself while spying on her nakedness.

Bloody bleeding hell.

He turned and fled like a murderer would flee the scene of a crime. It was the coward's way out but nothing he did would make this any worse. She already thought him the most shameful voyeur so he might as well do what he needed to do. As soon as he reached the protection of the trees, he tore at his braies. He was going to die if he did not relieve the pressure building in his body. Once he had granted his body the release it needed, he might be able to think straight and decide on the best course of action. At the moment, he was in too much pain to do anything other than ease the pressure boiling in his veins.

With a grunt of frustration, he took himself in hand and

started to pump his steel-hard shaft. Blood was drumming in his ears, rushing to his groin. He was so primed, it was over in a moment. The groan he gave when he came seemed wrenched from his marrow. Ah, if only he could expel his craving for the maddening Saxon as easily as he forced his seed out of his body! He had no idea where all this would lead but he feared he was not ready for it.

Panting, he tucked himself back into his braies. Now what? Dare he go back to the river and speak to Dunne, explain himself? No, of course not. What could he say anyway?

Forgive me, I got so hard watching your naked body I had to go stroke myself while I imagined you writhing under me. I hope you're not offended.

He had better run back to the hut and pretend nothing had happened. With luck Dunne would do the same and they would be able to get past the awful moment. He turned—and found himself staring into bright amber irises.

Dunne stared into Björn's sky-blue eyes as understanding dawned.

Not only had he needed to bring himself to climax now, after seeing her emerge from the water, but the previous day, on the horse, he had fled precipitously because he'd needed the same relief. He'd gone to stroke himself away from her, just like he had now. Now she knew why he'd been so embarrassed, so gruff when he'd come back from behind the bushes.

"You...When we rode together yesterday, did you jump down from the horse because you wanted to—"

"Bloody hell!" he exploded, going red to the roots of his hair. "No, it's not what you think, I—"

She stopped him with a raised hand. It was better if she put an end to this conversation. She should never have asked the question in the first place. But even if he had not brought about his release then, he had definitely done it now. As she had approached the clump of trees, she had seen his hand move frantically in front of him, she had heard his satisfied grunts when he'd reached his release. Though she had never felt pleasure herself, she was not so innocent as to mistake what he'd done.

Heat flooded her veins.

Why had he felt the need to relieve himself out in the open with such urgency?

Was it because he had seen her in a shocking state of undress? She could well imagine that a hot-blooded youth would find the sight of a half-naked woman arousing, especially if the imperfections of her body were hidden under her wet shift. Björn would have fantasized about what he couldn't see rather than lust after what he could glimpse. But then, what about yesterday, on the horse? She hadn't been naked then, or even close, she hadn't even been looking at him.

Then it all came back to her. They had been talking about Gertrud at the time. How could she have forgotten that all-important detail? His blood had become overheated imagining what he could do to the pretty girl, that was all. It had had nothing to do with her, a woman old enough to be, if not his mother, as Leodred had teased, at least his aunt. And right now, the sudden sight of her exposed curves had taken him by surprise, flooding him with uncontrollable desire. His body had reacted before his mind could comprehend who he was seeing.

"Why did you follow me?" Björn asked, getting over the embarrassment of the moment faster than her.

Dunne didn't know what to answer. She'd thrown her mother's blanket over her shoulders for modesty before following him, but she had no idea what had compelled her to go to him in the first place.

"I'm s-sorry," she stammered, unable to explain or understand the urge. "I shouldn't have."

"No, you shouldn't have."

For a long moment they stared at each other. Dunne's heart was drumming hard in her chest, fire was rushing through her veins. To think she had come to the river to cool her blood and forget about her lascivious dream! So much for trying to put the desire she felt for this man at the back of her mind! Now she would have to imagine him giving himself pleasure while he thought of her.

She turned and fled without a word.

This had been a disaster.

***

"I'M LEAVING THE VILLAGE."

When Ingrid stared at him, Björn wished he'd been less abrupt. "You're leaving?"

"Only for a time, don't worry. A few months at best."

Time enough for Dunne to find herself a new home and leave the Norsemen village. He could not stay here, not when the need for her was torturing him every moment of every day, not when he had embarrassed himself not just once but twice in front her. After the humiliating incident on the horse and what had happened this morning, he was never going to be able to face her again. He dreaded to think what she would think of him.

Nothing good, in all probability.

As far as the woman of his dreams was concerned, he was nothing but a randy, excitable youth who went around spreading lies about fathering children onto her, spying on her half-naked body, and touching himself while he thought of her. It was a disaster. And so he had to go.

Ingrid made a face, as if she weren't sure what to think of his decision. "What brought this on?"

He shrugged. How could he tell her that he lusted after the woman she saw as a friend and had most probably scared her away with his crudeness? "I should be back before summer," he said instead of answering the question. "Will you be all right here on your own?"

Was he being selfish? A few months after the shocking death of their parents, he was going to abandon her in turn. Should he not stay and find a solution to his dilemma? But Ingrid merely laughed.

"Me? Of course I'll be all right! I mean, what do you do here except make ale anyway? I'm the man of the house, in case you hadn't noticed."

He gave a reluctant laugh and kissed her cheek. They often jested that he was the one doing what was seen as a women's work and she was more independent than the average seventeen-year-old girl. Since the death of their parents back in spring, they had found a way to live together that did not fit the traditional model but suited both their temperament and abilities.

It had been good, but almost overnight this situation had become stifling. First his parents' son, then Ingrid's brother, Björn had never a man in his own right, in a position to have his own family. He had to leave, go somewhere where he could be himself and not just someone associated with somebody else. Here in the place where he'd been born, where people had seen him grow, he would always be Rorik's first born child. It was time for him to be Björn, a man with no past and a future of his own choosing ahead of him. In the village people treated him like a youth, dabbling with domestic chores, unable to speak their language properly and destined to marry one of their daughters, someone he had known all his life.

He wanted to erase that Björn and finally be the man he could be.

Most of all, he wanted to free himself of the hold Dunne had over him. When he'd found out she was widowed, he had started to hope she could see him differently. But she did not. Worse, the few days he'd spent in her company had shown him that after her unhappy marriage, she was not looking for a man, much less someone like him, who was constantly being talked of as a boy.

"I love you, sister, you know that?" he said, engulfing Ingrid into his arms.

"I do, and I love you too." She sighed against his chest.

"I'll go pack now."

"Where will you go?"

"I think I will go board a ship bound for Denmark." The further the better. He needed distance from the intoxicating Saxon filling his dreams and fueling his wildest fantasies. With luck he would come back home cured from his infatuation.

"Denmark!" This time Ingrid looked alarmed.

"You know I've always wanted to go to the land of our mother and father. It's time I did. In the spring it will be the anniversary of their death. I want to be on their native land when it happens. I wish to honor them that way."

"I understand."

They both went to bed in a pensive mood.

At dawn, after a restless night, Björn was ready to depart. But before he went there was something he needed to do. He walked over to Dunne's hut, hoping to find her daughter playing outside. He remembered Dunne complaining to Ingrid once that the child was an early riser. Luck was with him. The little girl was already out, and on her own.

"Bee?"

The little girl raised her head. "Bear?"

He smiled. The bear and the bee. That image never failed to amused him. Such a contrast between the two animals, just like between the two of them. He must be four times her size, as big and strong as she was small and delicate. Would she one day grow into a woman as beautiful as her mother? With those eyes and that dimple, it was almost certain. What fool of a man would long for her the way he was longing for Dunne, he wondered?

"I have something for you. Come."

Taking her by the hand, he led her to the hayloft. Barley was sleeping in her favorite corner while her brood tumbled about in the hay. The kittens had grown in the last few days and were now ready to be separated from their mother. Just like him, they were still young but strong enough to live their independent lives and have a chance at love. He reached out to the white female that had attracted Bee's attention the day they'd met. He smiled when he remembered how Dunne had struck him. It now seemed a lifetime ago. The bruises on his arm had faded and he hoped to repair his soul while he was away.

"This one is for you. You can take her home."

"For me?" The little girl was so stunned that she didn't even reach out for the animal.

"For you. On one condition. You have to promise to take good care of her. I think you will, because you love animals."

"I do," she said, finally taking the kitten from him and hugging her tight. The animal settled in her arms as easily as if she had always known her. "But why are you giving her to me?"

"Because she is now old enough to leave her mother and I want you to have something to remember me by. I'm leaving the village and we might never meet again." Simply saying the words out loud tightened his chest.

"You're leaving?" Bee sounded dismayed at the idea and suddenly he wondered if going to Denmark was such a good idea after all.

He steeled himself. It would be hard, undoubtedly, but it was the only thing to do.

"I'm leaving today. Tell your mother..." He cleared his throat. What would he want Dunne to know? He wasn't sure. Nothing he could tell an innocent little girl anyway. "Tell her I hope she doesn't mind you having a cat. I should have asked for her permission before I gave her to you."

The child nodded. "Thank you for the cat. I will call her...I don't know how I will call her. I've never had an animal before." Bee's face fell.

"It doesn't matter. You don't have to decide now. Take your time. The name will come to you when you're ready."

He ran a hand along the back of his neck to stop himself from lifting the little girl into his arms and giving her a hug. Damn it but he would miss her. Not in the same way he would miss her mother, but he would.

"Now, I have to go. Goodbye, Bee."

CHAPTER FIVE

"**B**ear!"

Dunne froze. Either her daughter had just spotted a bear baiter walk through the village with his animal on a chain, which she doubted, or she had just seen someone who bore the animal's name stand right behind her.

"Bee."

Oh, Lord.

It had to be him. No other adult called her daughter Bee. No one else had this rich, husky voice. No one else could make her shiver with just one word. It *was* him, she just knew it.

Slowly, she turned in time to see Dawn throw herself into Björn's arms. He lifted her up as easily as if he'd expected the demonstration of affection and was happy to receive it. Her heart flipped over in her chest at the sight of the two them entwined together. For a moment they looked like any father and daughter would.

"I have to go and tell the cousins you're back! They won't believe their eyes!" Dawn exclaimed, wiggling out of Björn's arms. He deposited her on the floor with a slanted smile.

"Run along. I wouldn't want anyone other than you to announce my return to the village."

All too soon, they were alone.

For a moment, they stared at each other. Dunne could barely believe her eyes, as Dawn had just said. After months away from her, Björn was back. And he looked different. Was it the beard? Was it the braids? Was it the newfound assurance? She didn't know. Or perhaps she didn't remember him properly. Had he always been so tall? He seemed to tower over her, which she did not remember. Had he always been so muscular? His chest seemed impossibly broad, even more chiseled than before. Dear. She had been struck by his beauty in the autumn, she was now overwhelmed by his masculine presence. And they had not even exchanged a single word. What would it be when he started teasing her, as she expected him to do?

"What are you doing here?" she asked eventually.

He arched a brow, as if the question was unwarranted. Or perhaps he had taken exception to the accusation in her tone. After all, she had not even greeted him before launching it.

"I live here, in case you'd forgotten," he said, tilting his head. "I think I should ask you what *you* are doing here."

She flushed. Her first words to him and she was already making a fool of herself. Indeed, why wouldn't he be here? Unlike her, the village was his home. "I heard you'd left for Denmark, is what I mean."

The blow had been as hard to deal with as it had been sudden. When Dawn had told her Björn had given her a cat because he was leaving, she had refused to believe it. Her daughter must have misunderstood, and he had most likely only gone to town for the day. But later that evening Ingrid had told Frigyth and Sigurd her brother had gone to Denmark and there had been no choice but to accept that he had really left.

Left without warning or even saying goodbye.

She had berated herself for the pain she had felt at the notion because after all, why should he warn her of his intent or tell her goodbye? She was nothing to him, and he had embarrassed himself in front of her more than once. He was probably glad to see the back of her. No, in the circumstances she should not have expected anything from him.

But she had been hurt all the same.

"I did leave for Denmark. But I always intended to come back. Now will you answer me? Why are you still here?"

Dunne refused to think she had delayed her leaving because she had known Björn would return eventually, and she had waited for him. Besides, it was not just that. She felt good here in the Norsemen village, amongst people who didn't judge her. For the first time in her life, she was free and there had been no reason to put an end to a situation that suited her.

She shrugged, deciding to be honest. "I see no reason to rush, since I am not accountable to anyone for my actions. And Dawn seems to like it here. She spends her days with her cousins, running around like a..."

"Like a bee?" Björn supplied when she faltered.

She could not help a smile. "Bees do not run, you know."

He smiled back. "No. All the same, I think you'll agree it's an apt image."

"It is."

That was what she had missed, she realized when he laughed, this inexplicable bond between them. The man was breathtakingly handsome, but he was first and foremost easy to be with. He rubbed at his chest absentmindedly, as if to scratch an insect bite hidden under his clothes. She found herself mesmerized by the movement. Dear God, he *had* grown stronger.

And she even more besotted.

Oh, this was not good.

By the gods, he had missed her!

For seven long months Björn had done his best to forget the beautiful Saxon and he had almost convinced himself he had succeeded. He should have known he was only fooling himself. If three years had not been enough to take out of his mind a woman he didn't know, how had he hoped to forget in a few months someone he had become friends with, someone he had seen all but naked? He was no impressionable youth anymore, but a man who knew it was not every day you met someone like Dunne. She made him hard and she made him melt at the same time.

While they were alone and he had the chance, there was something he needed to ask, something he had tortured himself over more times than he cared to remember during his time in Denmark.

"Did you come to an agreement with Leodred in the end?" he asked, running a hand along his jaw. It still felt odd to have a beard. Odd but good. It gave him confidence, a confidence he had not had before, especially in front of Dunne. It seemed to give him the legitimacy to address her as an equal.

"Yes. I went to see him about a month after our first visit."

"Alone?" The idea of her facing the man who had looked at her as a dog would look at his next meal made his blood boil.

She flushed, proving she had understood what he was getting at. "No. Wolf accompanied me. He had business in town that day, so I took the opportunity to go with him. I also..." The color in her cheeks reached all the way down her neck when she stopped.

"What did you do?"

"I placed some padding under my gown, to make it appear as if I was beginning to show. You know, just in case he started asking questions. I thought I might as well go along with the lie you told."

Yes...The lie that she had been carrying his babe. The idea of seeing her swelling with his child was enough to bring Björn to his knees. Because that would mean he had finally been allowed to do what he was dying to do and take her to bed.

No! He could not afford to weaken now, moments after he'd come back! He'd left precisely because he'd made a fool of himself where this woman was concerned. He would not make the same mistake on the day of his arrival. He would *not* start thinking of her writhing under him, he would *not* get hard!

"Did he bother you?" he asked, focusing on the topic at hand.

"No. Your stratagem worked. All through our discussion I could see him eyeing up my stomach with—" She flushed and he understood what she had not said out of consideration for him. Leodred had looked at her with revulsion. The man had thought he'd almost been saddled with a Norseman's bastard, a child that was half savage. "In the end we agreed on a compromise. He bought the hut from me for a reasonable sum."

Reasonable. No doubt she meant pitiful. Björn's nostrils flared. "You mean that you offered him a lowered price because he made you feel guilty about owning the hut?" Surely she knew the scoundrel was lying about Toland's supposed gift to him? She could and *should* have sold the house at a better price.

Dunne shrugged. It was clear she was not interested in justice as long as she was rid of the man. "He could well be telling the truth about Toland gifting him the hut. It would not surprise me in the least. It matters not anyway. I don't want to see it ever again, so he's welcome to it."

"Did you get your possessions back at least?"

"Yes. Sigurd borrowed the smithy's cart one day and came with me to get what little I actually wanted. I left the rest for Leodred." She shook her head. "I hated living there, and don't want anything to remind me of that time. I just want a fresh start."

His chest squeezed. He'd guessed by now that her marriage had been an unhappy one, but it gutted him to see how badly her husband had hurt her. Every time something or someone reminded her of him, she seemed to grow smaller, and the look in her eyes hardened. He would have to find out what had happened exactly. Perhaps he would ask Sigurd, who'd known the man.

Bee chose that moment to reappear and take him by the hand.

"Come, you have to see Hilda."

"Who is that?" He didn't know anyone by that name. But then again, he had been gone for months. New people could have settled in the village in the meantime. "A friend of yours?"

"No, silly!" A giggle left her throat. "The kitten you gave me. Well, she's not a kitten anymore. She's a big girl, like me."

In turn, Björn laughed. A big girl indeed! Bee was as fragile as a sparrow and utterly adorable. "And you gave her a person's name? When you prefer to be called by an animal name?"

"Yes." Bee was looking at him as if he were daft for not seeing the logic behind it. Perhaps he was, because he could not. "The only problem is, we think she's deaf," the little girl continued, looking crestfallen.

"Mm, she probably is. White cats with blue eyes often are, you know. It's not such a problem, as long as you love her."

The joy on her face, obstructed for a just a moment, returned. "I do love her! Come now, you must meet her."

With an apologetic glance at Dunne, he followed the little girl.

"Björn is back," Sigurd announced that night while they all sat at the table to eat.

Dunne stayed silent because she knew that already. In fact, she had spent the whole afternoon mulling over what his return would mean for her. It might well mean she would have to leave, because it had not taken her long to see that her feelings for him were not what they should be. But alas she would never be able to act on them. Nothing had changed over the winter. Björn was still the last man she should get involved with, and she was still determined to live her life on her own terms. She could not afford to have someone unsuitable put ideas into her head that would only end up causing her confusion and pain in the long term.

Sigurd sat down next to his wife. "I'll admit I won't mind not having to go to town to get my ale."

Frigyth let out a sigh. "I'm sorry, I just can't make anything that is beyond palatable, no matter how much I try."

"It's a good thing I didn't marry you for your ale-making skills then."

"Dare I ask why you—"

"No, you may not, wife, not while there are children present."

"What is the problem with children exactly?" Elwyn piped, quickly followed by his two brothers, Eirik and Little Halfdan, whom everyone called Moon. Dawn added her voice to the chorus of protests and soon a happy chaos reigned in the hut.

Dunne barely listened to the boisterous exchange. Björn was back. The three words drummed in her skull. What would she do now? She had no idea and she dreaded having to come up with an answer.

For months she had tried to persuade herself that the odd despondency tainting her days wasn't due to his absence. After all, they barely knew each other. But now that he was back and life had flowed back into her veins, she knew the truth for what it was.

She *had* missed him, in imperceptible ways.

When she had been forced to drink anything other than his wonderful, floral ale, she had bemoaned the change, every time the little white cat nestled itself on her lap, she felt gratitude to him for having gifted Dawn with her dream companion, whenever she greeted Ingrid, she thought back to the day she had repaired his shirt. The need for him had been constant, if fleeting. But in the same way a knife slash on its trunk poses no threat to a tree, the repetition of such little cuts cannot fail to compromise its integrity after a while. Each little nick whittled her soul a little bit more and after seven months of such treatment, it felt as if it had sustained significant damage, enough to make her dissatisfied with her life in a moment when she should have been unquestionably happy.

The day Frigyth had announced she was with child for the fourth time, Dunne had refused to let jealousy pierce through her. She never wanted to be married again, she'd had to remind herself sternly. For years she'd wanted to be free, and she now was. If that meant never bearing another child, then so be it. It was her decision and she was happy with it. Besides, her life was perfect as it was. She had been reunited with her sister, she was rid of Toland, and her daughter was thriving. Yes, she *was* happy, of course she was. She simply had not expected she would have to constantly remind herself of the fact.

"Dunne? Do you want more?"

Shaken out of her thoughts Dunne looked up at Frigyth, who was watching her with an arched brow. She noticed only then that the children had finished eating and left the hut.

"More?" she asked in a rasp. Yes, she did want more of the Norseman she had not managed to forget in seven long months. "More what?"

"Stew, silly." Frigyth laughed. "Where have you been? You look miles away."

"Oh, I...Yes. More stew would be lovely."

"I'll get this. You stay where you are, Birdie."

Sigurd kissed his wife's temple before standing up to go replenish the bowls. Frigyth smiled her thanks and placed a hand over her swollen stomach. She was now over seven months gone, and blooming. Dunne quickly repressed the pang of envy before it could twist her gut, another habit she had accustomed herself to these last few months. Perhaps she should leave the village, regardless of Björn's return. As much as she loved her sister and her brother-in-law, it was hard to have to witness their love day after day. Perhaps if she didn't have to constantly see what she could have she would not need to keep reminding herself about the happiness she already had.

"Do you know?" Sigurd said as he placed the filled bowls on the table. "Björn learned to speak Norse properly while he was in Denmark. He actually sounds quite good, as if he'd been born there."

Oh, was he trying to kill her?

She didn't need more reasons to be attracted to the Norseman! But if he now spoke Norse, he would not only look good enough to eat, he would also sound like one of his deities descended from the skies to strike mere mortals mute with awe. There was something intensely erotic in the rasping sounds of the Norse language, and she couldn't imagine what it would do to her to hear Björn speak it. It was bad enough when he spoke her language.

"If we'd known he would go to Denmark, we could have asked him to check on Rune and Eowyn while he was there," she heard Frigyth say. "Pity, but there was no helping it. He gave us no warning."

"Yes. I was surprised by his sudden departure," Sigurd

replied, sitting next to her. "What could have pushed him to leave so suddenly?"

Dunne knew the answer to that question only too well. Her. She stared at her bowl, her appetite for food quite gone, replaced by a hunger for something—someone—else.

What would she do now?

CHAPTER SIX

A̲rne slapped Björn on the shoulder and grinned. "Look at you, you mighty Dane! Have you grown even taller since you left? I swear you have! You look just like your father with the beard and the braids, you know." His friend ran a hand over his own smooth jaw. "Perhaps I should grow one as well. The women seem to like it."

"They like it on sturdy lads with square jaws, my friend, not on everyone. On you, a beard would look like moss on a craggy rock," Magnar scoffed. "Not as appealing."

"Oh? And what do you know about what girls want? At least I *can* grow a beard!" Arne jeered. "All you can do is sprout a few strands on your chin. I wonder how many hairs you've managed to grow on your balls. It must be a sorry—"

"You can stop wondering right now, or I will—"

"Well, you arrived just in time to join us, Björn," another of his friend added, cutting the pathetic argument short. "We'll drink to your return and then we'll celebrate. A group of us are going into town for a night of debauchery with willing women. Care to join us?"

Björn smirked. "You mean you're going to paid women?"

"Same thing. They are willing enough once you place a coin in their hand. The others don't seem to want us, so what else are we supposed to do?"

"Go without?" he suggested.

The stare the three lads threw him might have made him laugh if he had been in the mood to laugh. But he was not. Seeing Dunne earlier, realizing that the appeal she exerted over him had not diminished had been a blow. Had he sailed halfway across the world and risked being shipwrecked for nothing? It appeared so. He had hoped she would have found herself a new home by now. It was not an unreasonable assumption to make. Why would a lonely Saxon stay in a village of Norsemen? But she had not left, she had only grown more lovely.

"So what say you?" Arne asked, crossing his arms over his chest.

"I say no."

"Ah..." His friend smiled. "Found yourself a sweetheart, did you, while you were away, and do not wish to betray her? No wonder you're talking of going without! With your girl all the way back in Denmark, you'll have to see to your needs yourself."

"Don't I know it," he grumbled. That fool Arne had to rub it in, didn't he? Björn knew he would have to get relief by his own hand because the only woman he wanted in his bed was Dunne. No one else would do.

Why was he still so fixated on her?

He'd hoped to find someone in Denmark who would help him get over his obsession with Dunne, someone he might take back home with him to start anew. In truth there had been a number of women in the Danish villages he'd visited who would have happily let him tumble them into bed but that was not what he wanted. He wanted more, something long-term. He wanted *her*. Why she was the only one who stirred his interest, he wasn't sure. But in the same way he did not wonder why he liked autumn better than summer, he did not question his craving for her. It was part of him, had been since he'd been old enough to look at women. There simply was no one else like her.

And so, he had come back just as obsessed with the golden-eyed Saxon as when he had left.

On the boat he had concluded that his only hope lay with her. If she was nowhere to be seen when he entered the village, then he would have no choice but to forget her and try to find someone who could replace her if not in his heart, at least in his bed. But Dunne hadn't left. Not only that, but she'd been the first person he had seen, after her daughter Bee. The message was clear. There would be no escaping her. She was still here, still as beautiful as ever.

And his desire for her came back with a vengeance.

He gave a curse and stormed back to the hut. After his long absence, Ingrid would be waiting for him.

DUNNE KNEW AS SOON as she woke up that she would have to address what had happened with Björn that day by the river. She could not spend her days fearing it would resurface at the worst moment or risk a repeat of it when he walked in on her bathing again. The thought of exposing her body to him, this time without the protection of her shift, had her shiver with something akin to excitement. Even if she knew his reaction had been nothing more than a young man's normal response to an arousing situation, she could not help the satisfaction it had brought her.

He had seen her and he had felt desire. It was flattering, undeniably, to be proven she *could* be desirable, at least to some men.

She decided to go see him without further ado. If they were to cross paths every day, they could not have such a thing hanging over their heads. One of them had to clear the air and, as the one who'd been most embarrassed by the incident, Björn was unlikely to want to bring the subject up himself. It was up to her, whose masculine pride had not been hurt, to take the first step.

She found him outside the hayloft, almost in the place where they had first met, cutting wood. Dunne allowed herself a moment to observe him unnoticed while he swung his axe with enviable—and, damn it—arousing ease. Yes, something had changed within him while he'd been away, making him a veritable danger to her senses.

Now, no one in their right mind would call him a boy.

She moved forward before she could lose herself in the contemplation. Ogling him was not why she had come.

He looked over his shoulder when he heard her approach. "Dunne. Good morning."

"Good morning."

"What can I do for you? Let me guess. Sigurd is after a cask of ale. I wondered how long it would take." With a laugh, he split the log he'd just placed in front of him clean in half. It was all she could do not to gawp at the demonstration of strength. It would have taken her five or six blows to overcome such a monster. Björn made it look easy. She had been right the day before, something had changed within him. It was not just the physique, his whole demeanor was different. There was a new assurance about him, and she felt at a disadvantage, as if she were the young, untried one, not him.

"He has mentioned it, yes," she started.

"Well, he's going to have to wait. I made a batch yesterday but it's not going to be ready for another—"

"Forgive me," she cut in before she could lose her nerve, "but that's not why I'm here."

"Oh?" He placed another log into position and waited for her answer before swinging his axe.

She lowered her gaze to the ground. As much as she wanted to help them get past any embarrassment, this was still awkward. What if she was wrong and he had actually forgotten all about the incident? Then she would only be stirring up trouble for nothing. Was she not overestimating the place she took in his mind? Perhaps. After all, he did not seem half as ill-at-ease as she was. Well, it was a risk she would just have to take.

Taking a deep breath, she went for it.

"I came to see if you think we could forget what happened that day by the river when you w-walked in on m-me," she stammered. "You were embarrassed by the way you reacted but I understand. You were shocked to see a woman naked and—"

"I was not shocked!" he cut in, sticking his axe into the log before rounding up on her. "I was nineteen, I had seen naked women before. Just...Not you."

Unsure quite what he meant by that, Dunne carried on. This was not going the way she had anticipated. She had thought Björn would agree with her and brush the matter aside as quickly as possible. He did neither.

"What I'm trying to say is that there is no need for any awkwardness between us. I realize none of what happened was about me, merely an unfortunate coincidence. The day before on the horse you—"

"What do you know about what I did that day?" This time he did seem somewhat flustered. Still, she wasn't sure it was due to shame, rather than... She shook her head, preferring not to dwell on the reason. Whatever it was, the color in his cheeks had heightened.

She blushed in turn. "I think you went to the bushes to...see to your masculine needs. It's all right, I know you were thinking about Gertrud and it heated your blood."

"Who?"

Björn stared at Dunne in disbelief. What—and who—was she talking about?

"Gertrud. The girl every man seemed to, er, lust after. I'm sorry to say she married a man from town a few months after you left."

This time he blinked, because he knew who she meant. Ingrid had given him a thorough summary of the changes in the village since he'd left and Magnar's sister had indeed moved to marry a cobbler from town.

But Dunne was wrong to think he'd been sad to see the girl go. Unlike Arne and the others, he'd never lusted after her, and was not disappointed to hear she had married another man. He couldn't care less about the mean-spirited chit. She had been comely enough, but not so comely he'd forgotten—or forgiven— the way she'd teased Ingrid for years for being "scrawny and shy," in her own scathing words.

It was time to set things right and put an end to this whole farce.

He planted himself in front of Dunne.

"Seeing as you don't seem to want to understand, let me be clear. That day I didn't go behind a bush to stroke myself because I was thinking about a girl I have never been interested in, I fled in shame because I'd actually come in my braies." The confession passed his lips easily. What had been the biggest humiliation of his life now seemed insignificant compared to his need to make her understand the reality of what he felt for her. "And I came because of you. *You* were the woman I was thinking about. I came because I was holding you in my arms, because I could smell your hair and feel your body against mine, because you were rubbing your sweet ass all over my cock and I could not stop myself."

He could tell Dunne was stunned by his crude admission, and little wonder. He should not have been so honest or so blunt, perhaps he should not even have rectified her wrong assumption, and just let her think he had been imagining another woman. But he could not. He could not bear for her to ignore what he felt any longer, even if what he felt was shameful and crude. He had tried to run, gone all the way to Denmark, only to find himself right back where he had started. He had tried to hide his feelings, only to have her mistake his actions for something else and believe him in love, or rather in lust, with another.

Well, there would be no more running, no more hiding. He was not ashamed anymore. At least one good thing had come from the interlude abroad. Away from people who still saw him as a child, and Rorik's son, he had finally become someone in his own right, as he'd wanted. It was a complete transformation, one long overdue. He looked different, he felt different, like a man. And men told their women when they wanted them.

"I saw you that day by the river, naked and beautiful like a goddess and I wanted you so damn badly I thought I might explode. I had to go and put an end to the torture for fear of doing something I had no right to do."

By now Dunne was trembling. "Like what?" The two words were but a whisper.

"Don't ask me that," he groaned, "the answer will frighten you, make you think differently of me." He'd wanted to tumble her onto the ground and sheath himself so deep inside her she would never forget the feel of his body filling hers.

She stared back at him, cheeks reddening. "I'm not frightened of you, Björn."

"Good. I never want to see fear in your eyes when you look at me. I couldn't bear it."

"You won't."

At that moment Björn understood two things. One, it wasn't fear that made Dunne's face flush such a becoming color. It was desire. She wanted him, as much as he wanted her. Two, as a consequence, he could actually make his dream come true and take her, right here, right now. Couldn't he?

The hayloft was beckoning, offering them a fragrant nest in which to burrow together.

"Björn?" She took a tentative step toward him. "I—"

He turned on his heel before she could finish the sentence.

CHAPTER SEVEN

"I'm sure I can get up there," Dawn said, her head thrown back to look at the branches overhead. "It's easy."

"No, it's too high, sweetheart."

Dunne sighed, cursing her luck. What had the cat been thinking? Hilda had rushed up the tree in panic when a hen had started to chase her and was now mewling pitifully, as if knowing her little mistress would risk life and limb to get to her. In which she was right, Dawn absolutely would do that and more. Why, she was even now considering climbing up a thirty-foot tree on her own.

"We can't leave her alone up there. You know she can't even hear us call her. She will think we've abandoned her!"

"Dawn..." Dunne's voice trailed. She already knew her daughter would not budge until she had been reunited with her cat.

"I am not leaving until we have Hilda back," the child said, confirming what she feared.

There was only one solution. She would have to go get the cat herself. Dunne eyed up the oak, wondering how she was going to reach the lowest branch. Perhaps if she brought one of the logs she'd gotten ready for the fire to the foot of the trunk she could use it to hoist herself up. As soon as she had put her plan to execution, however, she saw that it was not going to be that simple. She was higher, admittedly, but the log she had managed to drag all the way here was not as stable as she would have liked. If she weren't careful she was going to end flat on her face. Well, she would simply have to be careful, wouldn't she?

She lifted her leg up.

"Bear! Oh! We need you!"

Dunne could have sworn out loud. Of all the villagers, *he* had to be the one walking by in this moment. Sometimes she wondered if fate was not working with the sole aim of making her uncomfortable, aided by a seemingly innocent white cat who'd chosen that precise moment to shoot up a tree. Only two days ago Björn would have been in Denmark and her dignity would have been safe.

She lowered her leg and turned in time to see him ruffle her daughter's mop of hair.

"What's the problem, Bee?"

"Hilda is up the tree. She didn't hear the hen until it pounced on her. Mama was going to climb up to rescue her, but I think she would prefer if you did it."

Yes, indeed Dunne would be very glad to avoid what would be an ordeal for her. She would have been even more glad if Wolf of Sigurd, or anyone else had been the one coming to her aid.

"Mm, yes, I think it would be better if I did it. We don't want your mama to be injured, do we?" Björn answered, taking in her precarious position. "Or worse."

Great. So he agreed she would only end up making a spectacle of herself if she tried to climb up.

A moment later she felt two strong hands around her waist, securing her position on the wobbly log. Heat flared through her at his touch. After their discussion of the previous day, when she had all but admitted to feeling desire for him, she was not ready for such intimate contact.

"Careful here. You don't want to fall flat on your face."

From her perch she was taller than him by a few inches, and so close she was able to observe him at her leisure. Details she had not noticed before captivated her attention. She could see that the lashes framing his amazing blue eyes were almost transparent at the tip, she could single out a few ginger hairs in his golden beard and tiny creases on his forehead. Just when she was wondering if she would have to ask him to put her down, he lifted her and deposited her onto the ground.

She took in a sharp inhale of breath, like someone who'd just swam under water for longer than she had planned to.

"Let me go get the cat," Björn murmured.

"I don't want to put you out," she whispered back, totally under the spell of the moment. Under *his* spell.

"Don't worry. It will be the work of moments. Besides, I feel I should be the one retrieving Hilda. After all, I was the one who gifted her to Bee. I'm responsible for the mishap." He gave her a slanted smile and heat flared anew in her body. It was just like the day before, when they had looked at each other after she'd told him she wasn't afraid of him.

Right before he had fled.

She knew if they had been alone right now, he would have kissed her. The hold around her waist was too tight, the look in his eyes too intense, the curve on his lips too pronounced to be innocent. He wanted more. And so did she. She almost leaned in, ready for his kiss. Another inch and she would—

"What do you mean by 'worse'?"

They both blinked and turned to look at Dawn, who was staring at them with a frown on her face.

"Sorry, sweetheart?" Dunne asked in a croak. What had just

happened? Had she really almost kissed a man in front of her daughter? It would seem so. Her body was humming in frustration at being denied what it wanted. She had never wanted to kiss anyone before and she was not best pleased at having had the delicious moment cut short.

"Bear said he didn't want you to get injured 'or worse.' What is worse than that?"

Björn gave a cough. His hold was still too tight but she didn't even consider moving away. His hands around her waist felt too good. "I meant she could fall flat on her back," he explained, looking at Dawn.

"How is that worse than being hurt?" the little girl insisted.

When Björn looked back to her, the look in his eyes had become incendiary. Dunne swallowed. "Well—"

"I think we should go and rescue Hilda," she cut in before he could tell her daughter that he was imagining her mother lying on the floor with her skirts around her ears.

While Dawn turned her attention back to the mewling cat, Dunne tried her best to ignore the hard rod pressing against her stomach. This time she could not fool herself. Björn was aroused because of *her*. His breathing was fast in her ear, his body was taut, his eyes were burning with a mixture of arousal and amusement—a most lethal combination. She took in a deep breath and finally stepped away from him.

He shuffled on his feet, obviously fighting the urge to palm his erection. Was he in pain? She couldn't imagine how he could not be, considering how hard he'd gone. It had to hurt.

"All right, time to go up the tree. Only, I will have to remove my shirt, I'm afraid," he said in a deep rumble. "Ingrid will not thank me for ripping her first creation on the day she gave it to me."

"No, I guess not." Dunne knew his sister had been working on that shirt for months. She could well understand that he didn't want to risk it tearing when it snagged on one of the branches. Ingrid would be heartbroken.

The only problem was, she was once again going to have to see him bare-chested. It seemed at this point that she had seen him more half-naked than she had seen him fully clothed. Not that she minded. Which was precisely the problem...

Oh, yes, fate was definitely using her as a toy.

A swift jerk, a twist of the hips and Björn was standing in his golden glory in front of her. Dear God, he *had* grown more muscular during his time in Denmark, she could not ignore it any longer. The proof of it was staring at her straight in the face. What had he been doing over there? Chopping wood for months on end, until every muscle in his body had gone as hard as iron? Perhaps. And what had she done here in the village? Gorged on Frigyth's famous oat cakes. A wave of self-consciousness washed through her. Björn had never been more taut and lean while she had failed to shed any weight since she'd been widowed, rather the opposite.

"If you please?"

Dunne took the shirt Björn was handing her and almost brought it to her nose to inhale the floral scent that seemed to follow him everywhere.

After one last look at her he hoisted himself up the tree and started climbing. He was as agile as he was strong, and he reached the cat in the blink of an eye. Extending a graceful arm, he plucked the little white body with one hand and started his descent with the fluff ball tucked tight against his chest.

The whole operation was over in a heartbeat, or so it seemed.

Björn jumped to his feet in front of Dunne, feeling like a cat himself. She was watching him with an expression he could not quite identify. Was she grateful for his help, or was it something else? Unsurprisingly, he felt his body stir under her gaze. He had not missed the look on her face when he had taken his shirt off. All night he had regretted not making the most of the desire she'd felt for him the day before. He had fled when he should have swept her into his arms. Well he was not going to make the same mistake twice. She seemed to like his body, so he would use it as a weapon. The opportunity to parade half-naked in front of her had been too good to resist. Besides, it was the truth he did not want to ruin the shirt Ingrid had made for him. It had been the perfect excuse and he could see he had struck a chord.

Dunne was ogling him shamefully, even if he could tell she was trying not to be too obvious about it. His groin stirred again. He would not be able to wait much longer to finally put an end to the torture.

For now though, any sort of seduction would have to wait. Bee was practically jumping on the spot with impatience, waiting to get hold of Hilda.

"There you are." He handed her the cat. "No harm done."

"Oh, thank you! But you're all scratched now!" The little girl gestured to his right side.

Björn shrugged, even if he could feel the sting of the cuts. Climbing bare-chested into a tree made it inevitable that he should be scratched. "'Tis nothing. It will heal quick enough, Bee."

"I'm glad you call me Bee," the little girl said seriously. "None of the grown-ups do."

"Well, I like that you call me Bear," he quipped back. "No one else does."

"They d. They call you Björn and Björn means bear."

The inescapable logic of the statement made him laugh. He would have to remember never to get involved in a conversation with the little Saxon. She would have his brain twisted into knots in no time if he weren't careful. She proved it with her next sentence.

"You know, bees make honey."

"Yeeess..." Where was she going with this?

"And apparently, bears love honey. The man with the bear told us so last year in town."

Ah. His lips quivered. Now he thought he knew what she was getting at. "They must do, if he told you as much. What of it?"

"Well..." Bee made a pout, as if she had hoped he would understand by himself what she was trying to say—or had just realized that there was no real point to the whole thing. "We make a good team you and I."

"You and me," Dunne piped, coming to stand next to her. In that moment the similarities between mother and daughter were glaring. "But really, Dawn, I think Björn has some work to do now. He's wasted enough time going up that tree, don't you think?"

"How many times will I have to tell you, Mama? Call me Bee! And him Bear!"

Bear.

Somehow the wild name suited him. Dunne fought the urge to stroke his chest and feel if the short hairs were as soft as she imagined. How had she ever thought him a boy? He...Well, he was all man.

And he wanted her.

His words from the previous day came back to her.

I came in my braies because I was holding you in arms and you were rubbing your sweet ass all over my cock. I wanted you so damn badly I thought I might explode.

A shiver went through her. She could tell he was thinking of the same thing, of how he had admitted to lusting after her.

Why had he left so abruptly after making the shocking declaration? To stroke himself again, and relieve the desire boiling in his veins? For a moment it had looked as if he were about to tumble her into his arms. And she would have let him.

Instead, he had fled, and the moment had passed. Now she wasn't sure they would ever have the chance to give in to passion—or even if she should want it.

"Come inside. We will have to wash your cuts before you put the shirt back on," she mumbled, "otherwise you will ruin it with blood stains."

Björn and Dawn followed her inside the hut. While they argued over who were the better climbers, cats or bears, she found a piece of linen and dipped it into the pot of fresh water waiting on the table.

She came to him and hesitated. Did he expect her to clean the cuts? It was possible, since they would prove hard for him to reach placed where they were, along his side and shoulder blade.

"I will do that, thank you," he murmured, taking the rag from her hand. "I seem to end up with bruises and scratches every time we meet, don't I?"

A whimper almost escaped Dunne's lips. Why did that sound so suggestive? Though he was obviously referring to the way she had hit him while defending Dawn back in autumn, he'd made it sound as if she liked to claw at his back while he made love to her.

It was all she could do not to collapse when he lifted his left arm to run the piece of cloth along the side of his chiseled chest. This wouldn't do, she had to get hold of her composure, and fast!

Just then a shriek pierced her ear.

"Bee! There you are." Elwyn and Eirik came bursting through the door. Dunne rolled her eyes, relieved at the breaking in tension. Apparently Dawn had finally convinced her cousins to call her by the animal name. She was not surprised; she had them wrapped around her little finger.

"Mama and *Faðir* are taking us to sleep in the forest tonight!" Elwyn told her excitedly. "We asked if you could come with us. Please do, you will love it there!"

Dawn's eyes widened with excitement at the prospect. "Can I go, Mama?"

"Of course. Run along. And don't forget to thank Auntie Frigyth."

It was only when the three children and the cat had disappeared in a flurry of limbs that Dunne realized she was now alone in the hut with Björn. Alone with a bare-chested bear of a man who wanted her so badly he had told her in the crudest of terms only the day before.

Heart in her throat, she waited.

Without a word he went to close the door the children had left wide open. Her whole body went liquid. Perhaps the moment had not passed after all, and the chance to give in to passion had arrived. Perhaps he would tumble her into bed *right now.*

"I should—"

"No." He came to plant himself in front of her, blocking her retreat. "Tell me about Bee's father."

She recoiled. It had been so long since she had thought of her dead husband; why was Björn asking about him now? She had been so certain he was about to take her into his arms. What a fool she really was for misreading his intentions so drastically.

"Toland? Why would you want to know about him?"

His nostrils flared. "Because I'm trying to imagine the kind of man he was and it's killing me. I would like to know once and for all so I can stop torturing myself."

Dunne blinked. Björn was torturing himself thinking about

her late husband? This she hadn't seen coming. She nodded slowly.

"Ask what you want to know." After all, what harm could it do?

"Did you love him?"

"No." The answer darted out of her mouth before she could think. Her late husband had stirred many emotions in her, but love had never been one of them. Björn must have picked on her lack of hesitation for he cocked his head.

"Did you hate him then?"

This time she did pause because that was a more complicated question. "No. Not anymore. He's been dead for months and I stopped caring about him long before that. But I did hate him at first." It felt good to admit it out loud.

Björn started to pace around her. What was happening? Why was she under interrogation? Why should he even care? And why was she getting all hot and bothered? They were just having a conversation, weren't they?

"Why did you hate him? Was he violent with you?"

"He never hit me if that's what you mean."

"I would be glad to hear it if I didn't sense there was more to your answer. What did he do if he did not hit you, Dunne?" he asked, coming closer.

Her heart skipped a beat. "He...was not kind."

"Mm."

Oddly, the non-committal answer made her want to tell him more. Had he pressed her, she might have balked but he said nothing, simply carried on pacing around her, his rhythm slow, his presence comforting.

"It was not a love match, as you can imagine, but one arranged by my father," she started, while Björn carried on his slow circles around her. "He was older than me, and he spent his time criticizing me, saying I couldn't cook for example, that he was fed up eating bread and cheese."

Björn grunted but he did not slow down or even looked at her. "Then he should have learned to cook himself."

Dunne shrugged. Her husband's constant complaining about the food had hardly been the biggest problem she'd had to face. "He never loved our daughter. Predictably he'd wanted a boy."

This time Björn stopped his prowling. "Yes. That is unforgivable."

The statement was uttered in a flat voice that somehow emphasized his disapproval. It was as if he didn't even think anyone could disagree with him. Dunne straightened her spine and carried on, warming to her theme. Admitting out loud to the pain she had experienced during all these years to someone who seemed to sympathize was cathartic. It felt as if she were purging herself of a poison that had been too long in her veins.

"He disparaged me in front of his friends, who laughed at his supposed wit. He prevented me from wearing my hair loose or cutting it shorter. He forbade me to leave the hut and go to visit my sister and friends. He called me..." She stopped because this, she could not reveal.

Björn walked over to stand in front of Dunne, not liking the way she had stopped talking. She had started to open and now she was closing up again. What was she hiding?

"What did he call you, Dunne?"

At first she didn't answer. When she finally spoke her answer was so low he barely heard it. Had she said...

"Did you say 'fat'?"

Surely he had misheard. But the way she hugged herself and refused to meet his gaze told him all he needed to know. He had not misheard. Her bastard of a husband *had* called her fat.

Before he could think, he lifted her off her feet, forcing her to wrap her legs around his waist for comfort.

"What are you doing?" she croaked, grabbing at his shoulders. The feel of her hands on his naked shoulders sent a spike of need through his loins. It was the first time she had touched him so intimately. He didn't want it to be the last. He wanted to feel her hands all over his skin. "Put me down!"

He ignored her protests. "That's how fat you are," he told her in a growl. "You're so fat I can lift you like I would a child. By the gods, you didn't believe him, did you?"

"Well, after I had my daughter, I didn't—"

"Enough," he cut her off. He was not interested in hearing more about her supposed weight issues. She was perfect the way she was and he should know, he spent enough time mooning after her. If she had put on a few pounds during her pregnancy, then there was nothing odd in that. And if she had still not shed them four years later, then it was hardly a problem. From what he'd seen all those months ago by the river, she had nothing to worry about. She was every man's dream.

His dream.

And he was finally holding her in his arms, just against his straining hardness.

"What else did the fool tell you?" he growled.

She bit her bottom lip. "Put me down, Björn."

"No. Not before you have told me."

He waited, relishing the feel of her legs wrapped around his middle and her cool hands on his heated skin. He was hard as rock but for once he didn't pay any mind to his desire. All he wanted was to hear the extent of the damage caused to her self-esteem by that damn Toland. He nodded his encouragement and saw her nod back. She would speak, even if it took her time to build up the courage.

"He said no man could ever find me desirable."

With a roar Björn marched her to the nearest wall. Spreading her legs wider, he positioned himself against her. Holding her under the buttocks he held her trapped between his body and the wall.

"Feel this?" He nudged at her, watching her eyes go wide when she felt just how hard he was. It was little wonder he should feel like a randy stallion to her, he was near to bursting. Again. "This is how undesirable you are."

"You—"

"Yes. I want you. I told you the other day. You send me wild with need every time I see you. I've wanted you from the moment I saw you at your sister's wedding. I think you are the most goddamn beautiful woman I have ever seen and this..." He gave another nudge and groaned when the friction caused sparks to shoot up his shaft. "This is the proof that I'm not lying."

"I see." He watched Dunne swallow and for a moment feared he would unman himself again. She was so hot against him, she would engulf him in flames if he ever managed to get between her legs. It could happen in a heartbeat. All he had to do was rip at his braies and lift her skirts. He was already between her spread legs. He could be inside her in moments.

"Your husband was the luckiest bastard in the entire world to have had you in his bed. He should have told you so every day."

She whimpered, as if the thought of her and Toland in bed was too much for her to bear. He could understand the feeling. It was too much to bear for him too. "He told me I was like a corpse in bed. That I should move and moan and not just lie there waiting for it to be over."

That was the last straw. The man had accused *her* of not bringing him pleasure when he'd been the incapable fool?

In the blink of an eye, Björn had Dunne flat on her back on

the pallet. Finally, he had her where he wanted her, under him, *finally* he was going to make love to her.

"I will take great pleasure in proving to you that husband of yours was wrong in every way. It's not the woman's fault if the man above her doesn't make her writhe and scream. A corpse," he said between his teeth, unable to believe it. Dunne was anything but cold and insensitive. She was pure womanly fire. He would make sure she moved and moaned, not because he wanted her to, but because she would not be able to help herself. "Look at you alive under me."

Alive.

Yes, that was exactly how Dunne felt right now. She was writhing, whimpering, rubbing herself against Björn. She could not help herself, she could not get enough of his warm, taut body above her, poised between her legs. It was so different from when she had lain under Toland. This time she wanted to be here, wanted to press herself against the hard length prodding against her center, making her melt.

Her hands started to brush along his back in a back and forth motion, and she relished the way his muscles twisted and shifted under her touch. Such power! Such beauty! And all for her. She wasn't sure what to do with it. She felt like a sailor about to face his first storm, both apprehensive and eager to test what his ship was capable of.

"This is all new to me," she whispered. She preferred to be honest because her inexperience scared her. What if Björn was disappointed by her lack of skills, like Toland? What if he expected her to do more than lie there? She had no notion of how to please a man. For the first time in her life, she wanted to, but she had no idea where to begin.

"It is all new to me too," he panted, his mouth at her neck.

"What do you mean?" Surely he had never been married to

someone he hated? Surely he was not afraid of disappointing her?

He seemed to hesitate then placed his forehead against hers. "I've never lain with a woman before." Dunne stilled at the unexpected admission. Björn, the strong Norseman, the epitome of male beauty and power, was a virgin? Not for a moment had she imagined that would be the case. He must have mistaken her surprise for displeasure because he drew back. "If it's too odd for you, I—"

She placed a hand at the back of his neck to stop him from retreating. "It's not odd." In fact, it reassured her. He would not be comparing her to his other lovers and find her lacking, which had been her biggest fear, he would not think her inadequate. "We will learn together."

Sensing it would be up to her to resume their lovemaking, she reached out to the laces at the front of his braies, eager to bare him to her then cursed her inexperience when she couldn't seem to be able to free his straining member.

"Help me," she whimpered.

While Björn fumbled at his crotch, she opened her legs wider, making her invitation clear.

"Wait," he growled. "This isn't right. I should undress you..."

Her gown was bunched around her waist and her breasts were not even exposed but it didn't matter. She couldn't wait another moment. "This will have to do. I'm not a virgin, so there will be no pain."

At least, she didn't think so. Being bedded by Toland had always been uncomfortable but she'd heard that it could, and should, be different. She could already tell nothing Björn did would hurt her. Quite the opposite.

A warm hand landed over her sex. She almost bit her tongue at the exquisite sensation then arched her back when a finger entered her, gentle and possessive all at once. She was liquid with anticipation and Björn seemed just as aroused as she was.

"Bloody hell, I will spill as soon as I get inside you," he said in a rasp. "It is inevitable. I want you too much, I won't be able to stop myself. You're too beautiful, too hot, you will feel too good, and I lack the control to make it last. But I swear I will make it up to you afterward, there will—"

"Hush. Björn, please, take me, I'm burning."

IT WAS BOTH BETTER than he could have hoped and worse than he had feared.

Björn bunched up every single one of his muscles, absorbing the wonder of being inside a woman's silken body, of being inside this woman he had wanted for years. It was torture and ecstasy rolled into one. He was going to die, but he was going to die a happy man. The heat, the softness, the slickness of her! He'd entered her in one smooth thrust that had almost caused him to erupt.

"Dunne," he whispered against her neck, both a plea and a thank you. "Dunne."

"Yes." She sounded just as breathless, just as overwhelmed as he was.

"Can I move?" He was going to expire from want if he didn't. But he was going to explode if he did. It was an impossible situation. The best moment of his life.

"Ah, please."

He reared up and plunged again into bliss. Then again. Under him Dunne was moaning, urging him on.

Björn lost all restraint. Swearing to himself he would do whatever it took to pleasure her later, he started pumping, closing his eyes, and gritting his teeth to try and hold on to some semblance of control. His seed was boiling in his spine, ready to shoot out of him. This was going to be like never before, nothing like the solitary pleasure he usually wrenched from himself.

"I can't..." he panted.

The moan that answered him was so filled with lust he could not hold on any longer. He tensed like a bow string and erupted in a series of spurts that caused his whole body to convulse in a shattering release. It was uncontrollable. Glorious. It blinded him and almost caused his heart to stop.

After a while the world shifted back into place. He was lying above Dunne, supporting his weight on his bent arms. At least he had not been so lost to all reality that he had crushed her under his bulk. She had stopped moving and seemed to be waiting for him. Then he felt her nudge at him. White sparks ignited in his spine.

"You...You're still hard," she rasped, holding him tight against her.

"Mm. Yes." He was still embedded inside her as well. Apparently, one soul-shattering climax was not enough to sate his need for this woman. Grateful that his age gave him at least one advantage, he hooked one of Dunne's legs under the knee to bring it to his waist, opening her up wider for his thrusts. "So let me give you more."

Now that the fire in his blood had cooled somewhat, he might be able to take it slower and bring her the pleasure she deserved. This second bout of lovemaking would be for her. He took her in long, leisurely strokes, finding a rhythm that suited both of them, marveling at how tight she hugged him, at how perfect this was.

"Björn, it's..."

He stilled. "What? Too much? Should I stop?"

"No. Don't. It feels too good."

Sharp nails scored his shoulders, spurring him on. It seemed he would end up with even more scratches. But these he would wear with pride since they were the proof he had pleasured her so well she had forgotten herself. Groaning, he swore to himself he would not stop until she had come apart in his arms. A moment later she did just that.

"Ah!"

He roared when her sheath seized and started to tighten around him. Only a moment ago he'd thought it impossible to feel more pleasure but incredible sensations starting to bloom in his body and his his heart. Never had he imagined he would derive so much satisfaction from watching someone else's pleasure. Clearly he had much to learn about lovemaking, and he'd found the perfect woman with which to do it. Dunne was his every dream come true, giving herself to him without hesitation, without making him feel inadequate for his lack of experience.

Throwing his head back, he came again, filling her with all he had.

Dunne was struggling to come back to reality. When she eventually did, she found that she was crying. Unstoppable sobs racked through her, making her eyes burn and her chest heave.

"Dunne, no! Please, don't cry." Björn sounded panicked. He slid off her, taking his wonderful heat with him. "Did I hurt you? I'm sorry, I'm so sorry. I told you, I don't know what I'm doing, you should have told me I was being too—"

"No," she managed to say through her tears. "You didn't hurt me. Only...It was too much, like nothing I ever—Sorry, I just need to let it out."

She was blabbering on but in his arms, she had experienced something she had never suspected could exist, much more than physical pleasure. She had hoped being bedded by Björn would not be painful, and it hadn't been. But how could she have suspected it could be so...The word eluded her. Wonderful? No, too vague. Overwhelming? Certainly, but not positive enough. Life-changing? Perhaps.

When Björn drew her into his arms she didn't even try to resist. She was a limp mess, and his to do whatever he wanted with.

"I'm here. Cry all you want. It's a different kind of release, I suppose."

Yes, that was exactly what it was. A release she had needed just as much as the explosion of pleasure, the ability to admit to herself she could be a desirable—and desired—woman. Being shown that she was not the worthless, graceless lump Toland had accused her of being was doing to her mind what Björn's possession had done to her body.

It took her a while to master the tempest wrecking through her soul but slowly, she came back to calmer shores. Pressed against a strong, smooth chest, she could feel her mind ease itself into a different reality.

"Now," Björn said in a low rumble. "I know I'm going about it all the wrong way but...Can I undress you now? I need to see your body."

Indeed, even if he was bare-chested, she was still fully dressed. Dunne's heart tripped in her chest at the thought of a man seeing her naked but there was such desire in Björn's eyes that she didn't hesitate. She could not refuse him, not when they had discovered pleasure together, not when he had called her desirable, not when...well, when she wanted to be naked in front of him. Earlier she had bemoaned the difference between them, but she could tell he didn't think her any less beautiful than she thought him handsome.

"On one condition," she said, looking at him under her lashes. "I want to see your body as well."

He was tugging at his braies before she had even finished the sentence. The boots quickly followed. Soon, he was standing nude and magnificent, in front of her. Her mouth dropped open. The member in its nest of golden curls was not the powerful rod she had felt ramming inside her earlier but neither was it a limp worm. Either it had still not gone back to its original state or it was lengthening again. Björn let her look her fill for a long moment, sensing she needed time to absorb the sight of him in his full glory, for which she was grateful. Then he knelt down by her side.

"It's your turn, beautiful." His voice was as husky as she had ever heard it.

"Wait, Björn." She bit her lip, suddenly nervous. "If we are both naked together we might wish to...you know."

It seemed inevitable. He was looking at her like a predator eyeing up its prey and his member had gone from mildly interested to raging hard, betraying his need for more relief—and her body was responding accordingly.

Björn smiled and reached out to the laces at her bodice.

"No 'might' about it. Bee is with Frigyth and Sigurd. Ingrid will not be waiting for me. We have all night." He slipped a hand under her gaping bodice and groaned when his fingers closed over her breast to find her hard nipple. "Once we are both naked and I have stroked every inch of your gorgeous body, I *will* fuck you again."

CHAPTER EIGHT

What had she done?

Dunne bolted upright on the pallet. She had spent the night in a man's arms, that was what, when she had sworn she would never place herself under anyone's control ever again. And she had not been with just any man. She had been with a man she should never even have thought of seducing, a man who could not possibly want a future with her, only a good rutting. His words came back to her.

Once we are both naked and I have stroked every inch of your body, I will fuck you again.

Oh, and he had. Over and over again, in every position conceivable. He'd been so crude in his speech, so bold in this touch...She had loved it. Would she even be able to walk today? Every muscle in her body seemed to ache, which was odd because he'd not been rough, just unashamedly male, unafraid of his desires and utterly indefatigable.

As for her...She had not recognized herself. Gone was the woman who'd lain passively under her partner, enduring his clumsy, unwelcome attentions. She had been wild, imaginative and she had surpassed herself.

But...

As wonderful as it had been, it could lead nowhere. It had been a feast of the senses, nothing more. It could never be more. A man as young as Björn didn't want to be attached, he wanted to spend his wild oats before settling down when he was well into his thirties and had no choice.

Last night, he had wanted to finally lie with a woman. If he had not lied about being a virgin, that was...Lost to the heat of the moment she had not thought to doubt his claim but now that she'd had time to think, she was not so sure. How could a man who looked like he did be still untouched? Surely he had exaggerated his lack of experience at the very least. How else would he be so skilled at pleasuring her if he'd been a virgin?

I've never lain with a woman before.

That was what he had said. At the time she had taken it to mean he'd never lain with anyone but he probably meant he'd only bedded girls for sport, and never women her age, never been serious about it, never gotten involved with someone who had a child and would be expecting some sort of commitment from him, commitment he was not ready for.

That had to be why he had fled before she woke up.

Which was a good thing, she told herself, because she didn't want commitment either. Just like him, she hadn't wanted anything other than a feast of the senses.

And by God, she'd gotten it and more.

Dunne stretched and saw that she was still naked. Shock had her reeling. She *never* slept naked. She had also never been more in need of a bath. Mortified by how debauched she'd become in just one night, she slipped on a fresh shift and looked for her dress. It was not on the floor where it had landed last night when Björn had all but torn it from her body. Before leaving he had folded it and placed it on the table. Her heart melted at this unexpected thoughtfulness. He might not want to get involved with a more mature woman but he was being considerate for all that.

Just as she was fastening the laces on her bodice, the door burst open.

"Mama!" Dawn bounded into the room and jumped straight into her arms.

Frigyth followed her niece at a more sedate pace, a smile on her lips. "Good morning."

"Good morning," Dunne replied, ruffling her daughter's unruly hair. "Thanks for having Dawn last night."

Thereby allowing me to spend the most wickedly sinful night of my life.

"You're welcome. I hope you made the most of your evening?" Dunne didn't reply. She certainly had, even if there had not been much rest. "I think the children enjoyed themselves anyway," Frigyth added when she remained silent.

"Yes, oh yes!" Dawn cried out, encircling her neck to give her a hug. "It was the best night of my life! I want to do it again!"

The innocently meant words found a strange echo within Dunne because, well, she too had spent the best night of her life and wanted to do it again. She hugged the little girl tighter, hoping to hide from Frigyth the heat she could feel burning her cheeks. Her sister was looking at her with an odd expression on her face, as if she'd guessed what had happened between her and Björn.

No, it was impossible, Dunne told herself, considering she had confirmed only a few days ago that she had sworn men off. "Never say never" had been Frigyth's infuriating answer. Well, one of them had certainly been proved right last night. Perhaps she should have made sure to include *Norse*men into the declaration.

"I came to see you yesterday before we went to the forest," Frigyth said softly. There was a gleam in her eye Dunne didn't like.

"Did you? I missed you. I must have been out."

"Oh no, you were most definitely in."

The heat on her cheeks reached alarming proportions. Now she knew why her sister was looking at her in that smug way. She had come to see her while she was in bed with Björn and she had heard them make love. Heard the wild moaning and the grunting and the screaming and everything in between.

"I want to go play with Hilda." In her arms Dawn started wriggling so much Dunne had to put her down. The little girl immediately ran outside, leaving the two women to face each other.

For a long moment they didn't say anything. Then Frigyth placed a hand on her swollen stomach and sat on the chair with a sigh. "This babe is getting heavy. I sometimes wonder if I'm not carrying twins." She grimaced. "Serves me right for pretending I had given birth to twin sons once. Believe me, it is no laughing matter."

Dunne sat next to her and poured them both a cup of ale. As she sipped the amber liquid she wished it were Björn's ale. There truly was none like it. Nibbling at his throat last night she had found herself thinking that his skin tasted as delicious as his ale. Would the rest of him be as good, she wondered? Would she ever get her mouth on it?

Hoping to distract herself from such licentious thoughts, she pretended they were here to discuss Frigyth lying about having twin sons. She was only delaying the inevitable but, with luck, someone would interrupt them before the topic of Björn came up.

"When did you pretend you were carrying twins? I've never heard that story before."

Her sister threw her a look indicating she wasn't fooled by the purpose of the question, but she answered anyway. "I helped a friend who didn't want to admit to a Dane called Rune that she'd borne him a child. I passed off her newborn son as Moon's twin when he visited unexpectedly."

"I see. And did it work?"

"For a time. Then, of course, he found out the truth and ended up falling in love with both Eowyn and their son. They are now happily married and living in Denmark." Frigyth paused and tilted her head. "Some things are inevitable, no matter how much you try to fight them."

"I don't know," Dunne said rather more sharply than she had intended. "Everything that happens has a way of appearing inevitable afterward, as we cannot imagine any other alternative. But I don't think what you're saying is true. I don't think it was inevitable I should marry Toland, for example. A different, more loving father would have asked my opinion about a union with him and I would have refused."

"Mm. You might have a point there. Forgive me, that was ill-considered of me."

"There is nothing to forgive. None of what happened was your fault." And she shouldn't have snapped at her that way.

"I know. Still." Frigyth stared into her empty cup for a moment and seemed to decide they had prevaricated enough. "So. Björn, hey?"

Dunne knew it was hopeless to refuse to talk about it, but she could not surrender so easily. "How do you know it was him?" she challenged.

Far from looking caught out, Frigyth smiled broadly. "Unless you like to moan another man's name while one holds you in his arms, which I don't advise you to do by the way, then I'm pretty sure that's who it was. I know no other man called Björn in the village."

Oh, Lord. Had she really moaned his name for everyone to hear? It was all too possible. She'd been out of her mind with pleasure.

"Please," she whispered, knowing she had gone bright crimson. "I'm not comfortable discussing this."

Her sister ignored the protest and winked. "I always saw him as a boy, but I guess he's changed. He's certainly grown more impressive since he's been back from Denmark."

"He's not a boy," Dunne mumbled. Even though she had thought the same thing once, it bothered her to hear him described thus. It only made the disparity between them more glaring.

"No, I guess not. You would know."

Oh, this was excruciating. There was a pause. "Do you think ill of me?" Dunne blurted out, loath to have her sister, her best friend, start to look at her differently because of what she'd done.

Frigyth instantly went serious and placed a hand on her forearm. "Of course, I don't. And I would kiss Björn the next time I saw him if I didn't think you—or, even more to the point, *Sigurd*—would object."

Kiss him? "Whatever for?"

"For showing you what Toland failed to. It was time you found out that lying in a man's arms is all about pleasure. It seems to me Björn's demonstration was masterful."

Masterful. Yes, it had been.

"I almost passed out," Dunne admitted, staring at the floor. She kept to herself the fact that Björn had claimed to be a virgin last night. That was between the two of them. "And then when it was all over, I made a fool of myself by crying. Both times. It was all ludicrous, really."

"Ah, sister. I doubt he thought you foolish."

No, apparently he had not. He had held her a long moment afterward, allowing her to cry to her heart's content but his gentleness had only doubled her sobs. Eventually she had fallen asleep from sheer exhaustion, her head pillowed on his soft chest. And then at dawn, before he'd left, he'd made love to her all over again. Holding her close to his chest with his hands cupped over her breasts, he'd slid inside her from behind while she was still drowsy, and taken her straight from delicious slumber to soul-ripping ecstasy.

It had been perfect. The only problem was, it should never have happened.

"I don't know what to do."

Frigyth frowned. "What do you mean? What is there to do?"

Dunne lifted both hands in a gesture of helplessness. "Well, you must see that I cannot be with Björn...in that way. I'm not sure he wants anything serious and even if he did, we would look ridiculous together. Besides, I don't want to be married again, I told you only the other day."

"Who said anything about marriage? You've only just started something. Just get to know each other, see where it goes."

Dunne gaped at her. "You're not suggesting I...take a lover?" The look in her sister's eyes made it clear this was exactly what she was suggesting. "Even if I could do such an outrageous thing, he's the last man I should chose. He's ten years younger than me. You just said yourself you thought him little more than a boy."

"I said he'd changed from the boy I thought he was. And

Toland was ten years older than you, and look how that went," Frigyth answered roundly. "Björn might be younger but he's not a child for all that. The difference in age would matter if he were ten and you twenty, but that's not the case, far from it. You are both adults now, he's capable of making his own decisions, choosing what he wants, and he made it quite clear when he thrust inside you last night that what he wants is *you*."

"Frigyth!" Dunne was shocked at the crudeness, but her sister only shrugged.

"I'm sorry for speaking thus but you need to see sense. You have done nothing wrong and you could allow yourself a few weeks of guilt-free pleasure. No one has to know. I'm sure if you asked him to be discreet he would understand."

"It's not all about me. I have my daughter to consider. Dawn will—"

"Dawn will be fine. It will do her good to be surrounded by men who are good role models after the father she's had. You could do a lot worse than bring a man like Björn into both of your lives. He's personable, hardworking, honest, and I think you may have discovered qualities about him that I haven't even started to suspect."

Was she trying to embarrass her? If so, she was going the right way about it.

Dunne bit her bottom lip. She had been confused upon waking up, and after that conversation with her sister, her mind had twisted into further knots. "I need to think."

Frigyth emptied her cup with decision. "Then think. As long as you don't end up making the wrong decision, I see no harm in it."

"I DIDN'T HEAR you come back last night."

Björn ran a hand through his hair. What could he say? He had never liked lying to his sister. Besides, she had always been able to tell when he was. Better not to pretend he had slipped in when she was too sound asleep to notice. She would only know the truth. "That's because I didn't."

Ingrid stopped stirring the pot of stew and wiped her hands on her apron. "Oh? And I suppose you won't tell me where you went?"

"You suppose correctly." He would not lie but he didn't have to tell her everything, did he? Especially if his answer involved another person, a woman he'd spent the whole night making love to. The thought of all he and Dunne had done together sent a tingle down his spine. The night had been memorable. He only wished there would be many, many more to follow.

"I see." If the grin his sister threw him was any indication, she'd guessed only too well what he'd been up to. Damn her ability to see through him so easily! The only mercy was that she could not know *who* had welcomed him in her bed. "You found yourself a sweetheart."

Was that what he had done? If only. He stayed silent, leaving Ingrid to draw her own conclusions. What would she say if she knew he'd bedded Dunne, who she regarded as a friend and mentor? She probably expected him to have gone to one of their parents' friends' daughter, someone he had known all his life.

"What about you?" he asked instead, leaning a shoulder over the door frame. "Have you found yourself a sweetheart yet?"

She reddened and started fidgeting with the apron pocket. "While you were away I started seeing more of Ivar."

Björn recoiled at her answer. Damnation, he had only asked the question to take the heat away from him. He had not expected her to say she had actually found herself a lover! "You..." He could barely speak for the shock. This was his little sister they were talking about. She could not be going to men's beds already! "Ivar! Leif's son? Are you jesting? Did he touch you?"

"Only to kiss me." She giggled when he bunched his fists in automatic response. "Come, brother, no need to appear so horrified. As if I didn't know you've been doing much worse than kissing for years!"

"I haven't."

At least he hadn't until last night, but he wasn't about to admit as much to his sister. Not that he was embarrassed exactly, but she didn't need to know the details of his love life. Then her words penetrated his mind. "Worse than kissing," she'd said. It hadn't been *worse* than kissing, it had been much better, more wonderful, much more meaningful.

Although he'd been a virgin only the day before, he'd not been completely chaste. He'd kissed a handful of women, both here and in Denmark, even fondled a couple of them and allowed them to roam their hands over his body. So no, he was not totally untouched, but never had the pleasure of those embraces compared to what he'd felt when he'd held Dunne in his arms.

It was then that he realized. He and Dunne had not shared a single kiss. As heated as their night together had been, he had not kissed her on the lips once.

How remiss of him! It just went to show he had much to learn about the art of being a lover. What man did not even think of kissing the woman in his arms? A selfish, inexperienced one, that was who, one who was too overwhelmed to do things right.

"Does Ivar mean to propose marriage at least?" he growled,

steering away from the uncomfortable thought. "Or do I need to have a word with him?"

Ingrid opened wide eyes that reminded him of their mother's. His chest unexpectedly tightened. "Don't you dare speak to him about that! I don't want to get *married*. I'm only eighteen!"

"So? Plenty of women are married at your age."

"And plenty of men are married at your age yet I don't see you rushing into anything. Or..." Her eyes widened further, betraying her excitement. "Are you saying you mean to propose to your mysterious sweetheart?"

As soon as the words left his sister's lips, Björn knew that was exactly what he wanted to do. She'd only meant to tease him but in doing so she'd made him see the light. He could not bear the idea that the night he had spent with Dunne would be the only one. Because if he didn't marry her, it would be, he knew it in his bones. He had been lucky once, but he sensed she would not let him bed her a second time without some sort of commitment on his part. Being used for a man's pleasure and discarded when the mood suited him was simply not what a woman like her would be looking for—or deserved.

Soon she would wake up and realize the enormity of what they had done, swear to herself it would never happen again.

Them ending up in bed together had seemed inevitable to him, because he'd been longing after her for so long that he could not see any other way, but she would no doubt feel differently. She might think this had been brought on by their discussion about Toland and her need to be shown she was desirable and could feel pleasure in a man's arms, nothing more. She might think he had used her to lose a virginity which was becoming a burden to him. The fact that he had not kissed her once, only used her body time and time again would certainly allow for the misunderstanding.

His heart and guts twisted at the same time. Right now,

alone in her hut, Dunne might be regretting their night together, thinking he didn't feel anything for her other than lust. It was not to be borne.

"Mark my words," he told his sister slowly. "I fully intent to get married before the end of the year."

Now he just had to convince his future bride.

CHAPTER NINE

"I will go and see Birgit."

Dunne's announcement was greeted with the disbelief it deserved. Her sister stared at her as if she'd grown a second head.

"You mean you are going all the way to Mercia?" Frigyth sat back on her chair and narrowed her eyes. "Why now?"

Dunne shrugged, trying to appear innocent when her cheeks were burning. "Why not? I have wanted to go for a while. We haven't seen her since her marriage to Hereward more than five years ago. Now that I am free to do what I want and go where I wish, I want to see her."

"Mm. You know, if you wait a few more months, I could accompany you. I, too, would like to see our sister." She glanced at her rounded belly pointedly. The babe was due in less than two months. It wouldn't be comfortable or wise for her to travel such a distance now, when she could go into labor at any moment. But Dunne could not wait. This was not about Frigyth, or even the sister she had not seen in years, it had everything to do with her inability to face what she had done with Björn.

"No," she murmured. "It has to be now. By the time you are ready to travel it will be winter and the roads will be treacherous."

"The roads!" With a snort Frigyth dropped the pretense that this was about anything other than the Norseman she was trying to avoid. "Listen, we both know that this has nothing to do with Birgit but with Björn. You are fleeing him."

Well, what if she was, Dunne thought irritably? Wasn't it her decision to make? "I need time, and distance. I can't face him after what happened between us, surely you can understand that?"

"Not really. There is nothing more normal than a man and a woman sleeping together. I face Sigurd every morning, don't I, regardless of what went on the night before?"

Dunne refused to meet her sister's gaze. "That's different. You're married."

"Well, yes, we are now," Frigyth conceded. "But we weren't always. We did sleep together before that, in case you don't remember. I told you as much."

"I know you did. But remind me, what did you do the morning after that?"

Frigyth closed her eyes. "I fled and went back home."

"There you are, so don't go telling me not to—"

"It wasn't the same at all. I didn't flee because I regretted what we had done, far from it! I had actually hoped we could start something from there. I only left because that same day he got involved in a fight with the man who...who..."

Feeling worse than she had ever felt, Dunne placed a soothing hand over Frigyth's arm. She knew all about her ordeal at the hands of the Norsemen who had since been sent away in disgrace and she should never have used that dreadful weapon to defend herself. "I'm sorry. I shouldn't have asked you that. Please forgive me."

Under her palm she felt Frigyth shiver. "In any case, this is not about me and Sigurd, even if I will add that fleeing didn't get me anywhere. I tried to fight the inevitable and look where it got me."

She stroked her belly, making her meaning clear. There was no point running away. Dunne swallowed.

"I'm sorry," she said in a breath. "But I was never as strong as you are."

"You—"

"No, I wasn't, and you know it." That was the truth. Frigyth had always been the strongest of the three sisters. Maybe it was because of her friendship with a neighbor called Caedmon, who had looked after her and thus protected her from the worst of their miserable childhood, maybe it was due to something she'd been born with, Dunne didn't know. Either way, Frigyth was more resilient than anyone she knew. She could have crumbled after what had happened at the hands of the evil Norseman, but she had not. Instead, she had found the life she deserved with a man from that same village.

As if he'd sensed his wife needed him, Sigurd entered the hut at that moment, strong and dependable. He went straight to her and placed a kiss on her mouth, before giving her belly a loving stroke.

"Are you all right, Birdie?" Concern made him frown. "You look—"

"I'm all right. Just a little weary."

"Carrying my babe isn't too much of a burden, I hope?"

Frigyth smiled and placed a hand over his cheek. "No. Never that."

Dunne averted her eyes. Such domestic bliss had always seemed unattainable and now it just seemed to taunt her.

"I will leave in the morning," she said, standing up. There was no point in delaying the inevitable. The sooner she left, the better. "Would you look after Dawn for me? This is not a trip for someone her age."

Seeing there would be no budging her, Frigyth nodded. "Of course."

Sigurd straightened back up. "You're leaving? Without your daughter? Where are you going?"

"To see Birgit."

His eyes almost popped out of his head. "Your sister, Birgit? The one who lives in Mercia? Well, you can't travel on your own," he ruled once he had recovered from the surprise. "It's too far. Too dangerous a journey for a woman on her own."

"There will always be an excuse for me not to go. It's been five years since we have seen each other. I miss her."

She did miss her sister, but she knew she was only using it as an excuse. Thankfully, Sigurd was not to know that.

He seemed to mull on this for a while. "Wait another few days. At the end of the week a group of villagers are going to a fair in Lincoln. You can travel with them for most of the way. They will drop you off when you're close enough. It's the only way I will let you go."

There would be no convincing him that she would be fine on her own. Her brother-in-law had always been very protective of her. And, in truth, she was relieved at the idea of having an escort. The journey to her sister's village would take four or five days in her estimation, longer if she didn't manage to find transportation and had to walk some of the way. If she could avoid being on her own for most of that time, it would reassure her.

Yes, it was better to wait.

The only problem was, she had no idea how she would manage to avoid Björn for the best part of a week.

IN THE END she could not even avoid him for a day.

As she rounded the corner of her hut later that afternoon, she found herself face to face with him. Evidently, he had come to see her. Cursing her ill-luck, Dunne came to an abrupt halt. If only she had stayed another moment with Frigyth and Sigurd, they would have missed each other. At least he was dressed today, not bare-chested, she noted wryly. Unable to meet his eye, she lowered her gaze to his hands and regretted it when the memories of how he had caressed her made her shiver.

"Dunne."

"Björn. How are you?" So dreadfully formal. She kept her head bowed.

"I'm very well. You?"

"I'm well." She shuffled on her feet. This was excruciating. "I'm going to see my sister Birgit next week."

Why was she telling him that? Because she was ill at ease and had no idea what else to say, that was why. The only other option was to talk about their night together and she couldn't do that.

Mercifully Björn followed her lead and pretended this was a normal conversation to have with someone you had last seen naked and hoarse from shouting your name in ecstasy. "Does she live in town?"

Could she lie? She sensed he wouldn't like the real answer, but she could not see a way to avoid telling the truth. "No. She lives in Mercia. Just before Lincoln."

"Mercia?"

Björn recoiled. Had Dunne told him Birgit lived in Denmark, he might not have been more surprised. She was going to *Mercia*? Now? Why?

The answer descended upon him like an eagle diving on its prey.

She was leaving because of him.

He had disappointed her. Not because he had been unable to ensure her physical pleasure. He had seen, heard and felt that her body at least had been sated by his attentions. But somehow he must not have given her what she expected, he had disappointed her by not being more tender, and not kissing her, by leaving her bed before she woke up.

"Have I done anything to upset you?" he murmured, although he already knew what the answer would be.

"N-no." Still she refused to meet his eye. Clearly he had, only she lacked the courage to tell him as much.

It was as bad as he had feared. Because he had not kissed her, she thought last night had meant nothing to him other than an opportunity to finally bed a woman. By the gods, she would resent him for using her for his pleasure, for pounding into her all night, and then leaving at dawn without a word. He'd possessed her one last time while she was still half asleep, without asking what she wanted, and then he'd left while she'd slept, too exhausted by his relentless attention to resist the lure of some well-earned rest.

She would have been hurt and humiliated to find herself alone in the morning, to see he had not given her any assurances of commitment and left as if what they had done didn't matter. It did matter. More than she knew, more than he could tell.

Appalled, he stared at her. "You think I should have—"

"It matters not what I think, what is done is done. Perhaps... Perhaps we should forget about it."

Everything within Björn protested. Forget about the best night of his life? Behave as if nothing had happened between him and the woman he wanted above all others? That was the last thing he wanted to do! He had come to her to talk about what they should do next, perhaps even mention marriage, *not* to agree to pretend nothing had happened.

He bunched his fists. How had he thought for a moment he would be enough for this woman? How had he fooled himself that she would want him after he'd treated her so callously, that she would be satisfied with an inexperienced, clumsy lover not decent enough to tell her what he'd felt in her arms, not thoughtful enough to kiss her while he took possession of her body and so stupid he'd made it all look like a meaningless fuck. It had been more, so much more than that. Dunne, the goddess he had hankered after for years, had allowed him access to her gorgeous body and he had lost himself in the delight of it, forgotten everything else, indulged his senses, and gorged on her like Geri and Freki, the two wolves the god Odin fed from his own plate, gorged on meat.

As a result, he stood to lose all he had hoped to gain only this morning.

"I don't want to forget about it," he said through gritted teeth. "Dunne, look at me, damn it!"

"I can't." There were sobs in her voice.

Ruthlessly, he lifted her chin up to him. Her amber eyes were brimming with unshed tears. The sight sliced through him. He was making her cry when all he wanted was to make her happy.

"We need to talk about this, I know I've not—"

"Not now. Please. I can't."

There would be no sense in pushing her when she was so distraught. He would have to wait until she was ready. "When then? Tell me when I can come to tell you what I need to tell you."

"I don't know." She shook her head. "I'm sorry, I can't do this. I have to go."

And he knew she didn't mean just now, to go to her hut. She meant she had to leave the village, get away from him, go all the way to Mercia alone, and put herself in danger as she did. All because of him.

He watched, powerless, as she slammed the door of her hut behind her.

CHAPTER TEN

Avoiding Björn was easy in the end, because he made sure to stay out of her way. Why? Dunne had expected having to find excuses for not seeing him, but she had not anticipated he would be the one avoiding her for days on end. What did it mean? Was he regretting their night together? Had he been offended by her suggestion that they should forget about it? Or perhaps it was even worse. Perhaps he had been piqued when she had refused to see him the other day because he had come to her hut for another wild tryst. If that were the case, then it meant he was only interested in her for the pleasure he could get out of her body, not a flattering or satisfying proposition to say the least.

Yes, Dunne reflected with a heavy heart, as awful as it was, he had to be avoiding her because he thought she would not indulge his senses anymore and he'd lost interest. In his mind, there was no point in coming to see her if she refused him access to her bed. He had found himself someone else and was too busy bedding his new lover to worry about her, a woman who had said she wanted to forget about what they had done.

The pain all this caused her was best not to be dwelled on.

The sooner she left the village, the better. Away from Björn's disturbing presence, and in a place where she was in no danger of bumping into him, where no one even knew him, she would be able to put all this behind her.

At least that was the hope.

Finally, the morning of her departure came.

Dunne stared at the group of people assembled by their carts, ready to leave. She didn't know any of them, except for one, one she had not thought would take part in the expedition.

"What is Björn doing there?" she growled in her sister's ear. Surely he was not joining the convoy, and had only come to bid a friend farewell? But then why was he hoisting a bundle of clothes onto the back of a cart?

Frigyth shrugged. "He's going to the fair himself, apparently, to buy new casks for his ale."

Dunne recoiled. After having avoided her for a week and given her the impression he didn't care about her, the wretched man was going to travel with them? What was he playing at? "Does he have to travel hundreds of miles to get new casks?" she snapped. "Can't he get any in town?"

"What do I know? I don't know anything about the brewing of ale."

She was not so easily appeased. Say what Frigyth might, this could not be a simple coincidence. "You are behind this, are you not?" Had her sister gone to Björn to beg him to travel with her? Had she wanted to give them a chance to talk about what they should do now?

"No, I swear. He came to see Sigurd the other day and they talked. That is all I know."

Dunned groaned. She could all too easily imagine how that conversation had gone. Björn had asked if it was true she was going to Mercia and Sigurd had told him he'd organized it for her to travel with a group of merchants. Perhaps he had encouraged his young friend to go with them. Why? Did he know about her and Björn? She wouldn't be surprised if Frigyth had betrayed her secret to the husband with whom she shared everything. Or was it worse than that? Had Sigurd been outside the hut that day as well, and heard them together? Was anyone else aware of what had happened? Her hut was not in the middle of the village but still, anyone could have walked by and heard her shout Björn's name over and over again.

Whatever the reason for it, her brother-in-law evidently wanted to ensure that she and Björn spent the next few days together, in the hope that it would force them to talk. Well, she would not be so easily manipulated. They couldn't talk if they weren't within speaking distance, could they?

Björn's eyes threw daggers at her when she climbed into the cart of a man she had never seen before. The man, who seemed all too glad to have her travel by his side, introduced himself as Harald.

"I live just outside the village, that's why we've never met," he told her as the cart just in front of them started to move, signaling the departure of the convoy. "I'm going to sell my wool. My sheep have the best fleeces around, so I should get a good price for them."

Not sure what to answer, Dunne smiled politely. Mistaking this for an encouragement, Harald started to explain his technique to get the fleece off from the animal as neatly as possible while he steered his cart onto the path.

A moment later everyone was on their way and she resigned herself to hearing all there was to know about the shearing of sheep.

Björn spent the whole morning ruminating to himself. Harald's cart was the second in the line and his was the last, which meant he was not able to keep an eye on the wool merchant and see that he behaved appropriately. He wouldn't put it past him to try and make the most of having a beautiful woman traveling by his side. There had been a glint in his eyes when Dunne had asked if he could have her in his cart, one he knew all too well. The man lusted after her. He couldn't blame him, but he could still fear the outcome of such interest.

Why had Dunne chosen to go to a man she barely knew in preference to him? Damn it all, he must have really committed some unspeakable offense the night he had bedded her because she had not only decided to flee him, she also seemed determined to make him pay for it.

His heart plummeted because he could guess all too well what this offense was. He had tried to avoid the truth all week, but he could not ignore it any longer. Not only had he behaved callously toward her, but he had not tried to protect her from the consequences of their lovemaking.

That had to be why she was so angry with him.

It was yet another proof of his inexperience that he had not understood before why she might be. It had taken a crude comment from Arne about him preferring to have women swallow his seed to make him realize what he had done. Instead of withdrawing when he was about to reach his release, like a careful lover should have, he had spilled inside her, repeatedly. It had been impossible not to, he had lacked the control—and worse, the will—to do what was needed to ensure that their encounter did not bear fruit.

No wonder she was furious with him. Lost to the moment, she had not thought about it, but upon waking up she had remembered how he had not even tried to spend outside her body, preferring his pleasure to her protection. And because of this she was now convinced he cared nothing for her or for the possibility that he might have made her with child.

Damn it, he should have offered his help in dealing with it all, thought to provide her with the means of washing herself, at least, instead of vanishing like a thief, assured her he would look after his child, if there was a child. Well, that was why he was here, to make sure they could talk about what to do next.

After what felt like an eternity, the miller, who was at the head of the convoy, called for a halt. Björn was down from his seat in the blink of an eye and heading for the wool merchant. He reached the cart in time to see him hand Dunne down. Predictably, she didn't even look in his direction, even if it was obvious she had seen him.

Anger, fueled by shame at his inadequacies, caused something within him to snap.

She was determined to behave as if he didn't exist? Let's see how long it would last.

"Harald, listen," he told the merchant in Norse to make sure she did not understand him. There was little point as she was already walking away but he preferred to take his precautions. "Your mare is limping and your cart is piled high with bags. My horse is young and my cart is empty. I will take the Saxon with me this afternoon."

"Ah, don't worry about it, the nag will manage, it's only wool in the bags and the Saxon's not that heavy. A bit on the plump side maybe, but—"

"She's not fat!" he instantly snarled, remembering how Dunne had been hurt by her husband's criticism. If Harald said one more word about her physique, he would throttle him on the spot. Anything to prevent him for reawakening her insecurities.

"Oh no, she's not fat, she's just right. I like to have something to hold on to while I—"

This time Björn grabbed the man by the tunic and slammed his back against the nearest tree. "You will spare me—and her— the tale of what you like to do to women in bed. She is coming with me this afternoon and that's that."

"Why should she travel with you?" There was nothing he could answer to that. He had no claim over her whatsoever. Seeing he had scored a point, Harald smirked. "I'll tell you what. We'll ask her what she prefers. It's only fair to give her a say in this, don't you think?"

Björn's heart sank. Dunne would never choose him, not when she was at pains to avoid him. Nevertheless, short of removing her bodily from the wool merchant's cart, there was nothing he could do but agree with Harald's suggestion.

They found her by the stream, filling her cup with cool water. She stiffened when she saw them together, as if she anticipated problems and he could not blame her. In the mood he was in, it would not take much to push him into a fight.

"Dunne," Harald said, tucking his thumbs into his belt like a man assured of his victory. "We're about to set off. Who would you like to travel with this afternoon? Me again, or the ale-making pup?"

Björn clenched his fists. The man was not only disparaging him for his age, but he was also mocking him for doing an activity usually reserved for women. He'd heard the jab many a time in the past few months and it had never bothered him. Now it did, because the last thing he wanted was to appear ridiculous in front of Dunne. Things were bad enough as it was.

He waited, doing his best to hide the pain in his chest.

Dunne's heart started fluttering. What could she tell Harald?

I don't want to travel with you, not when you spent the whole morning boring me to tears with your stories and touching my thigh every chance you got. But I don't want to be alone with Björn either. It would be a recipe for disaster. I would only blurt out something I'd regret later.

She might want to avoid him but that didn't mean it would be easy, not when her whole body was yearning for him.

A short woman Dunne recognized as the miller's wife chose this moment to approach. She most likely had seen the confrontation from a distance and thought the Saxon needed help in dealing with the two menacing Norsemen, for which Dunne was grateful, because well, she did need help.

"Leave the poor woman alone, you strutting cockerels!" the woman admonished. Her accent made the words barely understandable but there was no mistaking her intent. "She will travel with me and my husband this afternoon and for the remainder of the journey. At least that way she will be assured no one will try to get under her skirts. We will go make some room for her in the back of the cart right now."

There was no gainsaying the woman. Neither of the men said a word. Relief washed through Dunne. The last thing she saw before following her savior back to the convoy were Björn's eyes glinting with ill-contained fury.

After the company had partaken of a quick meal Dunne sat in the couple's cart, amongst sacks of flour of varying sizes. The journey was excruciating. She had to brace herself against whatever she could find to try to absorb the shocks every time the vehicle rounded a bend or jumped over a pothole. As if that was not enough, she had to endure the woman's endless questioning. Just before they stopped for the night, one of the sacks, the one that had threatened to fall for the whole journey, finally gave up and toppled onto her as the miller urged the horse to a trot. The sack was so heavy that it knocked her against the side of the cart. Her head hit the wood and stars exploded in her vision. When the company finally came to a halt shortly thereafter, Dunne could feel an egg-sized lump forming on her temple. No doubt she was bruised all over and covered in white powder as well, courtesy of the flour escaping through the rough sack material.

Everyone alighted, ready to set up camp. The miller's wife

came to see her and skidded to a halt at the sight meeting her eyes.

"What on earth happened here? You look as if you've been in the wars, my dear, all bruised and battered! Is that flour in your hair?"

"Yes," Dunne mumbled. What else could it be? Really the woman's heart was in the right place, but she didn't have the sharpest mind. "One of the sacks fell on me."

"Will you look at that! You poor girl!" The woman was fussing, tapping her shoulders, her back, her hair, ignoring her protests that she was fine. "Mind you, the cart is not meant to transport people. I suppose it is not as comfortable as one might expect."

"No." That was the least Dunne could say. Another three days being tossed about between planks of wood and rock-hard sacks of flour was more than she could contemplate. "I thank you for the help, but I think I will carry on with Björn for the rest of the journey."

She had tried her best to avoid him, but she had to concede defeat. She was not stupid enough to risk injuring herself just to stay out of his way.

"Well, if you're sure..." The woman made a face.

"It's all right. He's a good friend of my sister's husband. I'm sure I will be fine with him."

"Yes..." She still didn't sound convinced. Dunne had to put an end to the whole thing before she snapped. The miller's wife meant well but this conversation was the last straw. She was hungry, her head was throbbing, and her patience was running to an end more quickly than she would have liked.

"What threat can he pose to me, really? He grew that beard while he was in Denmark to make people forget the fact that he's only a boy, barely old enough to know what goes on between men and women."

The woman chuckled. "You're probably right there. Rorik and his wife always cosseted their children. His impressive physique notwithstanding, the boy might not yet know what delights he could find under a woman's skirts. My son Arne told me only the other day he refused to go with them in town to see to his...manly needs if you know what I mean. He clearly hasn't felt any urges yet."

Dunne could barely contain her disbelief. Was that what the woman thought? How blind could one be? Björn was all about virility, his beard didn't hide anything, it only highlighted his masculinity. And if he hadn't gone to the stew house with his drunken friends, then that only proved he was a whole lot more mature than the lot of them. Still, she had finally got what she wanted—a way out of another day at the back of the miller's cart, so she kept her mouth shut.

"So you see. I can sit next to him tomorrow without fearing for my virtue," she concluded.

The woman nodded.

He's only a boy.

Björn's fists tightened of their own accord while his blood started to drum in his temples. Was that what Dunne thought, even after all they'd done in her bed? That he had no idea of what should happen between a man and a woman? Was that why she didn't want to have anything to do with him, because she thought him too young? All this while he'd been worried she'd resented his callousness or thought him unwilling to commit to her, and now he was finding out that it was a lot more simple than that.

He's only a boy.

How dismissive she had sounded, how scathing! He suspected the wound she had inflicted with her hurtful words would fester until his dying day. She was rejecting him not for a mistake he had made that could be corrected for something he had no control over. His age. Of all the things she could have said, this was the worst. He could learn to pleasure her better, he could make amends for his thoughtlessness, he could offer to look after her if he had made her with child, but he could not make himself older. He would eventually grow into an old man, but all his life he would be ten years younger than she was. If she objected to that then there was nothing he could do.

Which didn't mean he did not feel the full force of his disillusion.

He remained hidden in the shadows, biding his time, knowing she would have to walk past him at some point or other. Then he would pounce and make her pay for the pain she had caused him.

The miller's wife ambled past, and did not see him, ensconced as he was in his hiding place. He waited. A moment later, it was Dunne's turn to walk past the bushes. Making sure to look as menacing as possible, he placed himself right on her path. She would have to rethink her definition of harmless little boys after today.

"Björn!" His name was little more than a squeal. "Lord, you made me jump."

Oh, he would do more than make her jump. He would make her squirm. He might make her cry. And this time he would not comfort her. If she was hurt she would have no one but herself to blame. She had brought it on herself.

He opened his mouth, ready to unleash his wrath on to her —and froze. Night had not quite yet fallen. It was still light enough for him to see that there was a mighty bruise on Dunne's temple, just above her delicately-shaped eyebrow. His fury vanished in a puff of smoke at the sight.

"Who did that to you?" he asked, glaring in the direction of the wool merchant's cart. Had Harald tried to touch her? He could not understand when the man could have attacked her, but someone evidently had. Who?

"A sack of flour. Or rather, the c-cart, it—"

"What are you talking about?" he growled, interrupting Dunne's mumbled explanation. Was she more seriously injured than he had first supposed? She wasn't making any sense, talking about sacks of flour and carts when he'd asked for the name of her attacker.

"No one hurt me. I simply bumped my head against the side of the cart when a sack of flour fell on me," she said more calmly. "The whole ride was horrid, really. I think I must be covered in bruises. That is why I would prefer to travel with you tomorrow, on a proper seat, if I may."

His nostrils flared. *Now* she wanted to make use of him? "So. Between another battering and time alone with me, you choose me. I'm flattered."

She recoiled at the ice in his tone but he didn't offer any apologies. If she knew she'd come a hair's breadth from the tongue lashing of her life, she would count herself lucky.

"If you prefer, I-I could—"

"I prefer nothing. You will travel with me for the rest of the journey, and no one else. I mean for you to reach your sister's home in one piece. There will be no more fighting against sacks of flour or a smithy's tools or wool merchants or anything else. Since apparently I can pose no threat to you whatsoever, you will stay with me."

He planted himself in front of her and had the satisfaction of seeing her inhale at his proximity. The "boy" had the power to send her weak with fear. Or was it limp with arousal? Should he remove his shirt to make sure? The idea crossed his mind before he rejected it as foolish. He didn't need to prove she liked his body, he already knew that she did.

What he now needed to see was that she could like him for something else.

CHAPTER ELEVEN

That night as she lay by the side of the fire with the other women, Dunne found she couldn't sleep. The stiffness caused in her body by the ride in the miller's cart didn't help, but she suspected her restlessness had another cause. Björn. He had been unusually sharp with her earlier and she could not account for it. And yet, angry as he had been, he had insisted that she ride with him for the rest of the journey. It didn't make sense.

But then nothing made sense where he was concerned, first and foremost her feelings for him. She shouldn't be attracted to him but he drew her in a way she didn't understand.

She turned onto her back and stared at the sky above, a dark, glittering ribbon framed by black trees.

It was odd to be outside at such a time. Raised in town, she had never slept outdoors before and could not completely relax, even if she knew the men would take turns keeping guard. Björn had been designated to be the first. For a moment, she toyed with the idea of going to keep him company, but then she forced herself to stay where she was. After their tense conversation earlier, she wasn't sure what his reaction would be if he saw her coming to him. But it felt wrong to be allowed to sleep while he had to stay awake.

High above them, a white blaze ripped through the velvety sky, a sudden, silent burst of light. Dunne blinked. She had heard about these shooting stars but had never seen one before. It was breathtakingly beautiful and gone in a heartbeat.

Just like Björn. He had been an unexpected, sudden burst of joy in her life, destined to disappear as quickly as he had come. Except...Unlike the star, he had not fallen from the skies, he was real, a man of flesh and blood. He was also here, just a few paces away. She could go to him, get more of the blinding pleasure he had offered her, and feel her body burst into flames once more. Or, she could have if he had not been so unsuitable for her and she could imagine a future with him. At the moment she could not.

It was hopeless.

When she saw him swap places with the miller and join the men sleeping under the trees for a well-earned rest, she closed her eyes and finally fell asleep.

In the morning a surprise was awaiting her.

"You've shaved your beard!" the miller's wife exclaimed, planting both her fists on her generous hips in amusement.

Dunne could only stare at the smooth chin Björn had revealed. Her fingers started to itch with the urge to stroke his strong jaw. It was difficult to decide which suited him better, the blond beard or the shaven skin. One made you want to stroke it, the other made you want to lick it.

Lick it? A burst of heat spread through her chest. Had she just imagined herself following the edge of his jaw with her tongue? Yes, she had. She really was going mad.

Björn skewered her with a lethal look before answering the miller's wife. "I was bored last night, keeping watch. This gave me something to do. And I see no need pretending I'm a man, when we all know that I really am nothing but a boy."

While everyone laughed, Dunne felt her insides wither. That was why he'd looked ready to shred her to ribbons when he had pounced on her last night, why he'd told her he couldn't possibly pose any threat to her. He'd heard her talk to the miller's wife. Her insides withered.

She had to tell him she hadn't meant a single scathing word.

But how? They were in full view of everyone and what could she say that he would want to hear? He looked ready to bite her head off. In that mood he would not listen to her.

"Come, pup," Harald said, slapping him on the shoulder. "Time to leave camp."

They set off as soon as all the furs had been rolled up and the horses fed and watered. Accepting Björn's hand to climb into the driver's seat, Dunne wondered if she had not better go with Harald after all. It was not hard to guess that the journey would be uncomfortable. Björn's face was like thunder and she could not blame him.

The only thing she could do to make things right was to apologize to him and explain why she had said what she had said.

As they exited the meadow, she braced herself. The more she waited, the more time she would give his resentment to churn. It would only make things worse.

"I..." Her voice came out as a whisper. "I never meant what I said last night to the—"

"I'm sorry?" Björn didn't even look at her. "You'll have to speak up if you want me to hear what you're saying."

She cleared her throat, wondering if she would have the strength to speak louder. "I only called you a boy last night because I—"

"I think I understand why you did it, thank you," he cut in, his voice as cold as winter snow. "You called me a boy because you think that's what I am. And why not? I'm ten years younger than you, I've never lived with someone other than my parents, who cosseted me by all accounts, I do chores reserved for women and children and up until last week I was still a virgin. I can see why people who have known me for years would think of me as a boy with no male urges. Except that *you* should know differently, shouldn't you?"

Blue eyes pinned her in place when he finally deigned to look at her. Oh, he was in a towering rage! But she could not be defeated so easily. She could not make him believe her, but she could at least try to.

"I do know you are all man," she whispered. "And I only meant to ensure that the miller's wife let me go with you by speaking thus. I'm not proud of it, but it was the best way to make her believe you didn't see me as a woman to be seduced."

"But we both know I do. And I do have male urges, even if I choose not to indulge them with whores. I've proved it to you, I think, more than once."

Dunne felt her whole body crumple. He'd only bedded her because he thought the alternative—going to paid women—was unsavory. She had not seen that coming. To think she'd believed he had bedded because he wanted her! It turned out he had only jumped at the chance to bed a woman. And who better than someone foolish enough to think she had provoked desire within him and be both flattered and aroused by the notion?

He had been hurt to hear her tell another woman he was only a boy? Well, she felt sickened by the notion that he thought her only marginally better than a whore.

It was only when Dunne's face went the color of chalk that Björn realized how she had interpreted what he'd said. He had made it sound as if he'd used her to find out what happened between men and women without having to pay for it, as if he'd thought bedding her would be less demeaning and more satisfactory for his male pride than going to the stew house. The fact that he had left without a word in the morning and had not even kissed her as he'd made love to her would only confirm this humiliating impression.

Appalled, he understood he had all but called her a whore.

"I didn't mean I—"

"You don't need to explain. It is very clear. You were tired of being a virgin but could not bring yourself to go to the women in town. I was there, and I was willing. Why would you not make the most of the opportunity? You lifted me in your arms and I did not push you away. You told me you wanted me and I let you bed me. You are not to be blamed in any way." The bitterness in her voice raked through his guts.

"It wasn't anything like that!"

She raised a hand as if it were not even worth discussing. "I think we had better stop talking. All we seem to do is hurt each other."

The rest of the morning was spent in silence. When they stopped to give the horses a break, Dunne climbed down the seat without his help. Once the convoy was ready to leave, he saw her hesitate. In that moment, he knew that she was contemplating going with someone else. Well, he wouldn't beg her to choose him.

He climbed on, and stared ahead until, at last, he felt her weight tilt the cart.

They rode on, the tension between them palpable. Björn could hardly bear it. He could see only one way of repairing what had been broken between them.

She thought he was too young, but he could do the mature thing and rectify the pain he had unwittingly caused her. He'd all but called her a whore; so he had to make her see that he actually wanted her as his wife.

"Dunne."

The voice, soft and tentative, could have been part of her dream, but not the touch of a finger sliding over her cheek. That had to be real.

When Dunne opened her eyes, she found Björn kneeling next to her. Around them, everyone was still sleeping. It was dark, but birds had started to sing, heralding the fact that dawn was not too far.

"What's the matter?" Instantly alert, she bolted upright. She knew Björn had been in charge of the last stretch of the watch. Why was he waking her up? Had he seen something worrying? She could not hear nor discern anything, but then again, she'd been asleep and Björn would not have disturbed her sleep for no reason.

"Come, there's something I need to do."

This made her frown. After the way they had spent the previous day, barely talking, accusing one another of the worst intentions, he wanted her to be with him when he went investigating a possible danger? What did he expect her to do if there were marauders in the woods, or a family of irate boars in the undergrowth? "Do you really need me for it?" she asked weakly.

"Yes."

Surprising her, he took her by the hand and led her behind some thick bushes. As soon as they were hidden from view from the group, her heart started to beat alarmingly fast. Could he mean to waylay her? It was possible, if he thought her little more than a wanton he could tumble at will. Did she want him to take her? No. Of course, not, she assured herself, ignoring the throbbing in her veins.

"What are you—"

Before she could finish the sentence, she found herself pressed against a strong chest and kissed with breathtaking urgency. The softness of Björn's lips was something of a shock. Considering how strong the rest of his body was, she had expected his kiss to bruise her mouth. It did not, and that was not the only thing she could not make sense of. The desire blossoming inside her frightened her as much as it caused her pleasure, the urge to stroke his tongue with hers puzzled her and yet she could not fight it.

Björn seemed equally torn. Even if he kept his touch gentle, she could feel an undercurrent of fierceness swirling under the careful gestures, as if he wanted to devour her but did not dare frighten her.

All in all, it was a thoroughly disconcerting experience.

And all the more intoxicating for it.

"What was that for?" she asked when he finally drew away from her.

It had been the first kiss they had shared, her first real kiss, and it had come out of nowhere. She didn't understand why Björn would have kissed her now, of all times. It was not as if it had happened in the heat of the moment, as if it had been motivated by irrepressible desire in the midst of lovemaking or even blistering anger, during yet another argument. Björn had planned this. He had woken her up for this exact purpose and taken her to a secluded place so he could kiss her without everyone knowing.

Why?

He placed his forehead against hers and cradled her neck between his palms. The heat of his touch was welcome in the chilly morning, as much as the reassurance of seeing that he wanted to make peace with her, even after their awful arguments. She closed her eyes.

"I should have kissed you the night I made love to you. I

should not have left so abruptly in the morning, and made you think I used you to lose my virginity, nothing more."

She swallowed. How had he guessed she needed to hear she had been more than a tool for him? "I know you don't want to go to wh—"

"I don't," he cut her ruthlessly. "But that doesn't mean I would ever use anyone in such a way. If all I wanted was a willing woman in my bed, I would have lost my virginity a long time ago." Yes. That much made no doubt. He could have had his pick of conquests. "I do not want you to think you were only an alternative to paying a woman to accept my attention, I do not want you to think that night meant nothing to me."

"I believe you." His kiss had been too tender for her to doubt his sincerity, and he sounded too desperate to have her forgive the pain he had caused her. She mattered to him, he cared for her, at least in some way.

"You do?" Relief swept through Björn. Dunne didn't resent him. She didn't hate him. All was not lost.

"I do. But why did you want to kiss me instead of just explaining what you felt?" she asked, placing a trembling hand against her lips.

"You said we shouldn't talk, as we only seem to cause each other pain. But I had to make you understand somehow that it hadn't been like that for me, make you see that I didn't touch you as I would have a whore." He clenched his teeth. Just saying the words felt like an insult. But he had to leave her in no doubt about his feelings. The idea that she could think such a thing, feel so soiled, was killing him. "I made love to you because I wanted you so damn badly. I thought I'd made that clear but let me say it again. I wanted you, and I want you still."

"Please, don't say such things," she whispered, lifting huge eyes to him. The sun had pierced the horizon and was sending its gold light straight into them, making them shine like molten honey.

"Why not, when they are true?"

Instead of answering, she kissed him. Björn moaned his surprise and delight into her mouth and tightened his hold around her. What was she doing by provoking him so? Couldn't she feel the hard ridge pressing between them? It would not take much to tip him over the edge.

"I swear I don't think of you as a boy," she breathed when he finally found the strength to release her. "I only wanted to convince the woman I could ride with—"

He cut her off by kissing her a third time. He couldn't get enough of her, of feeling her body pressed against his, of tasting her sweet lips. Why had he not thought of kissing her while he'd had her in his arms that first night? It did not make sense. Now it was all he wanted to do.

"We've both said things we didn't mean, things we regret or that were misinterpreted. No more."

"No more," she agreed.

Still holding her face in the cradle of his palms, he again placed his forehead against hers. "No more lies. From now on, we'll be honest with each other."

"Yes."

And yet at that moment Björn knew he was still withholding something from her. His intention to make her his wife. He would have to tell her, but not today. They had only just cleared the misunderstanding between them. They had kissed. They were talking again.

For now it would have to be enough.

"Don't shave your beard again," Dunne said, placing a tentative hand on Björn's jaw. It was rough with golden stubble that glittered in the dawn light. "Or..." she amended when she realized it sounded like an order. "Not on my account anyway. You have nothing to prove to me or anyone. You are just..."

You are just perfect the way you are.

He was. But she could not tell him as much. They had promised to be honest but there was a limit to what she was prepared to admit.

"I won't shave ever again." It sounded like a promise heavy with meaning. Her chest tightened.

"Why are you here, Björn? Why did you decide to go to the fair? You are no merchant, you didn't need to go all the way to Lincoln."

His blue eyes shimmered. "I'm here because you left me no choice. At the village you refused to talk to me, and you would have left before we could discuss what we needed to discuss. I had to come. There was no other way."

"Yes. I can see that."

And she was glad he had. Only now that the air had been cleared did she realize how miserable she had been, thinking everything had been spoilt between them.

Noises started to reach their ears. People groaning and laughing, pots and pans being cleaned, horses being hitched to carts. The camp was waking up. Björn took a step backward.

"I will go first, taking a detour in the undergrowth."

Dunne nodded. That way it would look as if they had each gone to see to their personal needs upon waking up. No one would know about the kisses they had shared. Her lips still felt swollen, but she guessed it would be imperceptible to the casual observer.

Silent as a shadow, Björn slipped through the bushes.

Her heart lighter than it had been in days, she walked back up to the camp.

CHAPTER TWELVE

The next couple of days were spent in a blur. Sitting together on the cart's driver's seat, Dunne and Björn got the opportunity to get to know each other better. There was little choice anyway, as there was nothing else to do but talk from morn till dusk. She found out more about his parents, what he had done during his trip to Denmark, she talked about Dawn and her antics, making him laugh.

It was perfect, but it was over all too soon.

When they reached the crossroads where they were to part ways, Dunne stared at the road ahead with a sense of foreboding. The farmer they had asked earlier had told her she had a two days' walk left before she arrived. It would be long, but if she just followed the road, she would eventually reach her sister's village.

Yes, easy enough. But suddenly the prospect was impossibly daunting. A heavy mist had stolen across the land that afternoon, preventing her from seeing what lay ahead in the distance, friends, or most pointedly, foes.

"Safe journey, dear," the miller's wife told her, hugging her tight.

Dunne nodded, hoping that would be the case. Now that everything had been resolved between her and Björn, she wondered what she was doing here in strange surroundings. She had left the village to avoid him but now she would have liked nothing more than to spend another day the way she had spent the last three, sitting next to him.

Instead, she had to go into the unknown alone.

Once the miller's wife had released her, Harald planted himself in front of her. For a moment it looked as if he was going to draw her into his arms as well. She steeled herself for it, but he merely leaned in to speak into her ear. "Goodbye, Dunne, I hope we'll see more of each other when we get back to the village. You'll want a man your own age in your life, not someone who needs a mother figu—"

"Come, Dunne," Björn said gruffly, interrupting the man's diatribe. "I want to make the most of whatever daylight there is left before we stop for the night."

We?

"You're going with her, then?"

Harald visibly recoiled at the news, but Dunne felt her chest expand. Björn wanted to accompany her? Please, let her not have misunderstood! His answer was unequivocal and caused her legs to go weak as gruel.

"Of course, I'm going with her. Who in their right mind would leave a woman on her own on the road for days on end? I know *I* won't have that on my conscience."

"But what about the fair?" the chandler asked, scratching the boil on his neck. "It's in Lincoln."

Björn sighed at the pointless reminder. "I know, and I'll join you there later, once I've seen Dunne safe with her sister."

"It's no small detour. What if you arrive too late?"

"Then I guess I'll miss it!" he snapped. "It doesn't matter, it's hardly a matter of life and death, but the way it's going, you'll all miss the fair! I said I wanted to make the most of the rest of the day to travel. I suggest you do the same."

With those words, he held his hand out to Dunne, who took it gratefully. She was not going to disappear into the mist alone. With Björn by her side she could face anything. Friends—and foes.

As they progressed, the mist became denser and denser, and silence descended upon the land like a shroud. Dunne could not imagine how she would have felt if she had been alone, wrapped in the shadows swirling around her. Terrified, probably.

"Thank you for coming with me," she told Björn, her voice barely above a whisper. It felt odd to speak out loud in such suffocating silence. "It is a great comfort to me."

He glanced at her briefly. "You didn't really think I would allow you to spend two days and one night on your own in such conditions, did you?"

"You could not have anticipated the fog."

"This has got nothing to do with the fog. It could be bright and sunny and I would still be here with you."

So he had planned it all from the start, even when she had been awful to him. Warmth spread through her. "Well, I'm grateful."

He only nodded and fell silent, focusing on guiding the horse through treacherous terrain. Dark shapes with fuzzy edges were looming overhead, looking more like skeletons than the trees she knew them to be. The moon was trying to pierce the thick gray fog surrounding it, creating an unhealthy halo in the milky sky. The whole world had turned eerie. All around them leaves were dripping their moisture to the ground with a sinister sound. Dunne shivered.

"It's too wet. We will have to sleep in the back of the cart," Björn declared when they finally came to a halt. "Fortunately, it's empty so we should fare well enough."

She nodded, unable to make any decisions right now. The oppressive landscape was numbing her senses and slowing her brain.

A moment later, after a light supper of bread and cheese, they settled under the covers on the hard wooden floor of the cart. It was not ideal but marginally better than the sodden, mossy ground. At least tomorrow they would wake up dry.

They were close enough that Björn could feel Dunne trembling and hear what he thought might be sniffles.

"Are you all right?" he asked, concerned. She had been awfully silent since they had left the convoy, not her usual self. Surely she wasn't afraid of being on her own with him, worried he might pounce on her now the others were gone? "What's the matter?"

"I'm cold, I'm scared, I miss Dawn."

That was three reasons, two more than he needed to take her into his arms. Björn didn't hesitate. He turned to his side and drew her against him.

As soon as they touched, she started sobbing against his chest. Damnation, it had been bad enough to see her cry after they had made love, but this was nothing like it. This time it was not brought on by an excess of pleasure but by despair. It was unbearable.

"What's wrong?"

He felt her shake her head against his chest. "I told you, I miss my daughter. We've never been apart for more than a day since the day she was born. And this fog makes me—"

"No, there's something else," he cut in. "Something you're

not telling me. No more misunderstandings, no more lies, remember?"

Although she didn't answer straight away, he knew she would not avoid the question, she was only trying to find the right words. "I'm not sure how to handle what happened between us," she said eventually.

"No. I noticed that."

She had preferred to flee hundreds of miles and risk placing herself in danger rather than face him after their night together. If that didn't prove she was ill-at-ease, nothing would.

"It wasn't meant to happen and I'm not sure it happened for the right reasons. Now I don't know what to think or what to do next."

He knew she was only trying to be honest, but her words were a dagger to his heart all the same. As far as he was concerned, it had been inevitable that they should end up making love, and it had happened for exactly the right reasons. He also had no problem deciding what to do next.

Bed each other again. And again.

And then marry.

But it was clear that Dunne was even more confused than he had feared. He sighed and drew her closer to him, understanding he would have to keep his intentions to wed her to himself for a little while longer. He'd thought to make the most of them being on their own to finally tell her about his hopes, but he could see she still wasn't ready for such a momentous step. For now, he would take what he could. There was no sense in scaring her away by making demands on her too early. There was no rush anyway. They would be spending the next fortnight together, away from prying eyes. In that context, she would have time to reflect on what she wanted and perhaps by the time they got back home to the village, she would have come to see him as an integral part of her life.

Nestled against Björn's body Dunne could feel her anxiety melt away. As the cold receded and the tightening in her chest began to ease, she became conscious of a different emotion invading her body. Desire.

Inevitably, the contact of a man's strong, virile body was creating havoc within hers.

Could they—

No.

She had just told Björn she had no idea how to handle what had happened the other night and that was the truth. Doing the same thing again now would only make her twice as confused in the morning. As if that was not reason enough not to surrender to her urges, just like the other day, she was afraid she would only give in to desire because Björn happened to hold her tight against his perfect body and she was grateful to him for having accompanied her. That wasn't why people slept together. They decided to share such intimacy because they loved each other or, failing that, because they knew that they would end up spending their lives together, and she wasn't in such a situation.

Wasn't she?

Right now, bathing in Björn's heat and wonderful scent, she wasn't sure of anything anymore.

"If we don't encounter any problems, we should reach the village late tomorrow afternoon," he said, cutting though the haze of lust. Apparently he was determined to be sensible tonight. There would be no lovemaking, no kissing either.

"Yes," she said, pushing her disappointment to the back of her mind. Damn, she was not supposed to be disappointed, she was supposed to be relieved! "Let's try to sleep, so we can set off early."

Despite this excellent idea, it was a long time before Dunne could fall asleep.

CHAPTER THIRTEEN

In the morning the fog had disappeared. Dawn unfurled its banner in a graceful arc over their heads. The contrast with the gloominess of the previous day was difficult to believe. Bathed in the rosy light, Dunne could feel a new energy coursing through her. A glance toward Björn only confirmed she had made the right decision in not sleeping with him. It would only have jeopardized the easy companionship they seemed to have found again.

By giving in to what were, ultimately, only carnal urges, she would only risk losing his esteem.

She saw to her needs while he harnessed the horse to the cart, and then they shared the loaf of bread in companiable silence. Soon they were ready to leave. But instead of handing her into the driver's seat as she expected, Björn brushed her cheek slowly. Dunne's heart started pounding unbearably hard. Was he going to kiss her again? Her body went limp at the thought. No, not now! Just when she was congratulating herself on her fortitude the night before, he was presenting her with irresistible temptation. She knew that if he leaned in she would not be able to resist. She would lift her mouth to him and they would kiss.

And if they kissed, they would end up making love on the forest floor. It seemed inevitable.

"Your bruise has almost faded."

Her bruise. Oh, she really was a fool. He had never meant to kiss her, he only meant to comment on the state of her injury! Not trusting herself to speak, she nodded and climbed into the cart.

A moment later they were off.

"Where does Bee's love for animals come from?" Björn asked as soon as they exited the forest.

"So you really are calling her Bee?"

He winked at her. "What harm does it do if she likes it? The name suits her as well. She's small and cute, always running around." He laughed as if he were imagining her doing just that and Dunne had to smile. The name did suit her. "Besides, it is not so odd for us Norsemen to have animal names. You know Wolf, of course, and there's Arne the miller's son. His name means Eagle. And there's me."

"Yes. Bear."

"Does it suit me?"

"I don't know. I've only ever seen a bear once and he was in chains." If she had to picture Björn as an animal it would be one that was wild and free, not reduced to such servitude. "I wonder what I would choose if I had to choose an animal name for myself," she mused. "Sigurd calls Frigyth 'Birdie' and I like that. But I don't think I'd be a bird."

"No? What then?"

"I have no idea."

There was a pause. "I think you would be a doe."

"A doe?" She arched a brow. He sounded as if he'd given

that a great deal of thought and she had to admit she rather liked it.

"Mm, yes. Your hair is the same color as its coat. You're just as graceful." He placed a hand on her thigh, causing her to flinch. "And just as skittish."

She pinched her lips, feeling caught out. "I suppose I cannot contradict you after that. Doe it is then."

"Yes," Björn said, chuckling to himself. "Doe, it is. Don't worry, it could have been worse. Like rat or worm."

"You wouldn't dare compare me to a worm!" she cried in mock outrage.

"No, not when you bear absolutely no resemblance to the slimy animal."

"Do bears eat does, do you think?"

The question had seemed innocent enough, but she regretted it the moment Björn's gaze burned a hole through her heart. "I suppose they would, given the chance. And I can't say I blame them."

Dear Lord. How could the conversation have veered off course so quickly or so dramatically? One moment they were jesting about worms and slimy skin, the next he was telling her he wanted to devour her whole.

Björn coughed, as if thinking the same thing. "So. Bee and her love of animals? Where does it come from?"

"I don't know. She has always loved animals. But Toland did not allow her to keep any pet. He went mad the day she rescued a sparrow and forced her to throw it in a ditch. She was not yet two but I don't think she has forgotten it, young as she was."

"Yes, well, we already know that the man was a fool. Apparently he had no idea of how to behave decently, in or out of bed."

Was it possible to blush all the way to one's toes, Dunne wondered? Apparently so.

"Were you born here or in Denmark, like Sigurd and Wolf?" she asked to change the topic. She had learned a lot about him over the last few days, but she didn't recall being told his place of birth.

"Wolf is an Icelander, not a Dane. But, yes, Ingrid and I were born here. My parents were amongst the first to settle in the village. They became a sort of role model for many." He paused. "They died just over a year ago, together. It was probably for the best. I can't imagine either of them being without the other."

"You're lucky to have grown up in such a loving environment."

"You mean you didn't?" He sounded surprised.

"No." That was the least she could say.

Björn sighed. "I am lucky, but all the same, it's been hard to forge myself an identity amongst people who only ever saw me as a child, and Rorik's son."

Dunne remembered the miller's wife telling her exactly that. "Yes, I imagine it was, but I think that people who meet you now won't be making that mistake."

He threw her a sideways glance that caused her heart to trip in her chest. "You mean Saxon goddesses who made a man out of me? Those kind of people?"

An intense heat suffused her chest. If he was jesting about being seen as a boy, it meant that he had truly forgiven her. She decided to answer in the same tone. "You mean that there are more than one?"

"No." The glint of amusement in his eyes was replaced by a fierceness that quite took her breath away. "Believe me, there is only one such woman."

"Dunne? My God, it *is* you!"

Birgit threw herself into her arms, laughing and crying at the same time. Dunne was just as emotional. She had finally been reunited with her little sister. How could it have been five years since they had last set eyes on each other? She swore to herself that she would not let so long pass before she visited again.

"I can't believe you're really here," Birgit said, between two sobs. Then she drew back to take a look at her and gasped. "But you're hurt! Don't tell me you were attacked on the road!" A careful finger landed on the place by her temple where earlier that morning Björn had told her the bruise was fading. Apparently it was still prominent enough to cause Birgit some alarm.

"Yes, I was attacked," she smiled. "But only by a sack of flour."

"A—"

"Don't worry, I'll explain later. I'm so glad to be here. Let me look at you."

She took a step back and saw that Birgit was not on her own. A little girl, about the same age as Dawn, was hiding under her skirts and looking at the scene with curious eyes. "Mama, who is this?"

"Edita, this is your aunt, my sister Dunne. I've told you all about my sisters, haven't I?"

"Yes."

In turn, Birgit glanced over to where Björn was standing and arched a brow. She was clearly wondering who he might be. With braided hair and the short blond stubble covering his jaw, he had never looked more like a Norseman, which would only add to her confusion. Indeed, why would her sister be accompanied by a Norseman?

"This is Björn, he lives in Frigyth's village." Dunne hesitated. How could she introduce him? Not as her lover, certainly...As a friend? It didn't seem right either. As if he'd sensed her hesitation, he moved forward.

"Since I was traveling to Lincoln's fair anyway, Frigyth's husband Sigurd asked me to accompany his sister-in-law, and make sure she didn't travel alone."

It was the perfect explanation. And yet...Her chest constricted because it made it look as if they were nothing special to one another and he had only accompanied her as a favor to another man. Was this the impression she wanted to give her sister? She wasn't sure. But what else could she say? That they had slept together? She would die of mortification.

"Come, you must be famished."

"Yes," Dunne answered gratefully. If she was hungry, she could not imagine how a man Björn's size would fare. They had not eaten anything since the bread they had shared that morning.

They followed Birgit into a small but clean hut that smelled of dried herbs. While they washed their hands, her sister started ladling nettle soup into four wooden bowls.

"Hereward isn't here?" Dunne asked once they had finished a substantial and delicious meal. After the soup, they'd enjoyed a piece of roasted boar and some wild berry tartlets. It seemed she truly was the only one of the three sisters who didn't know how to cook.

"No. He's gone to see his brother in the village beyond the valley. He will be gone a few days, perhaps even a week."

Dunne tried hard to hide her relief. She would have time with her sister away from her brother-in-law. To say that she had never warmed to the man would be an understatement. He was not as bad as Toland had been, granted, but that was hardly a recommendation. Very few men were.

"So, you can sleep here with me on the pallet," Birgit concluded. "As to Björn, perhaps he could—"

"Don't worry about me. I can sleep in the back of the cart or just outside the hut. The weather is warm this time of year."

"Well, let me go and borrow some blankets from my friend, at least! I don't have any spare ones. Wait here, I'll be just a moment."

She left with Edita on her heels. Björn turned to Dunne, who was finishing her last bite of tartlet.

"What's the problem with your sister's husband?" he whispered in her ear.

"What do you mean?"

"You appeared relieved we wouldn't have to see him." He hadn't missed her reaction and wondered what could have provoked it.

"Did I?"

His lips quivered. "You're doing it again."

"Doing what?"

"You're avoiding answering me and asking questions instead. You often do that, you know."

"Do I?" He arched a brow to indicate she was only confirming what he'd just said. A delicious flush crept up her cheeks when she realized he was right. "No one's ever told me that before. Is it so very annoying?"

"No," he answered honestly. It should be. But somehow, with her, it wasn't. It was just another one of her traits, almost endearing. Besides she usually ended up answering anyway. She proved it when she waved her hand and sighed.

"Hereward is...not the man I would have chosen for my sister. He drinks too much and seems woefully inept at providing for a family."

"Mm. In other words, he reminds you of your father and your husband."

"Yes. Exactly. Not a recommendation, even if admittedly, he doesn't seem to have a cruel streak in him. I only met him briefly, though, as I had already left the house when he married Birgit, so I hope I'm mistaken." She paused as if remembering something. "It was a shock when he announced that, now he was married, he would return to his native village all the way in distant Mercia. She is our little sister. Frigyth and I had hoped we could keep an eye on her, see how she was treated. But we were denied the possibility."

Björn nodded slowly. "So you did want to come here to assure yourself she was well?"

Something in his tone made her frown. "Yes. What else did you think I meant to do by coming all the way here?"

He skewered her with a direct stare. Surely she knew. "Avoid me?"

"Yes, that too." He had expected Dunne to demure or even deny it. But she surprised him by stiffening her spine and meeting his gaze full on. She seemed almost angry. "You would know all about avoiding someone, of course, as that is what you did when you left for Denmark last autumn."

The words were like a punch to the gut. He *had* fled. He simply had not expected her to throw it back into his face so blithely.

He straightened to his full height and returned the glare. If she wanted to play it that way, he would indulge her.

"It's not the same. I left because I had made a fool of myself, twice in as many weeks. I left because I struggled with the desire I felt for you, desire I didn't think you wanted to know about or shared. I left because I didn't want to make you ill at ease, not because I regretted something that had happened between us!"

She flinched, as he knew she would. He had hit a nerve. "I-I don't regret what—"

"No? It looks that way to me." He did not even pretend to

believe her. "Tell me, if I wanted to draw you in my arms again and kiss you, would you agree?"

He made to do just that but before he could touch her, Dunne took a step back. A glance toward the door made it clear she didn't want her sister to see them in a compromising position.

There was his skittish doe again. After all they had shared in the last few days, such behavior hurt. He'd thought they had made progress, he'd thought she had started to accept what they couldn't fight.

"I'm sorry, I just—"

"Yes. I understand." He bunched his fists. "You don't regret what we did in private, but you can't bear anyone else to know about it. You can't bear the idea of being seen with a Norse 'boy.' I was man enough for you when I was thrusting between your legs giving you pleasure, but you can't face people's opinion, you don't want your sister to know what we did together. Well, I care not what people think. Let them make lewd jokes about my supposed lustfulness. Let them mock me for wanting a woman old enough to be my mother, I care not."

Björn knew he had made a mistake the moment he saw Dunne's face turn ashen. He yanked at a fistful of hair in dismay. Not again! Why did he have to say this? She'd hurt him, but it was no reason to hurt her back! It was just like the day he had unwittingly accused her of being little more than a whore. Every time he lost his temper, he ended up saying something he regretted and hurting her.

Dunne felt all the blood drain from her veins. "Is that...Is that what people are saying?" she asked in a voice she barely recognized as her own.

But she already knew it was. Leodred had told Björn he could be her son the day they had gone to the hut. Even if it was not strictly true, as she was ten years older than him, not sixteen or seventeen, it was the first thing people thought when they saw them together. And Harald had warned her only the other day that she would want to be with a real man. That might well have been because he was jealous she had chosen to travel with Björn but still. He had said it. He would never have said something like that if Björn was the same age as she was.

"Well now you know why we can't be together," she whispered. If it had been only *her* facing disapproval, she might have been able to accept the situation. But she would not have Björn ridiculed for wanting to be with her.

"No, I don't—"

"Here you are. Two nice blankets for—"

Birgit skidded to a halt when she saw the scene in front of her, the two of them glaring at each other. Dunne inwardly winced. So much for not wanting to betray any intimacy between them. She hadn't wanted to be seen kissing the handsome Norseman but being caught in the middle of a heated argument was not much better. Either way it would lead to uncomfortable questioning.

"What happened?" her sister asked, coming forward.

"Nothing." Predictably, Björn was the first to regain his composure. He gave Birgit a smile and took the blankets she was holding. "Thank you. I will go and find a spot to sleep, if you don't mind. I'm rather tired."

TUCKED UP IN BED TOGETHER, Dunne and Birgit were whispering, just like they had as children. Only this time it was not through fear, but rather so as not to awaken the little girl sleeping in the next pallet.

"At Toland's death, I went to live in the Norsemen village with Frigyth and Sigurd," Dunne explained once she had told

Birgit all about her unhappy marriage. "You would like our brother-in-law. He's utterly devoted to his wife and children."

"I always thought Frigyth would end up marrying Caedmon."

"So did I, if I'm honest. But it's hard to think he would have been a better match for her than Sigurd." Because she didn't want to talk about Björn, she steered the conversation toward Hereward instead. "How about you? How have you been? Frigyth and I...well, we worry about you. That's why I'm here, really."

The chuckle her sister gave her was enough to reassure Dunne.

"No need to worry. I'm happy. I've been made welcome here in the village. I have Edita, of course, and every week I assemble the children in the village hall and show them various skills. Weaving, cooking, woodwork and the like. I play an important part in the community. It gives me purpose and satisfaction."

That was all very well, but surely that was not all? "Your husband..." Dunne's voice trailed off. What could she say?

Your husband is a drunkard, not a man anyone would want to be married to. Frigyth and I worry that he mistreats you. We worry you have to endure his attention in bed like our mother endured our father's.

This was no way to live. Dunne knew what it was like to be touched by someone you did not desire and even if Frigyth was now happily married to a man she loved, she, too, had suffered at the hands of a man she didn't want. They could not wish that on their little sister.

Birgit took her hand and squeezed. "Hereward is not the monster I feared he might be at first. You don't know him, but if you did, you would not object to him, I'm sure. He used to drink a lot when he lived in town, it is true, but I suppose it was inevitable while in the company of our father. He was alone in a strange town and unhappy. Since we've come back to his village, he's changed. He works hard and spends a lot of time helping his brothers. We have found a way to live together. And," she added, lowering her voice even further, "he doesn't bother me at night, which I appreciate."

"You mean...He takes his pleasure elsewhere?"

Dunne didn't know if that was better or worse. Certainly she had not minded Toland going to other women, as it meant he bothered her less. But it was also demeaning and had only encouraged him to compare her to other women and throw her lack of skill in bed back in her face.

Despite the darkness, it seemed to her that Birgit flushed. "He is near impotent, to tell you the truth. I know not the reason for it, but he has always found it difficult to perform his marital duty. When I found out I was with child, he was very pleased. I think he had lost hope of ever having children. He dotes on Edita. When she was born, Hereward and I agreed not to resume our marital life. It was a relief for us both, I think, and it brought us closer. You know I was never one to fawn over men. Unlike most of the women I know, I never feel desire for the men I meet. I much prefer to stay in the company of women and children. So you see," Birgit concluded, "you don't need to worry about me, I am content with my life."

After this confession, Dunne fell into deep musings. Even if she didn't have the loving marriage Frigyth had, Birgit had sorted her life in a manner which suited her and found content-ment. Sometimes your path was the one you least expected. Who could have predicted on the day of her wedding that Birgit would end up miles away from home and happy with the half-drunk man standing by her side? Who would have imagined Frigyth living amongst Norsemen and adopting a little boy? Who could have thought that, after years of misery, the third sister would be offered a second chance at happiness with someone so much younger than her?

No.

Dunne shook her head, not convinced that was the path for her. Did her future lie with Björn? She still wasn't sure she wanted a man in her life.

"Now, tell me about you," Birgit asked. "What do you intend to do now you're a widow?"

That was the question.

She turned to her sister and smiled. "Not now, if you don't mind. It's been a long and tiring journey. I would like to sleep."

CHAPTER FOURTEEN

"I suppose you will be leaving now."

Dunne watched as Björn finished brushing the horse with brisk, efficient strokes. They had not talked since their argument the night before, but she had brought him some bread and honey to break his fast as a peace offering. He straightened back up before answering.

"Desperate to be rid of me, I see, before your sister or anyone realizes how intimately we know each other?"

"No, of course, not," she said irritably. Even if she understood why he would be angry with her, she did not like being reminded that she had hurt him. "But aren't you going to the fair? You can't delay any longer or you'll miss it."

Wasn't that why he had come all the way north? He rubbed a hand over his stubbled jaw, not looking concerned in the least. Suddenly he didn't look angry or hurt, just full of mischief.

"Mm, you know, now that I'm here, I'm not sure I can muster the energy to go all the way to Lincoln."

Dunne narrowed her eyes as realization hit. "You never intended to go to the fair, did you, or buy new casks?"

Björn dropped the brush back into the bucket and gave her

a grin that was seduction personified. "No. Why would I? After all, I can buy ale casks in town. In fact, I know a very good cooper. He was my father's best friend. I would never buy casks at the other end of the country while he still lives. And besides, the original plan was never going to work."

"What do you mean?" What original plan?

"Because there was a serious flaw in it. I was to take you to Birgit, or near enough. Very well, but then what? Were you supposed to make your way back to the Norsemen village alone?" He crossed his arms over his chest. "Over my dead body. I always knew I would escort you back as well."

Dunne shook her head. Odd as it was, she had not given the return journey a single thought. Now that Björn had pointed it out to her, she was surprised that no one else had done so, not even Sigurd. Unless...unless he'd known Björn's intentions all along. Frigyth had said the two men had talked. Now she had an inkling of how that discussion might have gone.

"You are impossible. Why didn't you tell me you intended to accompany me from the start?" He had not even mentioned that he would travel with the merchants, only placing her in front of the *fait accompli* the morning of the departure.

"If I had told you my intentions, you wouldn't have gone to see your sister. Instead, you would have disappeared on your own somewhere I couldn't find you."

"How do you know that?"

Björn sighed. "Dunne. As I told you yesterday, I know you're embarrassed about what happened between us and want to avoid me." He kicked a stone, evidently trying to control his temper so as not to start another argument. "But there's no need. I'm not embarrassed and I don't regret anything."

"I don't either. Only...It can lead nowhere." There, she had said it. Something within her died at the thought and, for the first time, she wondered if she didn't want a man in her life after all, if that man was a Norseman who made her heart flutter and her daughter laugh.

Björn didn't appear in the least put out by her declaration. "Oh, I can think of one place it can lead to." He leaned in, all masculine intent and she didn't move, as captivated by him as a moth would be captivated by a candle flame. She could only hope the attraction would prove less dangerous to her. "When are your womanly courses due?"

Dunne's mouth fell open. Had he just asked her that? "That is a very private—"

"Not under the circumstances. We made love more than once and very thoroughly. As a consequence, you might well be carrying my child. I need to know if you are."

A child.

Everything within her froze. How could it be that she hadn't thought of that before? She had been so lost to pleasure during the act that it was perhaps understandable she had not worried about it, but since then she'd had more than a week to come back to reality and realize that her moment of folly could have more consequences than she'd anticipated.

What would she do if she found out she was with child?

Björn was looking at her with feverish intent. He was still waiting for the answer to his question and she had to admit he had the right to know about something like that. And it was not hard to think of the date. She had just finished bleeding the day Björn had made love to her.

"About three weeks," she finally answered, her voice little more than a whisper.

The blue in Björn's eyes became stormy. "Well, then, we will wait for a month. And if you haven't bled by then, I will make you my wife."

His wife! She bristled at the same time as her legs went liquid. He made it sound as if her agreement was a foregone conclusion, or even worse, not even required in the first place. Just like Toland. He had told her one day they were to marry, that her father wished it, and that had been that.

"Don't I have a say in this?"

"I'm afraid not." This was said with such fierceness that she shivered. His mind was set. "I will not let a woman carrying my baby out of my sight or anywhere near another man."

Of course, this had all to do with the baby, not her. Oh, and all too predictable male pride and possessiveness. She bunched her fists.

"And I will not have another husband who doesn't truly want me. I don't want another husband anyway," she informed him coldly. "When Toland died, I swore off all men, and chose never to marry again."

Far from being impressed, Björn closed the gap between them. "Well I'm afraid you should have thought of that before you allowed me to make love to you. *I* haven't sworn off women and I certainly have not decided never to marry or have children."

Dunne shook her head. This conversation had taken a shocking turn, and she was still reeling.

"You would only be marrying me because of the babe when you do not really want me."

She could not bear the idea that he would only marry her out of duty. To think she had once believed Björn was not ready for commitment! He was about to throw away a future with the woman of his choice to offer her and her unborn babe a respectable life. She should have been ecstatic. She wasn't. She didn't want anyone to marry her because he had to when all along he wanted another woman.

Like Toland had.

Björn placed a warm, possessive hand over her stomach.

"That's where you are wrong. I would want both of you, I already do. I want you, this baby, and Bee."

That he would include her daughter in this bargain was the most unfair attack on her heart. It gave a jolt of yearning, urging her to relent. Of course, if he truly did want her...If she really was his first choice, then it would be different, wouldn't it?

"There might not be a baby," she could only whimper.

"There might not," he agreed, not letting go of her. "But it makes no difference. I would still want you and your daughter to be a part of my life. And once you were, then there *would* be a baby, for sure, because I would bed you as often as you would allow me."

Dear Lord. Allow him? If it came to that, she might well be the one demanding to be bedded.

"Björn, this is too much. Don't talk like that. It's too soon. We've only known each other for—"

"Almost four years. Plenty long enough."

She groaned at his refusal to be reasonable. Strictly speaking, yes, they had first set eyes on each other at Frigyth and Sigurd's wedding four years ago, but that hardly counted. She had not really paid much attention to him at the time and well... he *had* been a boy then, not someone she could ever have imagined marrying.

"You know what I mean. And we only slept together two weeks ago. Before that, we didn't really—"

"Before that you had been haunting my dreams every night," he cut in ruthlessly. "I might only have held you in my arms a fortnight ago, but I have fantasized about doing so for four long years. And it felt right to be with you in that way. You must have felt the same."

Yes, she had. It had been as he said, *right*.

But that didn't mean anything. She could not base a decision that would affect the rest of her life and that of her daughter on what her senses told her. She had to use her reason.

"My husband's death gave me the freedom I'd craved for years. I can't give that up on a whim." She shook her head, remembering the misery her life had always been. Not just during her marriage but while growing up as well. Dunne had spent the first thirty years of her life feeling trapped. She didn't want to spend the remaining forty feeling the same. She had only just started to live, alone with her daughter in the Norsemen village and she didn't intend to give that up. "I need to be free."

"Free to do what exactly?" Björn scoffed. "And marriage doesn't have to be a prison. My parents were happier together than they would have been apart. Look at your sister. Do you think she would rather be on her own?"

"I'm not Frigyth," she protested. "Our circumstances are not the same!"

"No. But you must see that she is happy, not in spite of being married, but *because* she is married. As is Merewen, and other women in the village."

Yes, the two Saxon women were blissfully happy, and this because they were married to men they loved, men who had married them because they loved them, not because they were doing their duty by them. It made all the difference.

"It's not all about me. I have a child to take into account. Dawn might not—"

Björn cut off her objection with a gesture of the hand. "Bee loves me. She's loved me from the moment I told her my name was Bear and I'd saved a cat. And I love her. She's the most adorable little girl I have ever seen and she's yours. That would be enough to ensure that I want to be the one to look after her. I told you, I want her to be part of my life."

This time Dunne's knees almost buckled. There was such

conviction in his voice, such fire in his eyes...She had to get out of here and think, because she could feel her resolve weakening. "Do you always have an answer for everything?"

"Yes," he said flatly. "So there is no need arguing. We will wait for a month and if you haven't bled by then we *will* get married."

IT TOOK Dunne all morning to muster the courage to leave the forest and go back to the village. After her tense discussion with Björn she had needed time on her own to absorb what he'd told her.

He wanted them to marry if she turned out to be with child and he seemed as determined to have her accept the offer as she was to refuse it. How could they ever reach an agreement in those circumstances? They would either marry or they would not. One of them would lose.

But which one?

In any case, she didn't have to worry about it now. They didn't have to decide anything for another month.

Her sister was not in the hut when Dunne entered. There was, however, one person waiting for her. A tall Norseman who pierced her with his blue gaze as soon as she walked through the door. The notion that he could always be waiting for her thus if she agreed to be his wife hit her square in the chest and she lowered her head to the floor.

"Birgit asked me to tell you she has gone to the village hall with Edita and the other children and would be busy all day," she heard him say. "I've made some gruel if you're hungry."

Dunne nodded. She was famished, and all too glad to have a meal ready for her.

"I've spotted honey and bread as well," she answered. "And I found some berries in the forest. We'll have a veritable feast."

He was behaving as if he had not threatened her with marriage earlier and, as it was easier to pretend he hadn't done such an outrageous thing, she followed his lead.

They sat down to eat. The gruel was good, thick and creamy, just the way she liked it. She almost groaned in delight. It seems that everything the man did provoked pleasure inside her. But his skill at cooking did not surprise her. Except for sewing, the man showed a surprising aptitude in household tasks. She knew that many, men especially, mocked him for it, but she thought it endearing—and very welcome. A man who didn't think it was beneath him to help around the house and did not judge a woman for her lack of accomplishments would make a good husband, one that would only make her life better.

She started when the thought hit her.

Only this morning she had balked at the notion of marrying Björn. And here she was, imagining what life with him would be like. Exciting, pleasurable. The worst of it was, he had not tried to pressure her into anything, or even broach the topic since she'd entered the hut. He had only cooked for her. If she weren't careful, before she knew it, she would be the one begging him to let her wed him.

"I know all there is to know about your two sisters, or so it seems. But do you have any brothers?" Björn ripped off a piece of bread and chewed.

"No. We had a neighbor, Caedmon, who was like a brother to us, though. We all grew up in town. Our childhood was..." She hesitated, wondering how best to describe it. All the words that came to mind were depressing, which was little wonder. It had been dire. "Well, by all accounts it was nothing like yours in the village."

"Unhappy, you mean?"

Dunne swallowed. That was putting it mildly. She could not recall her mother ever laughing or her parents sharing a tender moment. There had barely been enough to eat, little in the way of amusement and very few opportunities to meet other people. The only moments of joy had been the ones spent out of the house. Their friend, Caedmon, had always been able to bring a smile to their faces but that had hardly been enough to compensate for the misery they'd felt at home. Besides, he'd always had a preference for Frigyth, spending most of his time with her. Dunne had not begrudged them the time alone. In fact, as she'd told Birgit last night, she had been certain they would end up marrying each other. Which only went to show that she could not imagine a life outside their small, predictable world. How pathetic.

"You said that your parents were happier together than they would have been apart." When Björn nodded, she gave a small smile. Such a thing was hard to imagine. "Mine were even more miserable together than they would have been on their own. My father was a drunkard. Not violent exactly, but still he..."

Björn's nostrils flared when Dunne's voice faded. What wasn't she telling him? What had her father done to her?

"He hurt you, you mean?" The mere idea twisted his guts.

"Never intentionally."

But he had. No longer hungry, he placed the piece of bread on the table. What would she reveal?

"Tell me."

She hesitated and stood up, before starting to pace around the room, her way of building up the strength to answer. He waited.

Eventually, she answered. "Most nights he was out, drinking and...possibly whoring with his friends. Being the eldest, I slept in Mother's pallet. On the rare occasions when my father did spend the night at home, I joined my sisters in the other bed and did my best to ignore what our parents did under the cover of darkness."

"Mm." Björn didn't know what to say but he could well imagine her unease. Having to witness their parents coupling would be uncomfortable for anyone.

"One night, he came back home earlier than usual. My mother was still out, visiting a friend. I must have been about sixteen."

She paused and a shiver of foreboding traveled down Björn's spine. "What did he do?" Had he taken exception to the fact that her mother was out, struck her in his anger?

"Usually when he came back home early, it was because he wanted to bed my mother. They didn't get on but..."

She shrugged instead of finishing the sentence. Björn understood only too well what she refused to say. Indeed, a man didn't need to be in love with the woman under him when he wanted to satisfy his urges. As for women...Well, a women would have no choice, especially if the man laboring over her was her husband. He bunched his fists. It seemed that both Dunne and her mother had had to endure marriages that made them unhappy by day, and caused them to be raped by night. Was that why she had not thought she could escape Toland, in spite of all he'd made her go through? Because she had not seen anything different as she grew up and thought it was the norm for women to be used and unhappy? Ingrid, he knew, would never settle for such an appalling arrangement, because of what she had seen as a child. He swore to himself if that he ever had a daughter, he would teach her she didn't have to submit to any man.

He waited for Dunne to carry on with the story.

"My father got in the bed and reached out for my mother."

"But..." He frowned. "You just said she wasn't there?"

"She wasn't. But it was dark and he was drunk, as usual. And there was one person in the bed."

All the blood froze in Björn's veins. "You."

Dunne stopped her pacing but kept her back to him. "I was woken up by his hands on me. Even drunk, he was a lot stronger than I was and I just could not push him away. I screamed and woke my sisters up. They helped me get rid of him. My mother arrived at that moment and he turned his attention to her. I don't think he realized what had almost happened or that he had grabbed the wrong person. He just...made her lie down and..."

She shivered. Björn's stomach churned. What an appalling way to live.

"You heard everything, as he took his selfish pleasure with her?"

"We always did. We had no choice."

"My parents never made love within hearing range of Ingrid and me." He shook his head. Why was he talking about this? Did he have to rub in how different his life had been? Couldn't he see that it would only make her feel worse?

Dunne sat back on the stool and hugged herself. "I wanted to leave that day. I could not bear to think he might make the same mistake again when we were alone, because then there would be no escaping."

Björn bunched his fists to stop himself from reaching out to her. "Why didn't you leave? At sixteen you could have; you were old enough."

"Maybe, but my sisters are younger than me. Birgit was only a child." Dunne shook her head. "As the eldest, I felt responsible. Even if my presence did not make much difference, I didn't want them to have to endure it all alone. I was trapped."

"And then you were trapped in your marriage to Toland."

He understood now why she had bristled at his offer of

marriage, why she valued her freedom so highly. All her life she had been forced to be in a place she wanted to escape, to live with people she wanted to flee, to place others' needs above her own. But now she was a widow, her parents were dead, her sisters were married and settled. She was no longer accountable for her actions or responsible for anyone except a daughter she loved, and she relished her situation.

If that was the case, he might never convince her to marry him, whether she was with child or not. His chest caved in at the thought because he would never be able—or willing—to force her into a union.

Which meant he might well lose, not only her but their child also.

"Do you know what the worst part about being married to Toland was?" Dunne asked in a small voice.

Björn tasted bile. There was worse than what she had already told him? Worse than being insulted, humiliated, and raped by one's husband? "What is that?" he managed to ask.

"It was all for nothing. We should never have married. He never wanted me. When he approached my father, it was to ask for Frigyth's hand. My father refused and answered the only daughter available for marriage was me. Perhaps he had realized what had almost happened between us and he wanted to get rid of me before it could happen again, I know not." Dunne shook her head. "All I know is that he was adamant and that Toland made my life a misery because all along, he'd wanted another woman. My own sister."

"By the gods."

"I have no idea if Frigyth knows about it," she said with a shiver. "But I will never tell her. She doesn't need to know my husband lusted after her."

"How do you know he did?"

"He told me himself, one night, while he..." A flash of

hatred sliced through Björn's chest when he understood what she was not saying. The foul man had told Dunne he desired another woman, and her own sister at that, while he'd pounded into her. "He said the same things as usual, that I was cold as a fish, and that he would curse my father till his dying day for having saddled him with one sister when he wanted another. He…"

"He what?" he asked, even though he wasn't sure he wanted to hear what else the man had done. It might well push him over the edge. But he sensed it would help Dunne to confide in someone, to rid herself of the memories poisoning her, so he would be here for her.

"He started to tell me what he would like to do to Frigyth, and how he was sure she would like it, how she would not lie like a corpse under him. The idea seemed to heat his blood and he became more aroused than usual. It was the worst night I ever spent with him. It was also the last. He died shortly after that."

Bloody bleeding hell.

"How did he die?" If only he'd still been alive, so that Björn could skewer him and show him what a corpse really looked like!

"He broke his leg coming back from town one night and froze to death in the mud."

Too good and easy a death then, Björn thought ruthlessly. The man should have suffered for days after some rabid dog had feasted on his entrails, not been lulled to eternal sleep by the cold. "I'm so sorry."

Dunne gave a mirthless smile. "You have nothing to be sorry about. None of this is your fault."

No. But it would be his fault if he trapped her in yet another marriage she didn't want and burdened her with a child she had not wanted. Damn it all, he should have withdrawn before he'd reached his release, he should have thought about the consequences instead of getting lost in the most wonderful moment of his life.

Well, there was no helping it now. They would have to wait and see if their heated night together had borne fruit. He knew which outcome he would prefer, but alas, he wasn't sure Dunne shared his opinion. What would he do if she wasn't with child? How would he keep her then? And what would he do if she was and still refused to marry him?

He had no idea.

"I'll go for a walk around the village," he told her, feeling more dejected than ever. "I want to see who lives here."

CHAPTER FIFTEEN

"Tell me straight." Orvyn winked. "What do you think of this brew?"

Björn barely repressed a grimace. In truth, it was awful, but he wasn't sure he should be honest when the man seemed so proud of his creation. The day before he'd wanted to meet some of the villagers, but as luck would have it, the first man he'd encountered was one he would have avoided in other circumstances.

When he'd crossed paths with the pompous, self-satisfied widower, their conversation, short as it had been, had made him decide to avoid him in the future. But as Björn had reached the wooden bridge leading to the second part of the village that morning, Orvyn had recognized him and invited him to have a drink. It had been impossible to refuse without offending him. Then, as if that was not bad enough, Björn had made the mistake of telling him he brewed ale.

Delighted, the man had exclaimed, "I've been widowed for six months so I've had to take over the making of it out of necessity and it's not easy. But I'm getting there."

Next thing he knew, Björn was handed a cloudy, unappealing beverage.

"So?" Orvyn was still waiting for a verdict on the ale.

"It's strong," Björn said cautiously. This, at least, could not be in doubt.

"Precisely!" A slap on the shoulder rewarded the answer, as if Björn had meant it as a compliment. He had not. "It's not for every day, I'll grant you that, but it has its uses. Do you know how I achieve such a result? I cram as much grain as I can in the vat and I—"

Björn raised a hand. He was not interested in trying to reproduce the foul mixture. "It's fine. I doubt I will want to make such a potent brew. The people in my village prefer a lighter drink."

"Yes. I bet they do. But you're a real man! You can take it."

The irony of finally being called a man for doing nothing more than pretending to like a strong brew twisted his guts. "Oh, I am a man, Don't I know it," he mumbled, staring into his cup.

Orvyn slapped him on the shoulder again, a habit that was quickly becoming tiresome. "I'll tell you what, Björn, a sturdy lad like you, who knows what he's about in all manner of things, is exactly what I need as a son-in-law."

"A son-in-law?" Had he heard that right?

"I'm looking to get my daughter Agnes married. I was thinking of a match with the miller, but I might prefer someone younger, who could help me and take over some of the chores in the house."

Oh, so not only was the man marrying him off to his unsuspecting daughter, but he was also assuming Björn would come live here in the village to look after him now that his wife was dead. Could any offer be less tempting?

"I thought the miller was married already?" he said instead

of answering. He must have misheard the other day when Birgit had talked about the people living in the village because a married man could not take a wife.

"John is, aye. But his father is widowed like me, and I know he's looking to remarry. He's offered for my Agnes, as he feels he deserves a pretty wife in his bed after being married to plain old Jane for years. He's a friend, so I was considering agreeing to the match but now I'm thinking I might have found better. You're not a Saxon, of course, but you seem civilized enough, for a Norseman." Björn didn't know what to say. As offers went, this one was as offensive as it was unappealing. Orvyn, however, was not deterred by his silence. "She is a couple of years younger than you, I would say, pretty, with all the curves a man wants." Another slap landed on his shoulder. He had to grit his teeth to stop himself from retaliating. "I wager you will enjoy pounding into her."

Björn blinked. Had the man really said that about his own daughter? Was he really considering selling her off to an old lecher who'd made no secret of his vile intentions? The exasperation he'd been feeling instantly turned to disgust. But he was not here to create problems, least of all for Birgit, who would have to live in the man's proximity once he and Dunne had left, so he thought it more prudent not to say anything, for fear of betraying his feelings. Besides, the man didn't seem to require an answer. In his mind, the deal was already sealed.

Orvyn poured himself another drink and raised the cup high in the air.

"Come, let's drink to your health."

"Thank you, no. Birgit is waiting for me," he lied. He had to leave before he told the man where he could put his unsavory offer or slap him on the back. Hard. His fists were itching something fierce. "I promised I would build a new chicken coop for her."

"Mm. Birgit is a lovely woman. She deserved better than to be married to that Hereward, who is barely ever here to see to her needs." A wink. "Her sister is quite comely too, is she not? I wonder if she—"

"Stop wondering," Björn growled under this breath. Was the man determined to have a fist rammed down his throat? Apparently so.

"Oh." Orvyn nodded slowly. "You mean someone in your village has got his eye on her?"

"Yes." Someone definitely had. Him.

"Well, they're not here to see what she's up to, are they? Perhaps the widow would like to make the most of her time in—"

"I don't think so." *Not with a goat like you, anyway.* "I have to go."

WHEN DUNNE CAME BACK from the river, clean and refreshed from her morning ablutions, she found Birgit in the company of three other women. They were making goat's cheese in a sunny spot right by the vegetable patch.

"Hi. I'm Agnes," a young girl said with a timid smile, as she settled herself at a milking stool.

"I'm Brona," her curly-haired friend piped, wiping her hands on her apron.

"And I'm Adaline." The third woman lifted a heavy-looking bucket as easily as Dunne would have lifted a loaf of bread. "Your help will be welcome. As you can see, the goats have been generous this day."

"So they have. Lovely to meet you all." She smiled. "Of course, I can help."

As they started working Birgit explained how Dunne had

traveled with a convoy of merchants on their way to Lincoln fair and had done the last leg of the journey with one of their brother-in-law's friends. The women congratulated her on her bravery. Dunne said nothing. There had been no bravery involved after all, since Björn had been with her all the way.

"How big do you want the cheeses to be?" she asked, as she started to mold one between two cupped hands. "I prefer them on the smaller side, that way they dry quicker."

There was no answer. She could tell the women were not paying attention to her. At least, Adaline and Brona weren't. Their gazes seemed focused on a point behind her. They exchanged a quick, knowing glance and smiled like two people sharing a secret. The girl blushed while the older woman wiggled a suggestive brow. What on earth was going on?

Abandoning her cheese, Dunne turned around in time to see Björn come to a halt next to Birgit.

Her mouth fell open. No wonder the women had lost track of the conversation. He was...well...He was bare-chested again, and utterly mouthwatering. An axe was resting over his right shoulder and a thin sheen of sweat covered his chest, delineating each of the lean muscles and making his skin appear even more golden than usual. Her insides started to quiver. She had seen him bare-chested before, of course, but this was really taking it up another notch.

"Have you got time to come see what you think of the coop so far?" Björn asked Birgit, oblivious to the way the women were ogling him.

By now Agnes had finished milking the last goat and was blinking in disbelief at the sight greeting her when she straightened back up. Birgit seemed to be the only one immune to the Norseman's appeal, for which Dunne was grateful. It was hard enough being jealous of other women and, after Toland admitting he was lusting after Frigyth, she didn't want to have to compete with yet another of her sisters for a man's attention. But it seemed Birgit hadn't lied when she had claimed not to be interested in men. If a half-naked Björn could not provoke any reaction in her, then she was truly lost to the cause.

"Who the devil is that?" Adaline asked as the two of them started to walk toward the other side of the hut where the coop was. "He's not from around here, that's for sure. I would have remembered seeing him."

"It's Björn. He's the one who accompanied me here."

There was a stunned pause as the three women stared at her.

"Are you jesting?" Adaline's eyes almost popped out of her head. "You mean you traveled alone for days on end with *him*?"

Though she could feel heat creep up her cheeks, Dunne pretended not to understand what the woman was getting at. "Well, as Birgit said, for the first three days we traveled with a group of merchants. Björn lives in the village where my other sister settled with her husband, Sigurd. He's a Dane, like him. He has a sister, whom I taught to sew. Her name is Ingrid." She was blabbering on, but no one seemed to mind. Apparently, the more information they could get about the Norseman, the better.

"Does this Sigurd look like your...friend?"

No. There was no one like Björn. The answer tore through Dunne's mind. Nevertheless, she nodded. Broadly speaking, he did. They were both tall, muscular, blond, with golden beards and braided hair.

"Pretty much."

"My. Your sister is a lucky woman. Are all the men so tall and arousing in that village of Norsemen?" Adaline was practically drooling.

"Erm...I don't know about that. Depends on your tastes, I suppose."

"No, in this case it doesn't. This man is positively mouthwatering and only a fool would disagree. You should try your luck with him, Brona."

Brona gave what sounded like a nervous laugh. "I have no chance against you. You seem to attract men like flowers attract butterflies."

Adaline sighed. "Not the young ones. Not anymore. Alas, those days are over."

"How old are you?" Dunne couldn't help but ask her. They seemed to be of an age. And yet the woman deemed herself too old to even think of dallying with Björn. Her chest tightened. Say what he might, they weren't meant to be together, least of all as husband and wife.

"Thirty-one summers. Practically an old crone!"

Though this was said in jest, Dunne received the comment like a punch to the gut.

"I'm thirty," she mumbled, feeling more like a hundred. Practically an old crone indeed.

"Ah, well, you know what I mean then. Those were the days, hey?"

Dunne toyed with the idea of telling Adaline she might even now be carrying the proof that Björn didn't think her past her best, of detailing all they had done in bed together.

She stayed silent. What purpose would it serve, save to appear as if she were boasting? She could not tell anyone what she and Björn were to one another when she had not even told Birgit. Why had she kept the secret? Frigyth knew...

Yes, Dunne reminded herself sharply, her other sister knew because she had all but walked in on them locked in the most intimate embrace. Would she have told her otherwise? She wasn't sure. Why was she so ashamed of it? She wasn't sure either. But she couldn't help it, she was, if not exactly ashamed, at least uncomfortable. No matter what, she simply could not rid herself of the notion that it was ridiculous for them to be together.

And everyone save Björn seemed to agree with her.

Without a word, she resumed the molding of the curds with renewed determination.

She was supposed to make cheese, not torture herself over a certain Norseman.

"THANK YOU, that's perfect. I've been telling Hereward we needed a bigger coop for weeks but I'm afraid he's been even busier than usual, what with his brother having broken his arm."

Björn waved Birgit's thanks away. In truth, he was glad to have helped her. The woman was kind and had fed him for days without asking for anything in return. He wished he could do more for her.

"It's no issue. I'm glad to be able to repay your generosity in some small way." Was there more to it, he wondered when she appeared unconvinced. Was he trying to earn one sister's approval by helping the other? He refused to consider the possibility, but a niggling doubt persisted. Perhaps he was.

Well, what of it? Trying to woo a woman was hardly a dastardly enterprise.

"Feeding you is the least I can do when you were kind enough to ensure my sister's safety during her journey here." Birgit smiled. "How well do you know Dunne?"

He cleared his throat as the honest answer almost escaped his lips. *I know her as intimately as a man can know a woman. I know how she feels under me, over me and around me. I know how she moans when pleasure overcomes her. I know I want to spend the rest of my life with her.*

"Not very well, really. I happened to be going the same way

as her so your sister's husband, Sigurd, asked me to make sure she reached you safely," he said gruffly.

"Mm. And yet somehow you seem to have forgotten all about your intention to go to the fair."

Damn it, of course, she would have picked on that fact.

Fortunately, he was prevented from answering by a loud voice coming from the other side of the hut.

"Agnes! There you are. Is your father home? I need a word with him. We have an important matter to discuss."

"Who's this talking?" he asked Birgit as his skin started to prickle. Agnes. One of the women making cheese with Dunne was apparently the brewer's daughter and the old man calling out to her the miller's father. The important matter he wanted to discuss with Orvyn had to be the possible union between them. A union she would be ignorant of, he suspected. After all, Orvyn had offered her to him even though they had never set eyes on one another.

"That's John's father, the miller," Birgit started to answer, as he stole a glimpse at a man with grizzled hair and a paunch. It was just as bad as he had feared. "He—"

"Forgive me. I have to see Agnes."

"I see." Birgit gave him a warm smile. "Someone caught your interest."

Björn wondered what the woman would say if he told her the truth. *Yes. Someone has caught my interest. Your sister. She is the most wonderful woman I've ever met and she might even now be carrying my child.* Would she be shocked? Happy for Dunne? Would she support him? Would she agree that he was too young for her? There was no knowing. But all this could wait. For now, he had to see Agnes. He had to warn her about her father's plans.

"Agnes?" he called out as he rounded the hut. Three women

were staring at him as they would to a supernatural apparition. Which one was Orvyn's daughter?

"Yes?" The girl to the left lifted beautiful green eyes to him. Her father had not lied. She was pretty. But he felt no flutter of arousal when he looked at her because she was not the woman he wanted to marry.

"Can I have a word with you?"

Agnes seemed too awestruck to respond. One of her friends, a woman with a generous figure and a smiling disposition, nudged her forward. "Go, girl, it's not polite to make people wait."

The girl followed him to the hut, where they would have some privacy. He closed the door and turned to her.

"Forgive me, I will be blunt. You don't know me, but I spoke to your father the other day. Orvyn, is that right?" Agnes confirmed his suspicions with a nod. "I understand he has plans to marry you. To me. Has he said anything to you?"

It was clear from the way the girl blinked that he had not. "N-no. But...forgive me, but you're a stranger."

"Yes, I know. And, to be perfectly honest, I have no intention of accepting the offer."

Agnes bit her lip and allowed her gaze to wander up and down his chest. Damnation, perhaps he should have put his shirt back on before coming to speak to her. He knew his looks appealed to women, especially Saxons, who seemed to like tall, blond men. With his beard and his braids, he looked markedly different from the men they were used to.

"I suppose I should not be surprised," she said eventually. "You could probably find all the women you want. Why would you choose an ordinary girl like me?"

"This is not against you, you seem perfectly lovely, but I cannot get involved with anyone right now."

She nodded slowly. "I see. You have someone waiting for you back in your village."

"Mm. Something like that."

The woman in question was not in his village at the moment and he was not sure she was waiting for him, but Agnes didn't need to know the particulars of his relationship with Dunne. He could not reveal what they were to each other when she had not even told her own sister what had happened between them, introducing him as nothing more than a helpful villager.

He had not expected any different, in all honesty. But it still hurt to see that she was not comfortable with what happened, to the point that she was not only hiding it from her sister but was also refusing to accept what there could be between them. No one knew that they were intimately acquainted. Sigurd might suspect it, given the fact that he had insisted he accompanied her to visit Birgit, but he was certain Dunne had not told either of her sisters about what had happened between them.

Because she could not accept it, and might never do so.

"Why are you telling me all this?" Agnes asked, bringing him back to the discussion.

"I wanted to warn you about your father's intentions, and make you understand why I will refuse his offer. As I said, it has nothing to do with you. You are anything but ordinary. At any other time, I might have accepted and counted myself lucky." This cost him nothing and the girl seemed in dire need of reassurance.

"Thank you. Now, if I may, I will return to the goats?"

He hesitated. Should he not warn her also about what the miller's father intended? Was it his place? Probably not.

He nodded. "Yes. Thank you for having listened to me."

CHAPTER SIXTEEN

Dunne spent the next day trying to convince herself that she wasn't falling for Björn—and failing.

She was plagued by unholy desires and shameful thoughts that made it impossible to focus on what Birgit said and caused her to behave like a ninny whenever he came anywhere near her. Every time her gaze landed on Björn she melted. Every time he looked back at her she melted. Every time they touched she melted. It was driving her mad. Any more melting and there would be nothing left of her.

What could she do to put an end to the torture?

There was one obvious answer. She craved Björn's touch? Then she should go to him and beg him to take her. She was melting for him? Then she should bed him and douse the burning in her body. Maybe then she would be able to think more clearly.

No, she could not be so weak, she could not go to him now. They had agreed to wait until they knew whether she was with child to decide anything. If they slept together now, it would only make that probability more certain and things would get even more complicated. Not only that, but she owed it to herself to not surrender to her urges.

She had decided she would place her freedom above all else. She could not go back on this decision after two days just because the man was infuriatingly handsome, could she? It mattered not how good he looked naked, or how much she wanted to—

"How long are you going to fight this?"

Dunne let out a squeak when the deep voice jolted her out if her musings. "Björn, heavens, you made me jump."

His smile was wry. "Yes, I seem to do that, don't I? And you still haven't answered my question. You seem to do that as well."

"I don't understand your question, that may be why," she replied tartly. "Fight what?"

He let out a small laugh, as if he knew she was being deliberately obtuse. Not that it was hard to guess. "Let me be clearer then. How long are you going to fight the desire you feel for me? How long are you going to pretend that there isn't something between us? How long are you going to lie to yourself and act as if you don't want me?"

She stayed silent. What could she tell him? That she had no idea how long she would be able to deny the truth? That she needed to fight the desire she felt, for fear it made her do something she regretted? That she could not base a decision that would affect the rest of her and Dawn's life on what her senses were urging her to do? She was attracted to him because she couldn't *not* be. He was too handsome for any woman to ignore; he had given her too much pleasure for her not to want a repeat of the performance. But she had to be sensible.

Because she knew that if she went to his bed a second time, he *would* marry her. There would be no more excuses, no more delaying. He would marry her to offer their child a home. And then in a few months' time, a few years if she were lucky, he would see what a monumental mistake their union had been. He would regret shackling himself to a woman past her best, just because she had borne him a child conceived in a mad fit of lust. She would rather deal with his absence than with his bitterness and resentment.

"I-I don't know."

Björn placed himself in front of her, overwhelming her with his presence. "Just tell me this one thing then. Do you think of me when you touch yourself at night?"

The shocking question made her gasp because she didn't do that. Had never done it. Wasn't even quite sure what he meant. "I do not touch myself!" was all she could say.

As she might have expected, he was not so easily deterred. "Well, do you dream of me touching you then?"

This time she could only stare at him because she did. She had. Twice. Once before he'd left for Denmark, and once... Once only last night. She had relived their wild night together and woken up panting and sweaty next to an oblivious Birgit. She had been mortified, and wished she could vanish into the ground.

Björn smiled wolfishly. Evidently he considered his question well and truly answered.

"Think of me tonight, Dunne, when you put your hands between your legs to try to alleviate the ache burning your body," he said, lowering his head to speak in her ear. "I will be thinking of you when I fist myself, just like I did that day by the river. I was ashamed of my desire then. I am not anymore. You are the only woman for me, always will be."

Dear Lord above.

Dunne let out a strangled cry that managed to convey her longing, her shock, and her despair all at once. As if satisfied with her reaction, Björn smiled and walked away, his gait impossibly feline. Once he'd disappeared from view she sagged against the fence post, drained of all energy.

What could she do to get this man out of her head? At this rate she was going to go mad long before they returned to the Norsemen village. She needed something to distract her, anything.

As if in answer to her wishes, a man appeared in front of her, holding a jug and two cups.

"Hi, you're Birgit's sister, are you not?" When she nodded, he poured a cup of the liquid contained in the jug as if to offer her a drink. "I'm Orvyn, it's nice to finally meet you. I've seen you around the village but haven't had the opportunity to say hello properly."

She mumbled something unintelligible then cleared her throat and tried again. "Nice to meet you, too."

"I'm looking for someone to try my new batch of ale. I'm not very good at it, but I have no choice but to try my hand at it, you see, since I am recently widowed." She could tell this comment was meant to elicit her sympathy, but she could not bring herself to offer her condolences because then he added, "I hear you're a widow as well. Isn't it hard?"

No. Being a widow was anything but hard for her. In fact, it was making the decision to marry again that was hard, even if the man wanting to make her his wife made her blood sing in her veins and her heart flutter with hope.

"I'm fine on my own," she said cautiously.

As if knowing he would only antagonize her by insisting, Orvyn didn't respond. Instead he handed her the cup he'd poured. "Would you try this and tell me what you think? It might be a trifle too strong, but I think I'm getting there."

"Strong, did you say?"

Dunne stared into the amber liquid in the cup. In it, oblivion beckoned, and with it the assurance of forgetting about the Norseman who was crowding her thoughts by day and invading her dreams by night. She could not resist. It was either that or go to bed right now and touch herself while thinking of Björn's hands roaming all over her body. Anything would be better than that.

She raised her cup and drank.

As HE CROSSED the wooden bridge Björn spotted a woman hurrying toward him. Birgit. She looked harassed, her attitude a far cry from her usual calm demeanor.

"What's wrong?" he asked, drawing closer to her. It seemed to take her a moment to recognize him, so lost in her thoughts was she.

"Edita is ill. She's delirious with fever."

His chest squeezed. He had taken to the little girl who reminded him of Bee. "I'm sorry, is there anything I can do?"

"No, thank you. I have everything I need, she is sleeping in my friend Ragild's hut. She's a healer and knows what to do. I just need to stay with her and pray for her recovery. Unfortunately, my daughter is used to these episodes. All I can do is hope she will get better, the way she usually does."

He nodded in sympathy. Watching over a sick child had to be the worst thing in the world. "Where's Dunne?" She would provide her sister with comfort better than he could. He felt woefully inadequate. But Birgit arched a brow in surprise.

"I-I don't know. In fact, I thought she was with you?"

His heartbeat instantly picked up in alarm. If Birgit thought they were together, that meant Dunne had not been seen in the hut all day. Where was she? Had he frightened her away with his bold talk that morning? How had he been so foolish as to order her to think of him while she touched herself? It was obvious he had shocked her, had gone too far.

He looked around in panic. Night was already falling. Now was not the time for a woman to be wandering around. So where was she? Had she fled? He would not put it past the infuriating woman. Had she decided to go back home on her own and avoid having to deal with him?

No, she would at least have said goodbye to her sister before leaving. Unless she didn't want him to set off after her and had asked Birgit to cover for her? No, the woman seemed too genuinely surprised by her sister's unexplained absence to be lying.

"Go to your daughter," he instructed Birgit. "I'll find her."

He set off at a run and almost collided with Adaline, who was coming round the village hall.

"Careful there!" the woman laughed as he steadied her. "You almost fell on top of me. Not that I would mind overmuch, you know..." She winked at him, but Björn was not in the mood to jest or even less, flirt with her.

"Have you seen Dunne?" he asked instead.

She frowned. "The last I saw her, she was with Orvyn. It wasn't that long ago, actually. They were heading toward his hut, and they seemed rather cozy, if you know what I mean, arm in arm and giggling. Well, good for them, we all deserve a bit of joy in our lives."

Björn almost retched at the thought of Dunne getting joy in Orvyn's bed. But Adaline was right on at least one thing. It was late, much too late for an innocent visit. If Dunne was in a man's hut at this time, there was only one reason for it.

Thanking the woman, he started running again.

As he came to a stop, a masculine groan, filled with lust,

reached his ear, confirming his worst suspicion. Dunne had not merely come to get a taste of the widower's foul ale. Disillusion churned in his gut. Hand already at the door, Björn hesitated. After all, who was he to interrupt the tryst? If Dunne had gone to the man of her own accord, and at the moment he had no reason to think she had not, she would not thank him for bursting in and interrupting them. Better to first make sure that his intervention would be welcome. He leaned in and pricked up his ears.

"Your skin is so soft." Orvyn's wheezy voice caused him to stiffen in anger.

"Is it?" Dunne. She sounded hesitant but he would have known her anywhere.

"Aye. Oh, I've missed this, you know. Being a widower makes it harder to indulge my senses whenever I want."

"Does it?" Now Dunne sounded tired, or bored, not the reaction of a woman filled with desire. Björn had heard her voice when she was overcome with need. It did not sound like this at all. What was going on in there?

"Yes. Stop questioning me. Have another drink."

There was a silence. Björn froze while everything clicked into place. Dunne wasn't tired, she was drunk. She'd been arm in arm with Orvyn when Adaline had seen them because she'd been unable to walk properly, and giggling because of the ale, *not* because she wanted a tryst. The blasted man was making her drink from his special strong brew, the one that "had its uses," namely making women unable to resist him. Literally.

"That's better. Now, let me see your titties. And then I'll show you my—"

The door shattered into dozens of splinters when Björn kicked it open. The sight that met his eye was even worse than the one he had feared. Dunne was lying on the floor, immobile, her eyes closed, her body limp. Bloody bleeding hell, the bastard hadn't even had the decency to take her to the pallet before pouncing on her! Her bodice was ripped open, exposing one perfect, rounded breast. And worst of all, Orvyn was bent over her, his mouth inches from her nipple.

Red mist descended. With a roar, Björn launched himself onto the man. In the blink of an eye, he had him pinned against the wall, his neck imprisoned in his hands. The urge to squeeze and end his miserable life caused his arms to tremble.

"Stay away from her, you worthless piece of shit. She's mine, do you hear?" The words felt as if they had been wrenched from the deepest part of his body. But Dunne was his, whatever everyone else, including her, thought, and that was all there was to it.

"I-I had no idea. Of course, if I had known that, I wouldn't have..." The man could barely speak with his throat caught in a vice-like grip. It didn't matter. Björn was not interested in his feeble protests anyway. Orvyn was only sorry because he'd been caught trying to steal another man's "property," not because he thought he'd done anything wrong by Dunne.

"Save your breath. And if I ever hear about you using your foul brew on unsuspecting women, I will drown you in it and laugh as you choke to death."

Leaving Orvyn to collapse to the floor, he bent down and gathered Dunne into his arms.

"Come," he whispered to her. "I'm taking you out of here."

There was no reaction. It was as if she had fallen asleep. As they exited the hut and chilly air wrapped around them, she started mumbling.

"I don't want to show you my ti—"

"No. Don't worry about it, I won't make you do anything you don't want to do." Björn growled. Bloody, bleeding hell. Orvyn had been let off too lightly. He would have to go back to him and give him what he deserved for preying on innocent women.

"Where is Björn? I want to see him."

His heart almost stopped. In her distress, she was calling to him. "I'm here. I'm taking you to safety. Don't worry, it's all over, you won't have to see that bastard ever again."

CHAPTER SEVENTEEN

I t was the comforting scent that told Dunne who was holding her in his arms.

For a moment, as she'd emerged from the mist she was drowning in, she had thought she was floating. She could feel that she was moving, but her feet were not touching the ground. How was that possible? Where was she? Who was holding her? And then she had smelled it. Yeast, herbs, fresh air, man. Björn. No one else smelled like him.

Where was he taking her?

"Björn?" Was that her voice? She barely recognized it.

"I'm here, I've got you. You're safe. I've got you."

Safe from what? Her mind was too fuzzy to think straight. She stopped fighting the pull of sleep and rested her head against his shoulder. A moment later she heard another voice. A woman, familiar as well. Birgit.

"Dunne! Dear God, what happened to you?"

"I don't know," she mumbled. What *had* happened? It felt as if something had, but she could not quite place it.

She felt Björn deposit her onto the pallet and heard only a few whispered words, pronounced in a deep masculine rumble.

Drunk. Bastard. Arrived in time. She could feel darkness invading her, stealing over every corner of her mind, but she fought it with all her might. She needed to understand what was happening, why she felt so wretched, why Björn sounded so furious and Birgit so worried.

A cool hand settled on her forehead. Her sister spoke again, her voice coming from just above her. "Someone should stay with her. I can't, what with Edita being so poorly. I only came back to the hut to get her favorite blanket, she—"

"I will stay here, don't worry. Go take care of your daughter."

There was a pause, then the sound of a door closing. Just as she drifted into oblivion, Dunne thought she heard Björn speak again.

"And I will take care of my woman."

HER BODICE WAS TORN, one of her breasts was exposed. Dunne covered it with a frown. What the—

"Good morning." Birgit was kneeling by her side. Though her sister was smiling, she looked pale and tired. "I'm glad to see you awake at last. Do you know where Björn is? I wanted to thank him for offering to stay here last night while I slept in Ragild's hut."

What was that? Björn had spent the night in the hut with her while Birgit had slept in Ragild's hut? Whatever for?

"Why did you sleep there?" Her heart started thudding as one explanation for this unusual decision crossed her mind. Had her sister meant to give her and Björn some time alone because she'd noticed something was brewing between them? Did that mean she approved of him?

Before she could work herself into a lather, Birgit answered.

"Edita fell prey to a fever yesterday. Ragild and I took turns looking after her."

Guilt invaded Dunne. All night her sister had been by her daughter's side, worrying herself sick while she'd been sleeping away, oblivious to it all. She tried to sit up and winced when a bolt of pain split her skull. "My God. Is she all—"

"She's better, thank you. The fever broke at dawn. But I was relieved to know you weren't on your own in the state you were in. Björn offered to stay with you when he saw I could not." Birgit tilted her head in consideration. "You probably don't remember any of it. You had drunk a lot, by all accounts."

Yes, she must have. That would explain the pounding in her head and the odd taste in her mouth. She frowned, then dread pierced though her. If Björn had slept in the pallet with her while she was out of her mind with drink, did that mean they...

Her heart started to drum in her chest. Had they slept together? Had she thrown herself at him, begging for another night of wild passion? She had been battling her desire for him for days, in fact, that was why she had started to drink last night. If they had made mad, passionate love, it would explain the state she was in, for she had not ripped at her clothes herself. She glanced down and found that her gown had moved during her conversation with her sister and her breast was exposed again.

Birgit nodded pensively when Dunne covered herself but didn't ask any explanation. That struck her as odd, but her sister spoke before she could ask anything.

"Let me get you something to wear while you repair your dress." She went to the chest under the window, extracted a bundle of clothes from it, place it on the table, then went back to the chest to retrieve a small wooden box that had belonged to their mother. "There is a needle and thread in the box. I will go back to Edita now. She will be asking after me."

Birgit spoke matter-of-factly. This only added to Dunne's

dread. Why was her sister not worried about her? She should be asking if she was all right and wondering how she had ended up with a torn bodice after spending the night alone with a man. It would be the normal thing to do. Unless...unless she assumed she and Björn were lovers, assumed that they had become so overcome with lust during the night that they had torn at each other's clothes. Yes, in that case, she would not wonder, and even try not to draw attention to it.

Except that they weren't lovers! She and Björn had not slept together since that day in the Norsemen village. Or...

Had they?

Considering she could not remember anything from the night before, it was all too possible they had.

When her sister left, she got up and swapped her dress with the one waiting on the table. It was too tight across the chest, but she did not let that worry her. She had to go to Björn without delay and find out what had happened last night. If he had slept in the hut, he might well have slept in the pallet with her. It was big enough to accommodate two people and more comfortable than the earth floor.

But had he only slept next to her, or had he drawn her into his arms, kissed her and begged for more? Had she agreed? The uncertainty was killing her. Never again would she drink to such excess! She had wanted to forget and she'd succeeded. Now all she wanted was to remember if she had made a fool of herself with Björn.

She found him almost immediately, soaking up the sunshine by the main hall. Taking in a deep breath, she walked forward.

Björn watched Dunne walk up to him. Despite the determined stride, she was pale and disheveled. She probably had a throbbing headache as well, courtesy of Orvyn's foul beverage. The russet dress she was wearing was not the one she'd been wearing the night before—and it was too tight for her. He forced himself not to dwell on the way her breasts were threatening to spill out of the low-cut bodice. The dress must belong to Birgit, who was not as well endowed as her sister.

When she stopped in front of him, he saw that her eyes were veiled with uncertainty, the gold in them not as vibrant as usual.

"Good morning."

She did not acknowledge the greeting and instead launched her attack. "Birgit told me you slept in the hut with me last night."

"I did." He waited, sensing something was troubling her. Perhaps she was embarrassed he had seen her naked breast. There was no need. The sight had roused his ire rather than his blood.

"Did you…Did we…?"

Björn stared at her in consternation. The questions she hadn't dared voice were not hard to guess—and offended him deeply.

Did you take advantage of me last night and rip my bodice open when I refused to undress? Did we sleep together while I was too weak to protest, even though I made it clear that's not what I wanted the other day?

"No," he said through gritted teeth. "We didn't sleep together. Who do you take me for? I only stayed to make sure you were all right. You were too drunk to be alone."

"I think I was. Which is why I cannot remember what happened."

He blinked. Didn't she have any memory of being assaulted? Evidently not, otherwise she wouldn't think to accuse him of any wrongdoing.

"Well, *I* have all my faculties, I remember everything, and I am telling you we did not sleep together, not in that way, at least," he said, articulating every word carefully. He could not leave any doubt about his conduct in her mind. "I did lie on the pallet next to you because I did not see any reasons not to, but I swear I did not touch you. I know you don't want me to do so, and, anyway, I wouldn't bed a woman who could not think straight."

"So what happened? Something must have. I didn't end up with my bodice ripped open by acci—"

"Something did happen but not with me! Bloody hell, do you really think I would..." He grabbed a handful of his hair and yanked at it. Apparently, she did. If she trusted him, she wouldn't have asked the question.

Dunne's bewilderment was not feigned, though. She truly had no idea what had happened to her. Perhaps he should tell her about the assault she had been a victim of. But he didn't see why he should help her when she was accusing him of such villainy.

And what was there to say she would believe him anyway? If she wanted the truth about what had happened to her dress, she would have to ask her sister.

"A word of advice," he hissed. "Next time a man who makes ale offers you a drink, refuse."

Before she could answer, he stormed away, aiming toward the lake. With luck he would be able to swim his anger off.

A man who brewed ale? Dunne didn't understand. The only man she knew who did that was Björn. So what was he saying? He could not at the same time be refuting what had happened and be warning her about himself?

While she was debating on her next course of action, a voice called out from the other side of the hall.

"Here you are, man. The cask of ale you requested. I hope you put it to good use."

Everything fell into place at the sound of that voice. A man offering her a drink he'd brewed himself, her back hurting on the cold, hard floor of his hut, her bodice being torn while she lay powerless under him. Orvyn. *He* had been the one trying to seduce her last night, not Björn. Björn had been the one carrying her away from her attacker. And she had gone and accused him of unspeakable deeds.

Oh, what had she done?

She set off in the direction he'd disappeared, hoping he hadn't gone too far. She had to apologize to him. Now.

She found him throwing stones into the lake. She had never seen anyone throw them in such an odd way before. He angled his body to the side as he threw the stones one by one with a brisk but elegant flick of the wrist.

This man really was like no other. He did everything other people did, but in his own way. And the results were always marvelous. Instead of simply falling into the water, the stones flew over it, skipping as they went, faster and faster until they sank under the surface in a flurry of ripples. It was beautiful. Like him. And she had accused him of an unspeakable crime.

"Björn, I'm so sorry."

A grunt answered her. He didn't look her way; he simply selected another stone and threw it even further than the previous one. Despite the discouraging reaction, she persisted. This was not about her and her pride, it was about him. She had to tell him she did not believe him capable of such villainy. If she had to beg for his forgiveness, then she would.

"It was not you, I know that now, it was Orvyn. But I woke up in bed with my dress ripped and the impression of something gone wrong. Then I was told you slept alone with me in the hut. What else could I think?"

Dropping the stone he had just picked up he turned to face her slowly. Ominously.

"I'll tell you what you should have thought, shall I? You were supposed to trust that I would respect your wishes. That I would never dare touch a woman without her consent." He bore a hole into her skull with the intensity of his stare. "We traveled alone together for two days and even slept in each other's arms one night. I could have tried to submit you to my will any time, even without the help of some awful ale. I am three times as strong as you, I could have done what I wanted with you while we were alone, but I did not, because I would never do or even think of doing anything like that. Damn it, Dunne, I thought you knew me better than this!"

"I do, I'm sorry. Only, I—"

"And another thing." He didn't appear to have heard her. Perhaps he hadn't, after all she had spoken barely above a whisper. "Why did you drink the man's foul concoction? You must have tasted how strong it was?"

"Of course, I did!" she all but shouted. "But that was precisely why I drank it! Because I wanted to forget."

He recoiled. Evidently he had not expected this answer. "Forget what?"

How much I want you! I wanted to forget how confused I was for a moment, forget the shame of having dreamed of you making love to me while I lay next to my sister, my daughter!

"Never mind," Björn said when she remained silent. "Just... promise me you'll never do anything like that again."

"I promise. I will never accuse you of wrongdoing again."

He pinched the bridge of his nose like a man praying for patience. "I meant trusting a man who brews ale when he—"

"I know. But I'm saying I trust you. Please forgive me for hurting you." She fought a sob. "This is such a mess!"

"Ah, Dunne." With a sigh Björn drew her into his embrace. "Don't cry. I'm sorry too, for shouting at you. Of course, upon waking up with a torn bodice after a night spent next to a man, you would assume he—"

"No. You're right. I should never have thought you capable of such a deed. I swear I will never doubt you again."

"Thank you."

For a moment Dunne allowed herself to bathe in the wonderful embrace. Then with effort, she left the comfort of his arms.

"What did happen last night then?" She now knew who had attacked her but there were still pieces missing. She needed to know.

Björn closed his eyes like a man in pain. "When Birgit told me she hadn't seen you for a while I guessed something wasn't right. While I looked for you, I ran into Adaline who told me she had seen you with Orvyn. As I reached his hut, I heard him threatening you through the door. I kicked it open and found you on the floor with your dress torn and that bastard slobbering all over you."

Dunned shivered, as much at the idea of being used so, as at the hatred on Björn's face. "Did he...Did he have time to..."

She could not remember anything; she had no idea if Björn had arrived in time to stop the assault or if she had been raped. How terrible.

"No," was Björn's soothing answer. "I arrived in time."

She took in a deep breath. She hadn't thought the irreparable had been committed, but, all the same, it was good to have it confirmed.

"What did you do to him?" The glint in his eyes spoke of murder and only the fact that she had heard Orvyn's voice earlier assured her that he had not killed him.

"Nothing. But I did warn him never to touch you or any unwilling woman again."

"You sound as if you regret it."

"I do. I should have—"

"No." She didn't want to think of anyone being hurt through

her fault, or Björn having murder on his conscience because of her. "You arrived in time, that's what matters."

Without him she would have been raped, just like her sister Frigyth had been four years ago. The only difference was, she would not have been conscious during the assault and would not have remembered it in the morning. Or...She shook her head. Surely she would have noticed something was not right. She would have felt the ache between her thighs, and the sticky wetness left from her attacker's release. How would she have borne it?

And then...If at the end of the month her courses failed to arrive, what would she have thought? She would have forever asked herself if the babe was Björn's, conceived in a moment of passion and unbelievable pleasure or if it had been imposed on her by a man she didn't even know, a man who'd taken her without her consent. The possibility was too dire to contemplate.

Frigyth had been through the pain of having to bear her attacker's child. But the little boy was now being raised and loved by her husband, Sigurd, who had refused to let her face this alone and loved him as his own.

"Thank you," she whispered, bowing her head. "I owe you more than I can say."

Björn placed a finger under Dunne's chin to lift her head up. "You don't need to thank me. I would have done the same for anyone. For you, I should have done much more."

How would he ever get the image of the foul man bent over her out of his head? He hadn't gone to see Orvyn this morning, knowing that if he caught even a glimpse of the man, he would hit him. And then he would hit him again when he tried to justify his unjustifiable deed. He would not stop until the scoundrel was lying in a pool of blood, dead.

Before he could think better of it, Björn placed his lips over

Dunne's. It was a kiss different from the ones he had given her the other day, not a kiss meant to seduce, but to reassure. He poured his soul into it and felt her respond.

When he drew back, he was trembling with the effort of holding on to his composure.

"Forgive me. I just said I would never take advantage of you and I—"

"You didn't take advantage of me. You kissed me, it's not the same. And, in truth, I wanted to be kissed."

She looked startled by the admission, as if she had not realized what she'd wanted until she had acknowledged it out loud. Was he finally making progress? He dearly hoped so because more than ever, he wanted to marry this woman. Last night when he had claimed she belonged to him, he hadn't lied. That was exactly what it felt like. She was his. And he was hers. If she was finally starting to accept that, then he would be the happiest man alive.

But then she bit her lip as if in regret. His chest tightened. Did she regret admitting to wanting to kiss him? Or was it worse than that, and she regretted allowing him to kiss her because doing so was only fanning false hope within him?

"Dunne, I—"

She placed a light finger over his lips. "Please don't. You said we should wait another fortnight to decide anything. It's...too soon."

It wasn't, not for him at least. He had never been more certain of what he wanted, but he had no choice but to agree to wait at the risk of frightening her away.

Instead, he kissed the tip of her finger. This innocent gesture seemed to confuse her even more than the kiss had, and he almost drew the finger into his mouth to suck on it.

"I will go and repair my dress," she mumbled, averting her

gaze. "This one belongs to Birgit and is too small for me. I must look ridiculous in it."

She looked anything but ridiculous, but he agreed she had better go change. With her breasts straining against her bodice, she was a walking provocation. The last thing he needed was another Orvyn thinking "Birgit's comely sister" could warm his bed.

"Go. Tell Birgit I will go hunting and bring something to eat for tonight."

With a nod, she left.

Björn picked up another stone.

CHAPTER EIGHTEEN

"Ouch!"

With a cry of startled pain, Dunne dropped her dress. Lost in thought, she had inadvertently pricked her finger with the needle. She watched, fascinated, as blood pooled at the end of her thumb before falling onto the table in a perfect scarlet drop. It seemed like a message somehow. The blood had been racing just under the surface of her skin all this time, since she'd been a child, had been part of her, and yet now that it had come out, it would never go back in again. Now that she had pricked her finger, a bit of her had been lost forever, in the same way that now that she had met Björn, a part of her had been revealed and she could not go back to being the woman she had been before.

She placed her thumb into her mouth and sucked pensively.

What would she do if she discovered she was with child? Even more to the point, what would she do if she found out she wasn't? She was dreading finding out that their moment of madness had resulted in a baby, but she was equally terrified of having to renounce a future with Björn. Because if it turned out she was not carrying his child, she would have to let him go.

She was not sure she could deal with that.

More lost than ever, she placed a hand over her stomach and let out a sob.

Toward the end of the afternoon, Björn came back to the hut, and deposited a rabbit and two birds onto the table. She knew he had spent the day hunting to avoid her after their kiss, probably thinking he had taken liberties. Birgit, however, did not see anything amiss and was delighted with the offering. The three of them started to prepare the meat for roasting in companionable silence. The meal was spent discussing the village children's next expedition.

Before Björn could leave and get to his cart for the night, Dunne walked up to him. She had been mulling on the idea all afternoon. It was time she told him.

"Can we go home tomorrow, please? I miss Dawn." It had been more than ten days since she had last seen her daughter. They had never been apart for so long and the need for her was gnawing at her insides day and night. Not only that, but she felt she would be better able to control her wayward urges for him with the little girl nearby. "I've seen what I wanted to see here. My sister is as content as could be. Now I just want to go."

"We can leave whenever you want." He paused, as if wondering whether to speak or not. "But I have a favor to ask of you."

Her chest felt uncomfortably tight. Without knowing why, she knew she would hate what he was about to ask. But she could not refuse, not after what he had done for her the night before and the hurt she had caused him. "Of course. What is it?"

"Can we take Agnes with us? There is room for her in the cart, since I never made it to the fair in the end."

He talked as if she knew who Agnes was. She didn't. But her hackles instantly raised. He wanted to take a woman home with him? Why? They had spent less than a week in the village. Who was she to him that he didn't want to leave her behind?

Dunne shook her head. She would only twist her mind into knots if she tried to make sense of what Björn was thinking. All she knew was that he wanted to take a woman with him when he supposedly wanted to marry her, and he had told her only the other day that he thought of her when he stroked himself to release. She didn't know whether to be crushed or outraged.

"Who is she?" she asked, doing her best not to betray her churning emotions. If this was a way of testing her resolve to wait for another fortnight before making a decision, then she would prove herself worthy.

"The girl who was making cheese with you the other day."

Oh, now she remembered. That sweet, pretty girl was the one he wanted to take home with him? Her heart plummeted further. It had to be someone like her, not a plain dimwitted fool.

"You see, she—"

"No need to share your reasons with me. If you think it would be better for her to go with you, then we'll take her. Now I need to go and tell Birgit we'll leave in the morning," she said, not looking at him. "Good night, Björn."

***

"Wait for me here, I'll go and get Agnes."

Not trusting herself to speak, Dunne merely nodded.

Once Björn had disappeared from view, she made to follow discreetly. Although she knew it was wrong, she could not resist. All night she had agonized about the possible meaning of his decision to take another woman home with him and not liked any of the explanations she had come up with.

She refused to ask Björn, but she needed to know where things stood or she would go mad with the uncertainty.

Dunne crept forward through the bushes, dreading what he would say if he saw her spying on him, then froze when she heard a girl's voice. Agnes.

"My father wants us to marry," she was telling Björn.

Shock froze the blood in Dunne's veins. Arrangements were already being made for a marriage between Agnes and Björn? It couldn't be. He wanted to marry her, Dunne, didn't he? He had told her as much only days ago, even threatened to marry her if she carried his child. Her stomach did a flip. Yes, he had made his intentions clear, but that had been before she'd refused him. Perhaps he'd thought it would be easier to convince her and he had changed his mind after seeing her reluctance. Then, having met someone who took his fancy here, he'd thought he had better ensure himself a future in case she wasn't with child after all—or persisted in her refusal even if she were. It was not impossible. Hadn't she warned him she didn't intend to remarry? Told him she had sworn off men? He would have reasons to doubt an agreement between them would ever be reached.

No, she was being silly. He's kissed her with tenderness only the day before. Such a kiss had to mean something. Perhaps...Perhaps he wasn't aware of Agnes' father's intentions? But his answer nipped that fragile hope in the bud.

"I know. That is exactly why you need to come with me."

Dunne's heart, which had barely started to beat again, stopped anew.

Reality slammed into her. Björn knew about Agnes' father's plans to see the two of them wed. Worse, that was the reason he wanted to take her back to the village with him. He had given up hope of her ever accepting his offer and had chosen another bride to replace her. Pain sliced through Dunne. She'd heard what she wanted to hear, she'd had her explanation, now she had to leave.

Slowly, she retreated back to the cart, moving like a mortally wounded woman.

Björn had abandoned her. But why was she so surprised? He had told her he wanted to marry her if she carried his child and she had thrown his offer back in his face, saying she wasn't even sure she wanted to marry again. He might well wish to make her his wife and look after her and the babe, but he couldn't force her to accept him. And apparently, he was preparing for the eventuality that she would not, like any wise man would do. If he couldn't marry the woman of his choice, then he would settle for a pretty girl who worshipped the ground he walked on and did not constantly challenge him.

And who could blame him?

Her heart breaking in her chest, Dunne took in a deep breath. When Björn and Agnes joined her, she would not cry, she would not ask questions, she would not ridicule herself. It would only make all this worse.

Numb with pain, she sat on the cart seat, but then reconsidered. She didn't belong by Björn's side anymore. Agnes did. Her lips set in a tight line, she settled herself in the nest of furs he had prepared at the back of the cart.

She would stand aside with dignity rather than she be pushed out like an inconvenience.

"My father wants us to marry."

"I know. That's exactly why you need to come with me." Björn answered, kicking a stone with a booted foot.

"I take it you haven't told him you wouldn't agree to the

match then?" Agnes was looking at him with wide eyes. He wasn't sure if she was hopeful or wary.

"No, and I won't. Because if I refuse, he will only find you another husband, one not at all suitable for a woman like you." That was the problem, and why he could not just walk away and forget about her. It felt as if she was his responsibility. He could not leave her behind, knowing she would be forced to marry someone else by a man who treated women as if they were on this earth to slake men's needs, nothing more.

"I did hear talk of an alliance with the miller," she said tentatively. "But I don't see how it could—"

"Not with John, with his father."

She gasped. "He's even older than my father!"

Björn sighed. Was it always a question of age? Was he the only one to think that it mattered not if people were not of an age? In this case, it was the man's character and motivations he objected to, not his age. "His age is the least of your problems. Believe me, you don't want to be married to a man who doesn't really want you." Dunne knew all about the pain that particular situation could bring.

"No." Agnes bit her bottom lip. "Please take me with you."

He nodded, glad she understood the peril awaiting her. "It is the best way. If we leave together, your father will assume we will wed once we reach my village. He will never know that we never actually married and you will then be able to choose a groom yourself, when you're ready."

Agnes flushed and, not for the first time, he wondered if she would not have liked to be his wife. He did not dwell on that uncomfortable thought. Hopefully she would get over the infatuation quickly enough. If she liked muscular blond men, then the village was full of them.

Björn glanced at the hut behind her. He would have liked to go confront Orvyn before leaving, make it clear that he had better keep his filthy hands to himself in the future and overturn the cask of strong ale while he was at it, but he knew it was better for Agnes if they just disappeared without trace. The man wanted this alliance mainly because of the benefit it would bring him, namely having a "sturdy" son-in-law he would exploit in every way he could. He would never agree to the match if Björn told him he was taking his new wife back to his village and would never be of use to him.

"Go and gather whatever belongings you want to take with you and meet me at the cart," he instructed Agnes. "Be quick about it, and discreet. We'll leave as soon as possible."

With those words, he went to join Dunne again. His heart skipped a beat when he saw that she was nowhere to be seen. Had she left, decided to travel alone? Or was it even worse than that? Had someone got to her? Orvyn? His heart started to drum hard in his chest.

Then he spotted a mop of chestnut curls at the back of the cart and life flooded back into his veins. She was here, she was safe.

"Dunne?" he called out, walking closer. "What are you doing sitting at the back of the cart?"

He got a flash of amber when she turned to glance at him over the wooden plank. As he always did when he caught a glimpse of the gold color, he inhaled sharply. There weren't two women like her, and soon they might be husband and wife. He couldn't wait.

"Aren't we going to travel with Agnes?" she asked instead of answering him, as was her wont. He could not help a smile. Why did he like this so much? "Didn't she accept your offer?"

"Yes, she did, but—"

"Well, then it's only natural I give her my place, considering."

Considering? He frowned. "What do you mean?"

For a long moment, she just stared at him. He thought he saw sadness veil her eyes and she looked about to answer. But then Agnes appeared, cutting the enigmatic discussion short. Before he could say anything, Dunne gestured to the place on the driver's seat.

"You can sit there, in my stead," she told the girl.

"But, I-I couldn't," Agnes started to protest. Dunne cut her off with a raised hand.

"You can. Now let us leave. It's already later than we had planned."

Björn had no choice but to help Agnes into the seat and settle himself next to her. Arguing would be pointless. Why had Dunne spoken so abruptly? She was always kind to everyone. What had happened? Why had she made Agnes feel like an imposition? Was it because she was Orvyn's daughter and she thought her as vile as her father? Surely not? Surely she would give an innocent the benefit of the doubt? He would have to talk to her as soon as they could find a moment alone, tell her she had nothing to fear from Agnes and ask her to show the poor girl kindness.

He clicked his tongue, signaling to the horse to walk on.

For the best part of the journey no one spoke. Björn was lost in thought, trying to make sense of Dunne's behavior, Dunne seemed determined to be unusually subdued and Agnes was no doubt mulling over the fact that she was leaving her village for good.

Eventually they stopped to have a bite to eat and water the horse.

"I feel uncomfortable having you sitting at the back," Agnes told Dunne once they had finished the bread Birgit had given them. "It should be me. Please say you will sit in the driver's seat when we set off again."

"Why should I be the one going on the seat?" Dunne

erupted. "Because I'm old, is that it, and my decrepit bones cannot endure the least amount of discomfort?"

Björn could only stare as Agnes dissolved in apologies.

"Of course, n-not, I didn't mean to—"

"Leave it," he snarled, grabbing Dunne by the elbow to drag her away from the mortified girl. "She doesn't know what she's saying."

What the heck had gotten into her? She wasn't being herself today and he would make sure to get to the bottom of it. Agnes didn't deserve to have her head bitten off for being solicitous.

"What on earth was that about?" he asked once they had reached the safety of the trees.

"What was what?" the minx had the gall to ask him.

"Don't even pretend not to understand what I'm talking about. What you just told Agnes. That you are *old*?" He was still holding her elbow and it cost him every ounce of restraint not to hurt her when he was incandescent with rage. He would not have anyone disparage her, including herself. She was not old, she was the most gorgeous woman he had ever seen, and also the kindest. So she had better snap out this madness right now. "You do remember what I did when you spouted nonsense about being fat? Are you trying to provoke me, is that what it is? Do you want to see what I'll do to convince you that you are not old? I will do it. Here. Now."

Dunne tried to disentangle herself from his hold. "Let me—"

"I will let you go if you stop being so damned unreasonable! What has gotten into you?"

She pushed at him, tears pooling in her eyes. "Don't scold me for saying out loud what everyone else is thinking! Leodred did say you could be my son, Harald agrees with him, he told me when we parted that I should find a lover my own age." She stopped and hid her mouth with trembling fingers. "You told me the other day that people mocked you for choosing a woman old enough to be your mo—"

"I was a bloody fool for repeating what those bastards said!" Björn erupted. Why, oh, why, had he been so foolish? He'd only been feeding her insecurities, which certainly didn't need to be encouraged. "Just ignore them, they have no idea what they're talking about!"

"I can't. And even if you had not repeated the words, they would still have been said. People watch us together and all they see are two people who should not be together."

"I care not what they think."

She did not answer, but he understood all the same. He might not care, but she did. Enough to make her throw away what they could have. How could he make her understand that what happened between them was about them and no one else, that he saw only her?

Her bottom lip wobbled and though his heart was breaking, he almost laughed. How could this woman think herself an old crone? At times like these she was nothing but a little lost girl. "I wish I could be strong like you," she breathed. "But I'm not."

No. But he could be strong enough for two, if the reward was the woman of his dreams. Dunne would come to see she could rely on him to protect her from malice, he had to trust she would. For now, though, she was too raw, she would not listen to him. All he could do was be there for her. He placed a kiss on her forehead.

"Let us leave. We need to find a more suitable spot for the night. And you *will* sit next to me on the driver's seat this afternoon."

By his side, where she belonged. Sooner or later, she would have to accept this was her rightful place.

CHAPTER NINETEEN

That night the two women slept side by side at the back the cart while Björn found a spot some distance away. The night was warm enough that they didn't need to start a fire that would signal their presence to any ill-intentioned individuals. Agnes fell asleep almost straight away, while Dunne stayed awake long into the night, worrying about what the future would bring.

She kept looking at the skies, hoping for a sign. *If I see another shooting star, it means I can accept Björn's offer of marriage. If a cloud passes in front of the moon it means I should remain firm in my resolve never to remarry. If a bat flies overhead it means I should leave the village as soon as we arrive.*

She never saw anything.

They awoke to a fine drizzle that didn't let up all day. On the wet roads the going was miserable, and they had to sleep in damp garments that night. But by then, Dunne was so exhausted that she fell into a deep slumber as soon as her head hit the makeshift pillow. Sky gazing in search for a sign would have to wait.

As they progressed on the road south, her chest became

tighter and tighter. Because of the argument with Björn she found it hard to go back to their earlier companionship and Agnes' presence in the cart made it impossible to discuss anything too personal. She could not talk about Orvyn's assault in front of a stranger, so she kept her gratitude for his help to herself. She would have liked to tell Björn more about her unhappy marriage, explain why she could not reconcile herself to the idea of being married again but she didn't want to betray any intimacy between them. And so they were forced to exchange meaningless comments about the weather and what awaited them when they arrived in the village.

Yes, soon they would be back to reality. In a few days she would know whether she was with child or not. And then a decision that would affect the rest of her life would have to be made. Dunne dreaded the moment.

The first person to see them enter the village on a sunny afternoon was Magnus, the village smithy.

"You're back before the others, I see," he commented, drawing closer to them. Then he spotted Agnes at the back of the cart. His eyes went as wide as if he'd witnessed a miracle being performed in front of him. "Good afternoon. I'm Magnus."

"I'm Agnes."

He cleared his throat. "Welcome to the village, Agnes. I'm the blacksmith."

Dunne had to smile at the look on Agnes' face when Sigurd and Wolf joined them a moment later. The girl was now faced with three Norsemen in their prime, in addition to Björn, and it was quite obvious she was overwhelmed by the sight.

"Good afternoon." Wolf smiled, totally oblivious to the girl's reaction. Either he had gone blind while she'd been away, or he was so in love with his expecting wife that he did not even notice other women's admiring looks. Dunne suspected it was the latter. "You must be glad to be home."

Home. The word sounded odd to her ears. Was she home? Not really. But where else could she call home? She still had not bought herself another hut with the money Leodred had given her, or even decided where to go. And did she really want to leave the village? It was far from certain. She didn't know anyone anywhere else. Slowly, she nodded at the Icelander, who had no idea his question had awoken a maelstrom of anguish within her.

"How is Birgit?" Sigurd asked once he'd helped unharnessed the horse. "Well, I hope?"

"Yes, she is, thank you. Very well. She has a little girl, Edita, who's almost the same age as Dawn, and just as mischievous," she blurted out. "We didn't see her husband, though. He has two brothers and one of them broke his leg so he—"

Sigurd interrupted her blabbering with a hand on her forearm. His smile indicated he'd seen her nervousness. "Come, you'll tell us all about it after you've had a drink. Frigyth is resting on the pallet. The babe is getting quite heavy, I'm afraid." Without waiting for her agreement, he took her bundle from the cart and made his way to the hut, expecting her to follow.

Dunne inhaled sharply.

This was it. After days of being constantly side by side, after two weeks away from their daily responsibilities and anyone who knew them, she and Björn were to go their separate ways.

She turned to him. He still had not said a word in answer to the various greetings. Behind her, Agnes was talking with Magnus and Wolf. From what Dunne could hear, the smithy had a room at the back of the forge he used when his brother visited and Agnes was welcome to use it until a more temporary solution could be found.

"Thank you, Björn, for your escort. And...everything else."

He stared at her, his face vibrant with all he could not say. "You're welcome."

"Frigyth is waiting for me. And Dawn is—"

"Yes. Go." The blue eyes gleamed. "But we'll have to talk soon."

"So you two really are involved."

Dunne almost jumped out of her skin. Lost to her ablutions, she hadn't heard Agnes' approach. "You made me jump! I didn't think anyone else would come to bathe this early."

"Forgive me. But I'm always up before dawn, and I saw you go to the river. I could not resist following you," Agnes said quietly. After a week in the village, she was still as shy as she had been when they'd just met. Which made her insistence on such a personal topic all the more surprising. But she repeated her question. "So, are you two involved?"

"Who?" When the girl arched a disbelieving brow, Dunne added, "Björn and I you mean?" There was no point playing dumb.

A crystalline laugh answered her. "Who else? Of course you and Björn. I had my doubts during the trip because you don't seem to want to show what you feel for him, but since we've been back..." Agnes shook her head as if unsure what she meant exactly but still did not drop the matter. "You must be the woman he mentioned."

Mentioned? Dunne's breath caught in her throat. When had Björn mentioned her to anyone? And what had he said? To hide her desperation, she wrung the piece of linen she'd used to wash her face and waited for Agnes to elaborate.

When nothing came, she had no choice but to answer.

"I do have feelings for him," she mumbled, before blinking. What had possessed her to admit to this girl she barely knew what she'd had problems admitting to herself? "But it's complicated."

Agnes sat on a rock next to her and nodded sympathetically. "You don't believe he returns your feelings, is that it?"

No, that wasn't the problem. Björn did feel something for her, she knew, desire first and foremost. She just wasn't sure that was quite what she wanted him to feel. Seeing that Agnes was still waiting for an answer, she gave her one that sidestepped the question.

"I have a young daughter from my marriage."

"Ah, I see. And she doesn't like Björn. I understand. That can be difficult."

Dunne bristled and realized she could not let Agnes believe such a thing. There was no helping it. Bit by bit she would be forced to bare the whole truth.

"Actually, Dawn loves Björn. If anything, she likes him a bit too much." After having given her a cat—and then retrieved said cat when she got stuck in a tree—the Norseman called Bear was her hero. If her daughter knew he wanted the three of them to be a family, she would rail at Dunne for refusing the offer and make her life a misery until she relented.

"But *he* doesn't like *her*, and would prefer you didn't have any children by another man?" Agnes suggested.

"No. He doesn't mind, and he's perfect with her. Kind, protective and amusing." He'd made Dawn smile more in a few weeks than Toland had in three whole years.

"Then..." Agnes seemed utterly at a loss. "What is it? Are you afraid to tell him what you feel in case he—"

"I am not afraid of him in any way," Dunne cut in. The

mere idea was ludicrous. "Björn doesn't pose a threat to any woman, would never hurt anyone."

"No, I don't think he would, and that's not what I meant." Agnes tilted her head, as if to indicate that, having exhausted her ideas, she was waiting for Dunne to finally give her a valid reason for refusing to acknowledge what was between her and Björn.

Dunne inhaled deeply and braced herself when she saw she would just have to expose all her humiliating thoughts. "He's too young for me."

"Is he? In what way?"

She had no idea what to answer. Was there more than one way? Up until this moment she had been certain anyone would agree with her when she claimed she couldn't be with Björn, but talking to Agnes brought home how confused and possibly silly her reasons were. If she told the girl that they'd slept together, that he had shown her pleasure beyond her wildest imagining, and that he had offered to marry her afterward, she wouldn't understand what the problem was.

Right now, Dunne wasn't sure she understood either.

At that moment, Frigyth appeared through the bushes, a smile on her face. "I bet you wouldn't say no to some oat cakes and hot pottage after your bath?"

Dunne smiled back at her sister, grateful to her for interrupting a conversation that was making her feel worse than ever. "No. I'm all cleaned and ready to break my fast. Is Dawn up yet?"

"Yes, and already asking for you. She missed you terribly while you were gone and thought you'd left again."

Guilt twisted her guts. She should be with her daughter right now, not trying to justify herself to a stranger. "Let me go to her."

The two sisters left Agnes to her bath and made for the hut. While Dunne hugged Dawn and promised her she wouldn't leave again, Frigyth assembled a veritable feast on the table.

"And look at this for a special treat," she said, holding two cups high in the air. "The ale Björn made when he returned from Denmark is finally ready. Sigurd tapped the cask this morning."

Dunne took a sip of the pale gold drink her sister was handing her and closed her eyes in delight. It was even better than the previous batch. Or perhaps it was simply that having had to do without for so long made her appreciate it even more when she finally had the chance to indulge. The bubbles danced on her tongue a moment, then slid down her throat with ease.

Mm. Perfection.

"He hasn't lost his touch, I'd say," Frigyth commented.

"No."

The following day, as they were finishing a quick meal, Ingrid came to show her latest creation, a cloak ready for the winter.

"What do you think?"

"It's wonderful!" Dunne enthused. It really was. Trimmed with rabbit fur, the garment was a masterpiece. "I always knew you would make a great seamstress."

"And I didn't believe you, but I am enjoying sewing, you know. I added some decoration to the hood yesterday. Agnes taught me a few extra tricks that came in handy."

Dunne's chest constricted. After spending the week watching Björn from a distance and worrying that he would eventually fall under the spell of the pretty Saxon he'd brought back, she didn't need to hear that Agnes was also replacing her in Ingrid's affection. But she knew that the two girls, who were of a similar age, had struck an immediate friendship. No doubt Ingrid would be delighted if her brother ended up marrying her new best friend.

"When Björn told me he intended to be married before the end of the year, I thought he was teasing me!" Ingrid chuckled. "But I guess he really meant it, if he jumped on the opportunity to bring a woman home so as to better woo her, and I have to say Agnes seems perfect for him, if a little bit shy. I would have imagined he would prefer someone with spirit."

Dunne stared at the eel on her plate and knew she would never manage to swallow the mouthful she had just taken.

"When did he tell you he wanted to get married?" Frigyth asked. No one would have suspected her to be particularly interested in the answer, but Dunne knew her sister had asked the question on her behalf and would be watching her with an eagle eye.

"A few days before leaving for Mercia."

Thunder fell at Dunne's feet. Björn had decided to marry before leaving for Birgit's house. In other words, *before* they had even discussed the possibility together. Which meant she had been right to worry that he had wanted to find himself a replacement bride in case she turned out not to be with child. If he was so bent on marriage, he would take the first woman who wanted him. If not her, then Agnes, who was, as everybody kept reminding her, "wonderful" and "perfect for him."

She stood up and excused herself. If she stayed another moment she might well be sick.

Björn watched Dunne storm away from Frigyth and Sigurd's hut as if the monstrous wolf of his parents' stories, Fenrir, was after her. But he could not let her get away, not when he had come to speak to her. There was a discussion they needed to have.

The month they had agreed on had finally expired. He

knew it because he'd been counting each excruciating day since they'd gone back to the village, but still she was avoiding him.

No more.

"Dunne, wait!" He set off after her, but she pretended she hadn't heard him and picked up her pace. Not to worry. Even if she started to run, she would be no match for him. He would eventually catch up to her. He had allowed her a few final days of thinking time but he would have an answer before tonight.

He reached her before she could slip behind the fence.

Seeing she had no choice but to confront him, she whirled around, eyes ablaze. His breath caught in his throat. In that moment her gold irises appeared lit up from within, like a roaring fire. He wanted that fire to consume him.

"We need to talk," he told her as calmly as he could. This would have to be handled with care. She already looked on the edge of an explosion and nothing would be gained from pushing her. But he had waited long enough.

"Yes, we do. Are you going to marry Agnes if I refuse you?" she asked, her voice little more than a hiss. "Your sister just told us that you intended to get married before the end of the year so I'm wondering."

Björn recoiled in shock. Here he was, about to discuss the possibility of a union between them and she was worried he was organizing a match to another behind her back? Everything made sense all of a sudden. Her odd, bitter behavior on the first day of the journey back home, her talk of being too old and not in her place by his side. She had followed him to Orvyn's hut, heard him and Agnes discuss the union the man wanted between them and thought he was considering it as replacement in the event that she wasn't with child.

"You think I took Agnes with me back to the village because I want to marry her?" he cried out, unable to believe she would think him so deceitful as to promise marriage to one woman while secretly plotting to wed another one.

"Why else?"

She said that as if that could be the only reason! He narrowed his eyes, feeling about to lose his temper. Knowing it always ended in disaster when he did, he tried to calm down. The last thing he wanted was yet another argument.

"I take it that you didn't stay long enough to listen to the whole conversation?" The way Dunne's face fell told him all he needed to know. She had not. "If you had you would have heard me tell Agnes that I didn't intend to marry her. I think you know why. Do I have to remind you I have asked *you* to marry me?"

"No, you do not. You have asked me, but only because you feared I might be carrying your child," she retorted with as much venom as if wanting to do what was right by her was the worst insult a man could pay a woman. "And you did warn me we would wed if I ended up—"

"Warn you? *Feared* you might be with child?" he roared, all attempts at calm forgotten. What did she take him for? "You make me sound like a heartless bastard and my proposal like a threat. You make it sound like I'm going against your will in this!"

"You are! I told you I didn't want to get married again, and certainly not to a man who doesn't really want me."

"But I do want you!"

"Yes. Now, and in your bed...But will it be the same in fifteen years time?"

Dear, this conversation was not going well at all. How could they be arguing again? Why were they talking about anything except what really mattered?

"I'm sorry," Dunne whispered. "But I need to understand why you told your sister you intended to get married before the end of the year before you even approached me."

"Because I do," Björn said through gritted teeth. If it were up to him, he would get married that very moment. "I want to marry *you*. It's been my intention from the moment I found out you were widowed, only I didn't know it at first. You think I bedded you in a fit of lust? I did not. You think I never thought about the future then? It was always on my mind. And so, fool that I am, on the morning after we made love, I told Ingrid about my hopes. I didn't name you because I didn't think it fair to you, but I was so certain what we had could not end after that one night that it made me see that marriage had been on my mind all along."

"And Agnes?" she asked, reddening a little.

He sighed. "Her father wants a match between us, that is true. He told me a few days after we arrived at the village that he was glad to have found a suitable son-in-law. He'd been considering an alliance with the miller's father, a lecher who wants a pretty wife in his bed to sweeten his last few years. I knew that Orvyn would marry her to him the moment I left. I could not let that happen. So I asked her if she would not rather leave with us to come here."

"Agnes is Orvyn's daughter?" Dunne appeared stunned and he was surprised himself. He'd not thought she wouldn't know the connection.

"Yes. I think you can see why I don't trust him to find an adequate husband for her."

She nodded slowly. "So you never intended to marry her?" There was relief in her voice. His heart leapt. Dare he hope now that her fears about his constancy were alleviated, she would come to consider his offer?

"No. The only woman I want to marry is you," he said, articulating every word so as not to leave any doubt in her mind. "I told you as much and I haven't changed my mind. I will still feel the same in fifteen or even in fifty years time. I want to look after you and our child."

Dunne shook her head, her eyes filling with tears. How was Björn to welcome what she had to tell him? He claimed he wanted her, but he didn't know what she knew. That there was no child, after all. Surely it would change everything?

Nausea roiled in her stomach, but she couldn't wait another moment to reveal the truth. The more she waited, the more pain she would cause them both.

"I'm not carrying your child," she said on a sob. "My courses started a few days ago. I didn't find the strength to tell you. Forgive me."

She had kept him hoping for days in vain but, coward that she was, she had been unable to bring herself to put an end to the whole thing. It was only when she had started bleeding that she had realized how much she had hoped to be with child, to have her decision made for her, to be forced to do what she secretly craved. No one would criticize her for wanting to give her child a father, whereas they would mock her for choosing a lover Björn's age.

The only way she could have lived with the idea of being his wife was if she'd been forced to. She wasn't strong enough to make such a decision when nothing obliged her to do so. But the moment she had bled, a future with him had been taken from her.

It was unbearable.

"So you see, it's all over now. There's no need to—"

"There's every need." He took her hand and gave it a hard squeeze. "Listen, Dunne, I want to marry you for *you*. Not because you might be carrying my child, even though I cannot wait to see you swell with my babe, or because I'm worried what other people might say if they think you are nothing more than a conquest I bedded and discarded, even if I hate the idea." His gaze burned a hole into her skull. "How many times will I have to say it? I want to marry you because I—"

Dunne's heart gave a jolt. He had stopped. Why had he stopped? But she knew all too well why. Because he didn't think she would want to hear that he had fallen in love with her, and he was right; she didn't want to hear it. Because it would make this parting even more difficult. If he said he was in love with her then she would have no choice but to say she was in love with him, too, and still she would have to leave him.

"You don't. You can't. I'm all wrong for you." Why couldn't he see it? Why did he have to make her spell it out?

"So wrong I'm out of my mind with the need for you," he growled, taking a step toward her, intent etched all over his face. He had never seemed more handsome than in this moment. "You're not fat, you're not old, or anything else you might think, you're just damn perfect. And I don't want to marry anyone else. I will—"

Suddenly Björn stilled, his gaze focused on a point above her head. Alarmed by the expression on his face Dunne turned around. A plume of smoke was rising in the air, right above where her hut was. After throwing a panicked glance at each other, they ran in the direction of the fire. A group of people were already assembled by the well, drawing water into various pots and buckets. Frigyth and her children were huddled together next to the smithy's hut, and Dawn was with them.

"What happened?" Dunne cried out, lifting her daughter into her arms. For a dreadful moment she had feared being told the little girl was still in the hut.

"No one knows. Magnus was the first one to spot the fire," her sister explained. "He instantly raised the alarm."

"Is anyone injured?"

"No, thankfully." Frigyth placed a hand over little Moon, who was clutching at her skirts. "Everyone is safe."

"Yes."

Dunne placed Dawn back down and watched the hut burn with a sense of fatality. This had not been her home, not really, only a temporary refuge, and only a moment ago she had been telling Björn they would not marry after all. It was all over. All her connections to the Norsemen village had been severed in one clean sweep of fate's scythe. With nowhere to live and no prospective husband, she would have to leave and make her life elsewhere, as she should have done months ago.

It would be good for her to start anew, away from the man she should never have fallen in love with.

"There's nothing of value inside," she heard herself tell the men desperately trying to reach the burning hut. The money Leodred had given her was safe in the purse tied to her belt and her mother's blanket was currently lining the floor of the tree house Sigurd had made for the children. It was the only thing she would have wanted to save. The rest did not matter. "Don't put yourself in danger for nothing."

Everyone retreated. The hut, which had been old anyway, was now beyond saving. All they could do was make sure the fire didn't spread to the other huts, an easy enough task.

Suddenly a cry pierced the air. "Hilda!"

Without warning Dawn let go of her hand and darted toward the hut, weaving her way through the crowd of onlookers.

"Dawn! *No!*" The scream tore through Dunne's throat as she started running in pursuit. What was the little girl thinking? She could not mean to enter the hut now!

Before she could get very far, two arms closed around her waist, stopping her so abruptly she almost went flying. Björn. No one else had moved, but he had set off after her. Just then Dawn slipped through the gaping door, straight into the flames engulfing the hut.

"Let me go!" Dunne screamed. She had to reach her daughter before it was too late. Couldn't he see?

"No. I'll get her." Without another word Björn deposited her on the ground and ran toward the hut.

As soon as he had entered the raging inferno, the roof collapsed, extinguishing any hope of rescue. No one would be able to get into the hut now. Or come out of it.

He and Dawn were trapped.

No! The word never passed her lips. Tears streaming down her cheeks, Dunne fell to her knees. She couldn't scream any more. Her throat had been ripped to shreds by her earlier screams. As if in a dream, she watched Wolf and Sigurd run to the side of the hut. They were armed with axes and determination oozed from them. Sudden, crazy hope surged through her, giving her the strength to get up. Of course, the window! Why had she not thought of this before? If the men could hack their way through the wall, then the two people inside might stand a chance. She ran and arrived just in time to see Wolf lift a little girl out of the window. In her arms was a white fluffy bundle.

Dawn. And Hilda. Safe.

Dunne would have gone to them, but her legs could not carry her anymore. She slid to the ground in a helpless heap and the little girl ran to her instead. "Mama!"

"Oh, my heart, what did you do?" Dunne sobbed, her voice reduced to a dreadful croak. "What did you do?"

"You know Hilda is deaf, she would not have—" Hiccups racked through the little body she was holding tight in her arms. Then Dawn stopped and shot back to her feet. "Bear! He lifted me up to the window. We have to go back for him now!"

Despair swept though Dunne. They did. But at the moment he was trapped. Trapped in the roaring inferno. If Wolf and Sigurd did not manage to get to him in time, once the flames had done their work, there would be nothing left of the golden man who had saved her daughter. The man she loved.

Tears stung her eyes. "We can't go, Bee, it's—"

Woosh.

Just then the whole hut collapsed in on itself in a shower of sparks.

Horror stole over Dunne, blinding her vision and she slid to the ground as darkness claimed her.

CHAPTER TWENTY

Where was she? Why was she lying on her back in the middle of the village? Dunne could hear women and children's voices around her; Frigyth, Merewen, Bee. She opened her mouth to call her daughter. Without knowing why, she desperately needed to hold her. She had the feeling something awful had happened, there was an unbearable weight crushing her chest. She opened her mouth, but no sound came. She tried again. This time a pitiful sound managed to escape. It was not much, but it was enough to attract Bee's attention.

"Mama!" The little girl fell into her arms. "You're awake!"

"Was I sleeping?" she whispered. Damnation! What was wrong with her voice? And why did Bee look so dirty? Why were they lying on the ground?

"You fainted," Frigyth's voice reached her from behind. Then her sister came to stand next to her. "Forgive me for not kneeling down. I can't manage it with my stomach. How are you feeling?"

"All right," she said cautiously. "But why am I lying down in the middle of the—"

In a rush of horror, everything came back to her. The hut, the flames, the cat trapped inside, the little girl rushing away to save her, the man lifting them both out the window. The man! *No!*

"Björn!" she screamed, bolting upright. "We must—"

"He's all right. Wolf and Sigurd got him out in time," Frigyth explained hurriedly, sensing she was about to lose her mind with anguish. "They hacked at the hut and managed to make the window hole big enough for him to get through."

"But the hut—" Her voice, tested to its limits, suddenly gave out.

"Yes, the hut collapsed. But from the opposite end. They dragged him out just as the last wall, the one with the window, came crumbling to the floor. You had already fainted by then, so you never knew."

Holding Bee tight in her arms, Dunne started to sob. If Björn was safe then she could start breathing again. How would she have borne to hear that he had died saving her daughter? It didn't bear thinking about.

A hand landed in her shoulder. Merewen.

"Apart from a few burns, he's fine. It's a miracle, really."

Incapable of talking, Dunne nodded. It was a miracle.

"Wait here a moment, I will call Wolf. He will carry you back to Frigyth and Sigurd's hut."

A moment later, Dunne felt herself being lifted into a man's arms. Because it was not Björn. she resisted the urge to lean her head against his shoulder. Once the Icelander had deposited her onto the pallet, she burrowed under the furs and drew her daughter against her, intent on finding oblivion. The little girl in her arms smelled of smoke and perfection. She was still holding Hilda tight against her.

Feeling more exhausted than she had ever felt, Dunne fell back to sleep.

Two DAYS PASSED. Dunne spent them inside her sister's hut, lying in bed, pretending to be asleep. Frigyth and Sigurd acted as if they could not see anything odd in her behavior, but she guessed they talked about her as soon as they were alone. She would not be able to put off reality for much longer. Soon she would have to find a place to live—and go see Björn, thank him for what he'd done. At the moment she simply could not face him. What do you tell a man who sacrificed himself to save your daughter? How do you behave in front of a suitor you just rejected? How do you deal with the shame of causing someone so much pain?

She had no idea.

On the evening of the second day, Frigyth approached her as she was helping herself to some cheese. She hadn't had much appetite of late but was trying to be reasonable. It would not help her or Bee if she fell ill now.

"Sister."

Dunne swallowed her piece of cheese with difficulty and braced herself. She could see from Frigyth's demeanor that the conversation would be difficult. She also knew what, or rather *who*, it would be about. Night was falling. Perhaps the darkness wrapping around them would help.

"Have you been to see him yet?"

The bluntness was no less than she had expected so she kept her gaze on her hands. "No."

"Why not?"

Why not? Had her sister really asked her that question? *Why not?*

"He nearly died because of me," Dunne said slowly, as if speaking to a simpleton. After days sounding like a croaking frog, her voice was finally back to normal.

"It wasn't because of you. The fire was an accident. One of Helga's boys stumbled on a rock and dropped the torch he was carrying back home. He told us so afterward."

"It matters not how it happened. The fire is not why I feel unable to face him."

"Why then?"

Dunne finally dared to look at Frigyth. "We were arguing when it happened," she said, keeping her voice low so as not to wake the children. "Do you understand now? I was telling him that I could not marry him, that I was not carrying his child and would never be his wife and the next thing we knew, he rushed into the flames to save my daughter, a little girl who should mean nothing to him! He risked his life for Bee, for me, when I—"

When I broke his heart.

She shook her head, tears filling her vision. So much guilt, so much pain. How would she deal with it all?

"I feel so ashamed, so wretched, so guilty. How can I face him after telling him we could never be together?" she sobbed.

"Why would you tell him something like that when we both know that you love him? Dunne, it's time you accepted what you feel for the man." Frigyth sighed. "Björn is dying out there, you have to go to him."

Dunne's whole body went liquid, stiff, hot and cold at the same time. Dying? Björn had saved her daughter from the flames and now he was *dying* because of it? And Frigyth had not thought of informing her of the fact before now, instead choosing to berate her for her lack of decision?

"Stay with Bee," she shouted, bolting toward Björn's hut like a mad woman.

She had to see him before he died, had to, even if she wasn't sure what she would say or where she would start once she was in front of him. By apologizing, by kissing him, by begging him to marry her before he died? She didn't know but she had to try.

"Björn?" she called out, pushing the door of the hut open slowly, dreading what she would find inside.

He was lying on his pallet, bare-chested. One of his biceps was bandaged, and the skin on his left shoulder appeared burnt. It was hard to see the extent of the damage in the near darkness, but one thing was certain. He was utterly still, and the sound of the door opening had not been enough to make him stir.

"No!" She fell to the floor next to him and started crying. Was she too late? How stupid she had been for not coming to see him before, for not fighting for their—

"Dunne?"

She raised her head when she heard him call her. "Thank God!" she whimpered. She wasn't too late, he wasn't dead yet, he had recognized her, and she would have the chance to tell him what was in her heart. Feeling ridiculous for her ill-timed outburst of grief, she straightened back up. Björn was looking at her in the moonlight, a thousand questions lurking in his eyes.

"Are you all right?" he rasped.

Oh, that he should be the one asking her that question!

"Yes. Forgive me, but you weren't moving when I entered and I thought…"

"I was sleeping. It is nighttime, you know." He sounded… Well, he sounded bewildered more than anything. Dunne wasn't sure what to make of it. Shouldn't he sound in pain if, as Frigyth had said, he was about to die, or at the very least look weak and wan? But no, he had never appeared better, or dearer to her.

In that moment, her decision was made. If he survived his injuries, she would ask him to marry her. When her sister had told her was dying, she'd had a vision of what life without him would really be like and it had caused her whole body to wither. Never would she place herself in that position willingly.

As long as he wanted her, she would stay with him, whether it lasted a hundred days or a hundred years. She would take what she could while she could, anything would be better than his absence and the need for him clawing through her.

Björn didn't know if he was dreaming.

After days ignoring him, Dunne was in his hut, looking pale and drawn, as if she'd been worrying herself sick. Why was that? Sigurd had assured him Bee had not suffered from her ordeal in the burning hut, thanks to him, and the only person Dunne would have lost sleep over was her daughter. As for him, she probably did not care. She had not visited him once, or even inquired after his health.

It had hurt. Hurt like hell. What did a man have to do to win his woman around? Was asking her to marry him not enough? Was declaring his love for her not enough? Even if, admittedly, he had been unable to finish the declaration, surely she had understood his intent, had seen it in his eyes. Was saving her daughter's life not enough? He'd been angry when he'd realized that no, it was apparently not enough.

And so he'd had to face reality. It was over between them. She was not carrying his child, she had refused to marry him and with no home in the village, she would soon have to leave. It was all over.

And yet, she was here now. Why? He resisted the maddening urge to draw her into his arms, knowing she would only balk and then stomp all over his heart again if he even hinted at his need for her.

"What are you doing here?" he asked, doing his best not to sound too accusatory. He could salvage his dignity at least, and behave as if he didn't care one way or another what her intentions were.

She made a face he found hard to interpret. Was she feeling guilty for not having come before? Perhaps. Regretting her decision to come to him? Very probably. "Frigyth said you were at death's door and I—"

"Did she?" He frowned. What had her sister been thinking, telling her something like that? She had visited him only that afternoon, she would have seen that, far from dying, he was almost restored to his usual self. Only the burns on his calf and torso continued to throb, but that was nothing.

"Well, she said: 'Björn is dying out there' and I..." Dunne's voice trailed away when he threw her a burning stare.

Because now he understood. Frigyth had seen all too well what was going on. She had seen the depth of despair he was drowning in and had wanted to shock her sister into revealing her feelings for him before it was too late. The fact that Dunne had rushed to him as soon as she'd heard about his supposed agony had to be encouraging, did it not?

She had to feel something for him.

And he had to speak out.

"I *am* dying. Inside. And only you can put an end to my suffering. I need..." He took her hand in his when his voice broke, willing her to listen, and finally give them a chance. "Dunne. Marry me. Please. You know I can't live without you. I will do anything to convince you. I will beg, I will remind you of the night we spent together, I will seduce you again and use your body against you, I will shamefully use the fact that I saved your daughter to sway you, I will make you—"

"Björn, please, it's not nec—"

"No, let me finish. I love you. I think I have loved you from the moment I saw you at Sigurd's wedding when I was only sixteen. That day I saw the woman I wanted to spend the rest of my life with. I love you. I should have told you so every day from the moment you finally allowed me to make love to you. I should have told you *while* I was making love to you, told you that this was why I was in your bed." What a stupid fool he'd been! He should have started there, instead of threatening her with marriage, and making it look as if he only wanted to do what was right by her and look after an elusive child. "I love you. Say you love me back, say you will marry me because I *am* dying without you. Not in the way you thought, but I am."

There was a pause. Too long, far too long for his liking.

He opened his mouth, but Dunne spoke before he could utter a word.

"Yes. I love you too," she sobbed, collapsing over his chest.

Happiness, as bright as a beam of sunlight, burst in his heart. He draped a hand over her neck, feeling her shudder under his palm. "You do?" He dared not believe what he had been told. He needed to hear it again. "Tell me again."

He felt a kiss land on his chest, just above where his heart was drumming fiercely. He closed his eyes at the tenderness contained in that gesture. Then Dunne said what he needed to hear.

"I do. I love you, Bear."

She did love Björn. And it had taken a near catastrophe for her to finally accept it. Dunne could have kicked herself. When she'd thought she would have to live without him, not because she had rejected him, but because he had died, when she had believed him about to vanish from her life forever, she had understood with painful, devastating clarity that she could not live without him.

Against all odds she had been given a chance at love, and she was not going to let it pass.

"I don't want to be free. I want to be yours," she whispered, her mouth against the smooth skin under his collarbone. "I don't understand how it could have happened."

"You don't need to understand. You just need to accept it."

"I had sworn off men."

He gave a rueful chuckle. "I guess it's a good thing I'm only a boy then."

Mortified, Dunne hid her face in the crook of his neck. "I'm so sorry. I should never have said that. In my defense, I swear I only wanted—"

"In your defense nothing. I was a boy for an awful long time, until I left for Denmark, at least. You weren't the only one to think that. And I don't mind you saying it, as long as you speak to me. It's your absence that was killing me, not your insults." He cradled her face between his two hands and forced her to meet his gaze. "Listen to me. I regret nothing of what happened between us, because it means we ended up where we are. And I think...I think from now on we will carry on together."

There was no hesitation in her voice when she answered. "Yes."

"Ingrid is not here, she's gone to see a friend. You will sleep here tonight, in my arms."

"Yes."

"And then tomorrow we will get married."

"Yes."

In the end it was that easy. As if to seal the deal, Björn kissed her. It was a tender, loving kiss. Despite the unusual gentleness, she could feel her body catching fire, readying itself for his possession. But to her surprise, he drew her into his arms and ordered her to sleep. Because she had not had much sleep in the last two nights, too worried about what could have happened to him and Bee, she did not try to resist and nestled herself against him. They had their whole lives to make love.

For now, it would be enough to *feel* loved.

CHAPTER TWENTY-ONE

When Dunne woke up, it was already light outside. She was shamelessly, possessively, indecently draped all over Björn. Her cheek was pillowed on his chest, her thigh was resting over his legs and her hand…Her hand was holding something warm, smooth—and hard as stone. Her eyes flew open when she realized what it was. What was she doing? Had she been stroking him in her sleep? It certainly appeared so.

Oh, God.

"Don't you dare move," Björn growled, clasping his hand over hers to keep her fingers in place when she made to release him. "I want to wake up with your hand round me like this every morning."

Ah, so she *had* reached out for him, and woken him up in the process. Heat flared in her chest.

"Do you always sleep naked?" It was a ridiculous question but if she behaved as if she was not mortified perhaps Björn would not see it.

"I do, and never have I had cause to congratulate myself on the decision more."

"I never meant to—"

"Ah, love, don't tell me that. I will carry on imagining you had a plan in mind when you reached out for me."

A plan! "Such as?"

"To send me wild with desire."

The heat in her chest crept down to the place between her legs. "I send you wild with desire?"

Something like a snarl answered her. At the same time, Björn drew her so that she could lie all over him. Yes, apparently she did send him wild. Positively feral. He forced her legs apart and she found herself sitting astride him, his hard manhood trapped between them.

"You make me lose my mind every time you're near, you infuriating Saxon woman."

"Then why didn't you make love to me last night?"

For the first time, he hesitated. "I...I thought you would not be comfortable with it, if you're on your monthly courses. Besides, I didn't want to give you the impression I only want you for your body, because I don't, even if I am dying to be inside you."

She blushed. Could there be a more thoughtful, perfect man? "I should have told you," she replied, leaning in as if to kiss him. "I've stopped bleeding."

"That is the best news I've heard all day," he growled, starting to grind his hips under her in a suggestive manner.

"That doesn't mean much, considering you've only just woken up!" Dunne muffled a giggle against his neck.

"No. *You* have only just woken up, beautiful. I, on the other hand, have been awake since well before dawn, watching you drape yourself over me bit by bit, starting with your calf and ending with your hand. It took all my control not to wake you."

He guided her hand to his hardness and wrapped her

fingers over it, mimicking the way she had been holding him earlier.

Her breath hitched. "Am I to understand that you want to want to—"

"Fuck you? Oh yes." Dunne groaned. Why did she love to hear that word in his mouth? She should be shocked! Instead she was aroused. And apparently he knew it, for he said it again. "I want to fuck you, preferably more than once, preferably before we get up to go get married."

Well, if that was the case, who was she to refuse him?

"I would like to try something," she breathed, her mouth on his skin.

"You can try whatever you want," he growled. "As long as you're naked while you do it."

In the blink of an eye, she was. As if moved by an invisible force, they had both started to tear at her clothes, throwing them all over the hut in their haste. Once she was naked, Björn took a moment to look at her. Sitting astride him as she was, there was no place to hide. But she didn't want to hide, not when he was looking at her with such passion, causing her insides to convulse.

Then with a supple jerk of his hips he reversed their positions so that he was the one looming over her, awe in his eyes. "Look how beautiful you are, wife."

"I'm not your wife yet," she rasped, overwhelmed by the love in his voice.

"No, but soon."

He brought a hand to her breast and cupped the aching fullness. A groan escaped Dunne's lips when he started to tease her nipple with his thumb and forefinger, pinching it slightly. Then the groan became a whimper because he took the nipple in his mouth and swirled his tongue around it as if to soothe the burn. For a long, delicious moment he suckled her, running his hands over her hips in a loving caress. When he released her, his lips were red, both her nipples were hard, and she was more desperate than she had ever been.

"What is that thing you want to try?" he said in deep rumble. "Tell me before I lose my mind and just take you."

"I heard that lovers could use their mouths to pleasure each other," she said, hiding her face in the crook of his neck. She would never have the courage to have this conversation if she looked at him. She felt him swallow against her mouth.

"I heard the same thing."

She ground her hips against the hardness prodding at her. "I-I never thought I would want to do such a thing before."

"I did. I imagined kissing the sweet place between your legs, and licking you until you screamed my name."

Oh. The place he had just mentioned went slick with need, giving its unequivocal approval to the plan.

"I never imagined doing something like that but right now, I'm imagining kissing you there and it..." She stopped. Dare she say it? Would Björn not be appalled? Probably not, considering what he'd just told her. She threw caution to the wind. This was the man she would marry and they had tiptoed around each other for too long. "It makes me desperate to try. If you agreed, we—"

"I do. I agree. I told you, I would do anything as long as it is with you and you're naked. Do what you will. I'm yours."

Never had any agreement been more enthusiastic. Dunne smiled. He was not appalled, or even shocked, but rather exited by the prospect. "I'll need you to free me then."

In the blink of an eye Björn had flipped onto his back and taken her with him, reversing their positions once more. She was now astride him and free to explore. Kissing her way down his magnificent body, taking care to avoid the damaged shoulder, she went to kneel between his spread legs. My, he was so hard, so unashamedly ready. For her. She couldn't wait to start her daring exploration.

At the last moment, a doubt seized her. "I don't know what I'm doing. I might do it all wrong."

He gave a chuckle and stroked her cheek in a soothing caress. The pad of this thumb came to rest at the corner of her lips. "I doubt there is a wrong way to do this, sweetheart," he rasped, brushing slowly along her lower lip. She knew he was imagining her kissing him intimately and heat invaded her. "Just make sure you don't bite me."

She nodded and lowered her head, stopping a few inches from the straining manhood waiting for her. "You'll tell me if it's good, and what I can—"

"Dunne, please. Just..." He didn't seem to dare ask for what he wanted but he sounded on the verge of madness. She placed her puckered lips on the tip of his crown to kiss it. With a curse Björn bucked and jerked upward, the brusque movement causing his shaft to push past her lips and into her mouth.

The shock of the intrusion made her freeze. But Björn didn't seem to think anything was amiss. Quite the contrary.

"Ah, yes, just like that, take it in!"

In? Did he mean she should behave as if her mouth was her—

A furious blush invaded her cheeks. She hadn't imagined doing that, just placing a few kisses on the head and maybe lick along the length, but, well, she *was* doing it, he was in her mouth already, or, at least, part of him was. And it wasn't bad, not bad at all. In fact, she had the odd urge to start suckling the way he had suckled her nipple earlier. His words came back to her.

Just make sure you don't bite me.

Mm. No biting. That didn't seem too hard. She sheathed her teeth with her lips and, gripping the base of his shaft, slid lower down. The hiss of pleasure she got in return made her groan.

"Ah. Do that again," Björn rasped, placing a hand over her nape in encouragement.

What did he mean? The groaning? The gripping? The sliding? Not sure what he wanted, she did all three. Moaning in delight, she gripped him tighter and slid as far as she could. Then, because she could not think of anything else to do, she dragged her head back up and did the same thing again. And again, going a fraction lower each time. The hand at her nape tightened, accompanying her movements. It struck her that, in that moment, her mouth was used exactly as her—

"You— Too good. Dunne...need to stop." Björn's voice had gone all raw and he wasn't making any sense. Why should she stop if he liked what he was doing? Wasn't that the point? Besides, the hand at her nape had not released her, quite the opposite. His fingers were now fisted into her hair, holding her in place. She wasn't going anywhere. Except down. And up again. Down. An agonized moan reached her ears. "I'm going to come!"

That must mean she was doing something right. Dunne increased her speed and closed her eyes. She had gone all wet between the legs and more desperate for him than ever. She was going to erupt as soon as he entered her.

It all happened at once. Björn shouted, his fingers seized around her neck, his shaft started to pulse, and heat flooded her mouth. Unsure what to do, Dunne waited, while he emptied himself with what felt like agonizing jerks against her tongue.

Then he released her hair and lay still as a corpse while his limp manhood slipped from her lips, causing some of the seed to dribble down her chin.

Björn felt Dunne shift a bit and opened his eyes in time to

see her wipe her chin. The gesture was so evocative that he groaned in lust.

Then reality caught up with him. This was not yet another of his lewd imaginings. This had been real. He had really used Dunne's mouth for his selfish pleasure.

"Bloody bleeding hell. Dunne, I'm so sorry."

Dunne looked at him, appearing nonplussed. "We did say we would experiment with our mouths. Why are you sorry?"

He blinked. Why was he sorry exactly? It had been the best release of his life, and she didn't appear outraged. "I..."

"Do you regret it? Did you not like it?"

"I loved it." Too much. That was the problem. He had reached his release with humiliating speed—and he had not withdrawn in time. "I came in your mouth."

"Mm. Yes, you did." She flushed.

"You're not disgusted?"

"No!" *Now* she looked shocked. "I love you, how could I be disgusted by anything you do?"

He rewarded this answer with a deep, lingering kiss. "I love you, too, you know that? You're one extraordinary woman."

"I'm not sure about that but—"

"I am, and as I will be the one marrying you, we'll take my word for it."

Dunne gave a sigh. She loved how determined he was to have her love herself. This was the greatest gift he had offered her, along with mind-numbing pleasure. How had she ever thought that she would feel trapped in a marriage with this man? He had set her free. Free from her crippling doubts and the prospect of a lonely life.

Now she had so much to look forward to. Wild nights in bed, love and other children. She couldn't wait.

"Very well," she said, nestling herself in his arms. Dear God, he was so warm, so strong, so soft! "I'm extraordinary."

He grunted and flipped her over onto her back once more. Before she could say anything, he lifted one of her legs and settled it over his good shoulder. The position was shockingly intimate, but she didn't even try to cover herself. This was her husband, or would be soon. She was his to look at and love.

"I believe it is my turn to experiment with my mouth." The smile blooming on Björn's lips was pure wickedness. Imagining those perfect lips nibbling at her core caused her to spasm in anticipation.

"Whatever you do, don't bite me."

"I won't. Not too hard anyway." He flashed his teeth in a wicked smile. "Now. I have it on good authority that bears like honey. Well, this bear is going to feast. And you are going to come for him."

"Yes." She suspected she would. Probably more than once.

He looked at her straight in the eye. "And then when I'm finished, I'm going to fuck you."

She whimpered. Oh yes, he did know how much hearing that word in his mouth aroused her. "I thought we were going to get married this morning?"

"I don't believe I mentioned the morning." He swirled a finger around her opening. She was wet, and desperate. "We'll have plenty of time to get married in the afternoon. Now, enough stalling, Doe, I'm starving."

"She's so beautiful."

Gazing at the baby girl asleep in her arms, Dunne wiped a tear from her cheek. Was there anything more moving than a newborn child? She couldn't think of one single thing. Bee snuggled closer to her and sighed with contentment.

"Finally I have a girl cousin!" her daughter whispered in her ear, doing her best not to wake up the sleeping babe. "I only had boys before."

From the pallet, Frigyth smiled the radiant smile of new mothers. "Elwyn is happy as well, you know. He's wanted a sister for years."

"A sister!" The little girl's eyes went round as coins as she turned to look at Björn, who was standing by the door. "Of *course*, that's what I need! It's even better than a girl cousin! Bear, please, could you give Mama a little girl? Husbands are the ones who give their wives children, aren't they?" Suddenly she didn't sound so sure.

"They are," Björn growled, crossing his arms over his chest. "And believe me, I'm doing my best to give my wife a little girl.

Or a little boy. I'm afraid that's something not even us husbands can choose."

Dunne knew she had gone crimson. Indeed, he was doing what was required to make her with child every night, and sometimes even during the day. At this rate it would be a miracle if she did not give birth to their first babe before the spring. But as they had been married for just a month, it was too early to tell, even if she had started to wonder whether her monthly courses were not overdue.

"Are you really doing all that's needed?" Her daughter came to face him and planted her fists on her hips, looking remarkably like a disapproving matron. "You had better ask Uncle Sigurd where men find babies because he has found plenty already. I'm not sure *you* know what you're doing since Mama is not yet—"

"Talking of Sigurd, Bee, would you go get him for me?" Frigyth asked, interrupting the mortifying conversation. "I need a word with him but I'm too tired to get up. He will be in Wolf's hut."

"Of course!" The little girl left without a backward glance.

"Thank you," Dunne told her sister with a sigh, handing her the baby back. "She is getting far too bold, I'm afraid."

"She's perfect, just like her mother." Björn came over to place a kiss over her temple. "But all the same, I have no wish to be harangued about my ability to...find babies ever again. So I will have to redouble my efforts to make you with child," he added, whispering in her ear.

Dunne's heart skipped a beat—or two. "Heavens, Bear, have mercy! A woman needs her sleep."

"Mm. And a bear needs his cubs. I cannot wait to see you hold our daughter or son. I only wish they have your eyes."

Björn gave her cheek a tender stroke and her heart threatened to escape from her chest. It was too much love for one person.

"We'll see. As long as they are cherished and happy, I care not."

"No, me neither. And they will be loved, whether in fifteen or fifty years' time."

ABOUT THE AUTHOR

As far back as I remember, I have been attracted to the Middle Ages, to knights in shining armour and their ladies in spectacular dresses. Now I get to write about them, I feel like the luckiest woman in the world. Being French and married to a Brit makes each book I write extra special, as our countries share a long and sometimes painful past. But in the end, in life as well as in fiction, love conquers all!

I have published several medieval romances under my own name, including series, and also have a pen name, Judith Falcon, for spicier projects, still in historical romance.

Join my newsletter and check out my other books on virginiemarconato.com.

The Noble Norsemen

Taming the Wolf

Soothing the Beast

Wooing the Devil

Baiting the Bear

Tempting the Saxon